Finders
KEEPERS

ALSO BY K.T. FINCH

The Girl in the Snow
Good Girl Gone

Finders
KEEPERS

K.T. FINCH

bookouture

Published by Bookouture in 2018

An imprint of StoryFire Ltd.

Carmelite House
50 Victoria Embankment
London EC4Y 0DZ

www.bookouture.com

ISBN: 978-1-78681-343-5
eBook ISBN: 978-1-78681-342-8

To my husband, Kevin, thank you for always believing in me.

To Tristan and Skylar, without you two, this book would've been completed twice as fast but with half the fun.

PROLOGUE

My heart pounds as I start the engine of my 2002 Dodge Neon and pray that the car will not fail me tonight of all nights. It doesn't. It roars to life and I am on the highway within a few moments, taking me further away from that place.

I step on the gas and drive faster and faster. As the road winds around the narrow highway, trees and housing developments whip by me. I don't know what the speed limit is and I don't know where I'm going. All I know is that I can't go back there and I definitely can't go home. No matter how fast I drive, my thoughts keep going back to what just happened.

His hands on me.

The sound of the gunshot.

The buzzing of my head.

Blood everywhere.

No, I can't think about it. Not now. Not ever. Not if I want to get away. None of that matters now. Dwelling on it won't solve anything. I need to get away from here. As far away as possible. All I see is the empty black road illuminated by my headlights and snow flurries whizzing by and colliding with the windshield.

I glance back in the rearview mirror. There's no one there. I haven't seen another car for miles, but it still feels like someone's following me. Watching me. They are coming for me. I know. If not now, then soon. No one gets away with what I've done.

Suddenly, I realize that I'm grasping the steering wheel too tightly. My knuckles are white from holding on so hard, and it's not just because the heating in this car barely works. I take a deep breath. I inhale slowly. In and out. *It's going to be okay*, I say to myself. Everything is going to be okay. You just have to stop freaking out and think.

I glance over at the bag on the seat next to me. I touch it to make sure that it's real. I can't believe what I have done. What the hell was I thinking? Still, I am a little proud of myself. For once, I had enough guts and I wasn't going to take all that shit anymore. For once, I stood up for myself. And now, everything in that bag is mine. All mine.

I take another deep breath and try to decide what I should do. All I want to do is go home and curl up in my bed with my cat. But that's an impossibility. *They* know where I live.

The road curves and I turn left. It's an unfamiliar route, but I'm pretty sure it's the straightest way out of town. I slow down a bit since the snow is getting heavier and I can barely see more than a few feet in front of me.

Maybe this is as good a time as ever to go somewhere I've always wanted to go. I was born and raised in Alaska and I've never been out of this state. Perhaps now is the best time to make a change. Well, if I could go anywhere, I'd go somewhere warm. Somewhere where the beaches are perfectly white and the water is crystal clear. Somewhere I can wear flip-flops all year round. And, of course, it would have to be a place that I can drive to.

I lose myself for a few minutes, imagining a life that I could have in Florida. When I finally come back from my daydream, I realize that I've taken a wrong turn. The banks are covered entirely by snow, stacked five feet high. Pine trees tower on both sides and the road continues to narrow. What was two wide lanes only a few hundred yards ago suddenly merged into one rather narrow lane. Shit, I say to myself. This road hasn't been maintained for days. How did I end up here?

I have to turn around. I step on the brake to slow down, but the car starts to slide. I pump the brakes, quickly and deliberately, but it's all to no avail. The car continues to skid forward. I've hit ice and the brakes are useless. My heart jumps inside my throat. I grab onto the steering wheel with all of my might. I take a deep breath, breathing in and out, trying to keep my cool. I put the car in neutral. This has worked hundreds of times before, but not tonight. The ground underneath feels like an ice skating rink. I turn the wheel from side to side, but it's doing nothing to control the direction of the car.

My headlights illuminate a large pine tree ahead.

Oh my God.

Everything fades to black.

CHAPTER ONE

NOAH

I'm following Ava up the hill behind our house. The sun is barely up, but we've been awake for hours. She runs ahead, grasping her round saucer of a sled in her little hand with the endless energy of a five-year-old.

'C'mon, Dad!' she yells for me. I struggle up the hill, my feet sinking deep into the dry snow. This is my ninth ride down, and I doubt I have another one in me.

'Let's race,' she announces at the top as if it's something new. We have raced all the other times, and each time it was a struggle to lose. This race is not unlike the rest. I dig my heels into the side of the hill and brave the pounds of powder that hit my face, barely managing to slow down just in time before reaching the finish line.

'You lost again!' Ava laughs, heading back up the hill.

'I guess I did.' I shrug, digging out the snow, which found my neck despite the zipped-up parka and scarf.

'I'm not sure if I can do another run, Ava,' I yell after her.

'Oh c'mon, please, please, Dad. Just two more,' she yells without waiting for an answer.

I can't help but smile. Though she doesn't know what a lawyer is, something tells me that this might be a perfect career choice for her. Her negotiating skills are second to none. Instead of arguing for just one more run, she asks for two. This way, we can both win by settling for one.

Two runs later – I can't say no to those big brown eyes – we come back inside. As I help her get out of her coat and boots in the mud room, she smiles at me and tells her mom how she won every single time.

'The last time, I really thought that Dad was going to win, but then at the last moment, he slowed down,' she says. 'Dad, I was thinking. Maybe you should put your feet up. I looked over and saw that you have so much snow going around the sides of your sled.'

'Yeah, maybe I'll try that next time,' I say with a shrug.

Emily pours us our cups of hot chocolate, shaking her head.

'You shouldn't let her win every time.' Emily turns to me when Ava's head is buried in a *Minecraft* video on YouTube on Emily's phone. 'I know your dad never let you win at anything, but that doesn't mean that she should live in a world where she thinks she's invincible.'

Emily and I don't disagree on much, but we do disagree on this point. She thinks the world is a tough place and the best way to prepare Ava for it is to be tough on her. I think that the world is a tough place and the best way to prepare Ava for it is to wrap her in a cloak of confidence and self-assuredness.

'I'm building her self-esteem,' I say.

'You're making her cocky,' Emily responds.

'Cocky and outgoing, hopefully. There's nothing wrong with boys being confident and outgoing, but somehow it's a bad thing for a girl to be. Well, not my girl. Ava's going to grow up thinking that she can be anyone she wants to be.'

'It's not that I don't want that, Noah,' Emily says with a sigh. She has always been the more realistic, grounded one. 'It's that I want kids at school to actually like her. I want her to fit in.'

'You want her to be popular.'

'So? What's wrong with that?'

'Nothing. But take it from me, the most popular girls are the most confident girls. They're the ones that don't take shit. They're the ones that aren't afraid to talk to guys. To state their opinions. I know. I see them walking the halls with their heads held high. I see the way all the guys fall over themselves just to talk to them.'

Emily sighs. A sign of defeat. We've had this conversation a million times before. We just see the world differently, and there's no way either of us can convince the other that we're right.

'She's a good girl, Ava. And we're raising her just fine. Don't worry so much.'

Emily flashes me an unconvincing smile and gets up for her purse and keys. Ava looks up from the phone and frowns.

'I have to go to work, baby.' Emily gives her a hug.

I hate to see this sad look on Ava's face every time her mom leaves to go to work. Especially for her weekend shifts.

'But it's Saturday,' Ava pleads.

Emily shrugs. 'I have to go to work, honey. We're short staffed at the hospital. Two nurses are sick.'

'Why can't you be sick?' Ava asks, already thinking like a lawyer.

'Because they need me there.'

'But I need you here.'

Emily pulls on her boots, apologizing over and over.

'But Ellie's mom is always home. And so is Levi's. And Logan's.'

Emily kisses Ava on top of her head, rolling her eyes at me. Even though she will never admit it, I can feel her resenting me. We both know why Ellie's, Levi's, and Logan's moms are home. Their dads aren't tenth grade English teachers. Ellie's dad runs a trucking company, Levi's dad is a lawyer, and Logan's dad owns a luxury fishing outfitter that requires him to work fifteen-hour days during the summer, taking tourists from the lower forty-eight around the best fishing spots in the state, and then lay around the house and drink beer for the other nine months.

Ellie, Levi, and Logan live down the street, in the same development as we do, but their houses, just like their fathers' salaries, are much bigger than ours.

'I'm really sorry.' I walk up to Emily and give her a warm hug.

'For what?'

'Just that you can't stay home with Ava like the other moms can.'

Emily shrugs.

'I may not love working twelve-hour shifts on weekends, but I love being a nurse.'

That's Emily's go to line. That's how she always explains away the long hours she works and the fact that she almost always volunteers for overtime. Back in the day, I used to believe her, but that was many years ago. Back then, I also believed that I loved being an English teacher. As if there were nothing better than going to work and coming home in pitch darkness, giving the same lectures year after year to practically the same bored students who couldn't care less about Scout Finch or Huck Finn or Hester Prynne. As if there were nothing better than grading eighty papers at a time because the other English teacher was conveniently sick and the school didn't have a budget for any more assistants or substitutes.

Of course, admitting any of this, even to your spouse, your best friend, the person who has been with you through thick and thin, the person you love most in the world, besides your daughter, seems impossible. Admitting this would mean that your life has been a sham. A mistake. It's like we already have all this invested in our life, and to say that maybe it's not what we want seems daunting to say the least.

Ava and I follow Emily to our four-car garage. Four-car garages are considered a necessity in our subdivision because they're meant to store your two sport utility vehicles as well as an assortment of toys: an all-terrain vehicle, a boat, a motorcycle. The type of toy varies, but everyone here has at least two toys. Our two SUVs and boxes of summer clothes don't even come close to filling up the garage, not that we have any more credit to buy anything anyway. The mortgage and the two car payments have pretty much stretched our credit to the limit.

'Are you going to work on your book today?' Emily asks.

'No, Dad's going to watch TV with me,' Ava announces. To tell the truth, that sounds like a much better way to spend the afternoon than staring at a blank page thinking of something to write.

'Noah?' Emily asks.

'I'm going to try.'

'Please do. You're already way behind on your schedule,' she says, opening the door to the garage and pressing the ignition button.

The thing is, I've always wanted to be a writer. I've always loved books. That's the main reason I majored in English in college and ended up becoming an English teacher. Naively, I thought that I would actually make an impact on the lives of the kids I teach. Unfortunately, I quickly realized that kids these days are more interested in YouTube videos, Instagram, and Facebook than in reading.

Eventually, about a year ago, I got it in my head that I could write a novel. I've written short stories and some poems and read about a million books on my Kindle. So, of course, I could do it, too, right? Well, that's when the writer's block started up. There are so many different kinds of books that someone can write and I couldn't quite decide on one. Emily, being the practical soul that she is, of course tried to focus my attention on the books that actually make money. She read all these blogs and listened to all these podcasts about self-publishing from indie authors so she is practically convinced that I, too, can be one of these people that make six-figures from writing. Inundated with her enthusiasm, I actually took a six-month sabbatical from teaching, and a significant pay cut, to focus on writing my book. Well, no, not just a book. According to all the self-publishing lore, I have to have at least a novella and two novels in a series before I can start making any real money. Well, a month into my sabbatical, I only have a thousand words on a novel that I have no further interest in writing.

I follow Ava upstairs and decide to take a break from the hectic morning of sledding by relaxing with a good thriller on my Kindle. Ava flips on the television and takes out her tea set. She rarely watches TV a hundred percent of the time, but she likes to have it on in the background as she plays. Given that she's an only child, she's actually quite independent. Unlike a lot of Emily's nurse friends' kids, who need to be entertained every second of every day, Ava really likes her alone time and knows how to keep herself company. The only thing she really requires is that I'm present in the same room. But still, watching her play by herself, makes me a little sad. Even though Emily doesn't particularly love her long shifts at the hospital, I'm not sure that she would do that great as a stay at home mom. She really thrives on energy and excitement, and I have a feeling that she finds spending time with Ava a little boring. She's always pointing out how fun Ava's going to be when she's a little more grown up and how glad she is that we don't have a baby anymore.

I guess that's what they call the irony of fate. It was Emily who actually wanted us to have a baby. We met in college, got married the summer after graduation, but didn't have Ava until we'd been together for ten years. We lived in a two-bedroom house with a mortgage that we could afford, had two used cars, and went on vacation three times a year. I was pretty happy with the way things were. But Emily wasn't. She said that our life wasn't complete without a child and that she would leave me unless we had one. I didn't *not* want to have one bad enough so I thought, what the hell? What's the worst that could happen?

Well, what actually happened was amazing. We had this little creature who I suddenly love more than anyone else in the world. She became the reason that I get up in the morning. I couldn't wait to get home to spend time with her. She became everything that I never knew I needed or wanted. But the experience was completely different for Emily. At first, she struggled with postpartum depression. She barely got out of bed or touched Ava. She said that she regretted having her, that our life was completely different now, and that she wanted to send her back. Her words frightened me, and I scoured the Internet reading horror stories about women whose depression was left untreated and they killed themselves, their spouses, and even their kids. When she finally agreed to go to the doctor and got a prescription, things had slowly gotten better. But five years later, she still doesn't have the same connection to Ava that I do. I know that she feels terrible about it so I agree to get things that will make her happy. She wanted the big house in the best neighborhood, she got it. She wanted two new cars to match our neighbors' cars, she got them. She wanted the large garage that we can't afford to fill and the acre of land that we can't afford to landscape, she got it. But still, there's a void. I know that Emily's jealous of my relationship with Ava. She's jealous that Ava loves spending time with me and that she doesn't feel the same way toward Ava as I do. But there's nothing that I can really do to fix it. I'm not sure that there's anything Emily can do about it either. You simply love someone as much as you can, or you don't. There are no in-betweens.

A few minutes later, I hear a car pull into the driveway of the house next door. Our neighbor Jim owns it, but he moved to Arizona for the winter, and it's now rented to four girls in their early to mid-twenties. The sound of their laughter reverberates around our silent bedroom community. I hear them park their cars in the driveway and gather their bags, slamming the trunk with abandon the way only teenagers or people whose teen years are not that long behind them do. A few seconds later, I hear the jingling of the keys and the bang of the front door hitting the doorframe.

That's my cue.

I head to the kitchen and position myself in front of our quartz kitchen island. This spot gives me the perfect view into their kitchen.

The perfect place from which to watch *her*.

CHAPTER TWO

NOAH

Her name is Charlie Easton. She's twenty-five and twelve years younger than I am. She has been my next-door neighbor since October seventeenth, for almost five precious and wonderful months. Her bedroom window is directly across from my office and one of the reasons why I may not be as productive at writing my novel. She doesn't believe in closing her blinds, and she doesn't own drapes. I don't know much about her except that she's a 911 operator, a fact I learned after finding her on Facebook.

Believe me, I hate being the creepy old guy next door who stares at my next-door neighbor. I never thought that this was who I would end up becoming. But I can't help myself. She's beautiful, charming, and fun in every way that I've forgotten that women can be. At least, she seems to be. She has shoulder-length ash blonde hair that she likes to wear in a messy bun at the top of her head. She wears just enough makeup to accentuate the gorgeousness of her big hazel eyes and red lips. Her skin is tan from spending time outside even in a place that only gets six hours of daylight in the winter.

I do the dishes that I specifically saved for the occasion, so that I can have a good reason for staring into her kitchen. Charlie lives with three roommates, two of whom are probably more attractive by objective standards than she is. But that's the thing about beauty and attractiveness, isn't it? There is no such thing as an objective standard. There are cultural standards, TV and magazine standards, and personal standards. All the men on the street – Levi's, Logan's, Ellie's, and about five other dads that I've spoken with – agree that Jim is one unlucky guy. He had to move out so that we could have the hottest young girls move in. Logan's dad thinks Eleanor is the hottest, and Levi's dad likes Elizabeth and Sarah the best. But it's Charlie who is my favorite. There's something more serious about her, even though she laughs louder than the rest. She has this look about her. It's like she has been through something. Not that she's damaged, just that she has been around. Overhearing a few conversations with her roommates, I also know that she isn't one to put up with shit. She's not a doormat. She's a woman with strong convictions and opinions, and she doesn't let guys run her life. I like that in a woman. It reminds me of the woman I married.

Despite the fact that I'm an old creep who peeks at her through my window, I do not have any bad intentions. I don't have any intentions at all. I'm not going to cheat on my wife. I just like watching Charlie. I like watching her laugh and dance and talk. I like watching her fall asleep to Netflix on her iPad. And most of all, I like watching her have sex.

I've only seen Charlie have sex once. It was a late afternoon. Emily was about to get home. I was upstairs in my office, staring at a blank computer screen. Snow was just starting to fall and the world had this mysterious twilight quality to it, the kind that will make you believe in magic. Suddenly, the door to her room opened. Charlie ran in, laughing and stumbling over her feet. A tall, slender guy about her age followed close behind. He was dressed in his official uniform and, squinting, I could make out the name on his jacket – Officer Silko. I'd never seen him before, but I'd seen his Alaska State Trooper SUV parked outside of her house a number of times.

Charlie and Officer Silko were clearly having a good time. Neither seemed to even be drunk. No one else was home and they were talking so loudly that I could even make out some of the words through the double pane windows. She sat down at her desk and opened her laptop, like she was going to show him something. He leaned over her and kissed her neck. She was facing me. She closed her eyes and breathed in. The guy gently pushed away her hair to one side and ran his finger down her arm. She tilted her head back. A smile formed on her perfect luscious lips. Suddenly, he pushed her up to her feet and knelt down in front of her. She crinkled her nose and furrowed her eyebrows until she finally got what he was doing. Slowly, he unzipped her jeans. They're tight fitting, hugging every curve, and they struggled a little trying to get them off her. After tossing them on the floor, he reached up and ran his tongue along her hip bones. She tossed her head back, letting her hair cascade off her shoulders. With each breath, her breasts rose up and down. Smiling, she bent her knees to try to stop him pulling down her panties, eventually giving in to the passion. He kissed her along the top of her black lace panties, turning her around just enough to show me that the panties were in fact a thong. At this point, I had a raging hard-on. After dropping her panties on top of her jeans, the guy pulled her close to him. He buried himself in her and didn't come up for air for some time. At first, Charlie stood upright, but as she got closer and closer, she leaned on the desk for support. A few moments later, she lay down on the desk completely with her legs up in the air and the guy's ass facing me.

Emily came home abruptly, and I never got the chance to see the rest of what happened. To this day, I don't know if Charlie actually had sex with that guy. All I know is that I haven't seen him again. Maybe he was just a one-night/one-afternoon-stand. Maybe something else happened between them, something that I was unfortunately not privy to. It's likely that I will never know. Much to my own disappointment, that was the one and only time I've ever seen Charlie have sex. Every day, I keep looking and hoping that today will be the day, but unfortunately, it never comes. If she's seeing someone, then maybe they're going to his place. Or maybe they're doing it at night, like regular people, when I'm asleep next to my wife.

I've never cheated on Emily. I've never even come close. I've always loved her, and we've always had good sex. And yet, something about Charlie is pulling me toward her. I've spoken to her maybe a handful of times. I don't know anything about her except that she doesn't like to take down her Christmas lights, and she doesn't think that anyone can see into her windows. But I can't stop thinking about what it would be like to taste her.

CHAPTER THREE

CHARLIE

Nana just got back from the salon and her hair is permed and colored a light shade of blonde. I'm not sure why she lives here in an assisted living facility; she's fully capable of taking care of herself. But she prefers it this way. And it's a relief for me. Here, she has friends, activities, and someone to watch *Murder, She Wrote* with in the afternoons.

While she goes to the bathroom to check on her immaculately perfect makeup, I glance at the nightstand and pick up the top book. It takes me a few moments to realize that it's a journal and that I probably shouldn't be reading it, but by then I'm already too engrossed to put it down.

Dear Julie,

When you first disappeared, your brother-in-law warned me about finding out exactly what happened to you. He went on the searches. He watched the news. He waited by the phone. But somehow all that was still easier on him than actually finding out.

'I don't want to know the details,' James said back when we still talked about you every day. 'You watch all those crime shows – Dateline, 20/20, 48 Hours *– you know what happens to pretty girls who go missing. Nothing good.'*

I know that. Of course, I know that. But I still need to know. If there's a body to find, I want it. No matter how cut up, abused, or decomposed. I have to lay you down to rest next to our mom so I can visit you both.

The winters are getting tough on James. He wants to move away from this icicle as he calls our state. But our mother is in the cemetery, and if we find you dead, that's where I want to put you, too. And if you're ever there, next to her, there's no way I'm ever moving to Arizona. No matter how bad my arthritis gets. No matter how bad my knees ache.

I have to find you, Julie. You're the only family I have left. You're my little sister. You're the little girl I loved when you were born and the teenager I hated when you became rebellious. You're the little girl I resented because Mom always treated you better and bought you nicer gifts. You were the baby, and I both loved and hated that. Then when Mom died, you came to live with me and James, and we formed a whole new kind of bond. You were older then – sixteen. Still a rebel. Still not prone to listening to the rules. Still prone to doing whatever the hell you wanted to do.

Remember when you came to me with tears in your eyes, terrified that you might be pregnant? Terrified that I would kick you out if you were pregnant. I was so mad at you then, Julie. I hated what you've done to your life. Mom and I had big dreams for you. Not just going to a few semesters of community college like me, but a real university. Four years. School was always easy for you. You could've gotten in anywhere. But you and I both knew that it was actually too easy. You got bored and did what most kids who get bored do – drink too much, smoke weed too much.

Remember when I held you in my arms and said that I would be mad at you if you were indeed pregnant, but I would still be there for you and whomever else happened to come along? Well, I meant that, Julie. I meant every word of it. Even if you were pregnant with his baby.

His baby. The thought of that sends shivers through me even now. Jonathan. He started out a friend. James actually met him at the Rite

Aid where he was an assistant manager. He was twenty-seven when we first met him, ten years younger than I was and ten years older than you were. We all fell in love with him, didn't we? Other people wouldn't understand. They'd think that something was off, but he became something of a best friend to all of us. James loved watching football with him. You loved to flirt with him, innocently at first, or so I thought. And I loved talking to him. I loved the way he listened to me. Really listened to me. He hung on every word I said, Julie. He was there for me when you went out to parties you weren't allowed to go to and James went to work the night shift. I was lonely, fat, and married for way too long. But he didn't see that person when he looked at me. He saw me as I once was. A long time ago. He saw me as the twenty-year-old who was outgoing and fun and single, the girl you never really knew. I don't want to admit it – hate to admit it – but I fell in love with Jonathan. Me. Thirty-seven-year-old, five-foot-four inch, two hundred and five pound Holly with swollen ankles and wrists.

Jonathan wasn't the only one there for me. I was also there for him. Through all that garbage with Megan. Man, she really did a number on him, didn't she? Crashed his car and sued him for child support? You knew how much he missed his daughter; you knew how hard it was for him to see her because Megan started an altercation practically every time he came by. Remember how many times she called the police on him? Of course, you do. It was all he could talk about for weeks. And I was there for him. I held his hand through the court cases. I held him when he sobbed on my shoulder.

I don't know if you know this, Julie. I never told you, but you might've heard from Jonathan, but there was one night when he and I made out. I know you'll think I'm a hypocrite. I know you'll think I'm an unfaithful and ungrateful bitch. Maybe I am. But the thing is that James and I hadn't had sex in almost a year. With his back surgeries and my knee surgery, we were just under a lot of stress. We fought all the time. We screamed at each other. We called each other awful things. You know that, of course. You were there for all of it. I know that I didn't tell you this then, but I'm going to tell you this now. I'm sorry about all that, Julie. I'm so, so sorry. You deserved a nice, peaceful place to finish high school. And I couldn't provide you with that. Instead, you got a chaotic, crazy household where people yelled at the top of their lungs, hit each other with canes, and the neighbors called the police. I know you worried about me, Julie. That's why you asked me to press charges against James that one time he left a mark on my face using my cane. I know that you didn't understand then, but when you love each other, Julie, you forgive each other. That wasn't abuse. He was just tired. Exhausted. Worried about his job. He loves me, Julie. I know that. I just don't see his love very often.

But when it came to Jonathan, I hated you, Julie, for what you did. You knew that he and I had a special bond. You knew that we spent evenings together, when James was at work, watching horror movies and talking. You knew he was my special friend. Even if you didn't know what happened that one late July night when James was at work for the weekend and we had the house to ourselves, you still shouldn't have gone after him. I didn't have sex with him, Julie, if that's what you're thinking. I'm not a total slut. We just made out. For close to an hour. He touched my breasts. For the first time in years, I felt like someone actually wanted me. I've thought about that night every night since. That's my happy memory, Julie. That's the place I go to when I need to escape my life.

Then, two months later, when Jonathan started growing distant and telling me that he was hanging out more with Megan, I caught you. You thought I was out grocery shopping. But I forgot my wallet. I came home and I caught you in your room. You were in bed. Being loud. You didn't care who heard you. He was on top of you. You shouted for me to get out. I screamed at you. He apologized over and over. Fuck, I can still hear his sorry ass whimpers.

It took everything in me not to tell James what happened, Julie. He would've kicked you out immediately. And where would you have gone then? Did you ever have sex with Jonathan again after that? I guess I'll never know. I'll never forgive you for this. Jonathan is my one true love and you know that, but I still hugged you and kissed you that day you came to me and said that you might be pregnant.

I didn't tell you this, Julie, but I sort of wished that you were. I loved having Jonathan around, and if you had his baby, then we would be tied to each other forever. Even if I couldn't be with him in any real way, he would still be around. I would still have my crush. My love. And maybe, you would still be with us.

But then, less than a month later, you disappeared. Poof. Vanished. Where did you go, Julie? Come back to me, darling. I miss you more than words can ever express.

CHAPTER FOUR

CHARLIE

'This is intense, Nana,' I say. My grandmother nods.

'Why do you have this?'

'Holly came to visit me this morning and left one of her bags here by accident.'

'So, you read her journal?'

'I wasn't going to. But I picked it up to glance through it and I couldn't put it down. Every entry is like that. Addressed to Julie. Talking about their life together. About all the things that she could've or should've done differently. It breaks my heart.'

I nod and sigh. Julie Reid is the nineteen-year-old sister of my nana's next door neighbor, Holly Donaldson. She disappeared one night about six months ago. It was all over town. Even the Anchorage news ran stories about it. Holly tried to get all the national crime shows interested in doing the story on Julie, but once they found out that she did some drugs and hung out with the wrong crowd, it didn't matter how pretty she was anymore.

The fact that Julie is missing is still surreal to me. I babysat Julie a few times when I was in high school. My only real memory of her is the way her bright yellow pigtails swung from side to side when she danced to Taylor Swift. Does she still like to listen to her? I wonder. Are her eyes still as blue as they were when she was little? Is she still alive?

One thing is for sure though. Julie was pretty. Is pretty. Maybe she's still alive. Maybe she did run away like some people say. There were rumors that she was pregnant, but until they find her body, there won't be any way of knowing for sure.

'Julie always hated the cold,' Nana says, looking out of the window. 'She had these large posters of palm trees, turquoise water, and white sandy beaches all over her room. Once, I talked to her and she told me how much she wanted to move to Florida. She told me about this little island called Siesta Key on the Gulf Coast somewhere and her dreams of living there. She was just going to buy a one-way ticket to Tampa and then take the bus down.'

'That sounds nice.'

'I asked her what she was going to do when she got there.'

'What did she say?'

'She said, she was going to get a job at one of those little crab shacks right on the beach that served drinks with little straw hats. She said, that's when I'm finally going to live.'

I take a deep breath and watch large snowflakes fall from the sky.

'That sounds nice,' I say. 'Really nice.'

'She told me that the day before she disappeared.'

My grandmother lives in an assisted living facility on the outskirts of Wasilla. My parents died in a car accident when I was twelve and I went to live with her then. Even though I was an only child, my parents never really had too much time for me growing up and I spent all available weekends and summers and school vacations with my grandmother. So, after they died, I went to live with her.

When she broke her hip a few years ago and needed more help, it was her idea to go to an assisted living facility. Nana is a firm believer in young people having time on their own and living the lives of young people. She was the oldest of eight kids and always resented the fact that her childhood was 'wasted' on taking care of her younger siblings instead of being a kid herself. So, when she started to need more help, she found this place and announced that she would be moving in a month, catching me completely off guard.

'You are a twenty-two-year-old girl. You have no business wasting your time taking me to my appointments and spending your Friday nights playing Scrabble,' I remember her saying. 'I want you to find a few nice girls to share a house with and have fun, the way that single girls are meant to.'

In addition to raising her younger siblings, Nana also missed out on being young and single, one of the biggest regrets of her life. She got married before she was twenty and was immediately 'strapped with two babies' even when she was still 'a baby herself' – her words, not mine. My grandfather worked as a fisherman and was away at sea for long stretches at a time, leaving her all alone with two babies she resented and no social life whatsoever.

'But I'm not you, Nana,' I would say. 'I love hanging out with you and this house is more than enough space for us to live together and for me to have my own life, if I want.'

Of course, Nana wouldn't hear any of it. 'You can't have a proper social life living with your grandmother, no matter how liberal or enlightened I am. You need to learn to live on your own and not waste your time taking care of the elderly.'

That was pretty much the end of the conversation. Once my grandmother makes up her mind, there are no more ifs, ands, or buts about it. The decision was made and she moved into this assisted living community two years ago. The nursing home is pretty expensive. Nana was a teacher most of her adult life, after her children started school, and did not have much in terms of savings. So, in order to afford this place, she had to sell her house. But the money from the sale was quickly eaten up by the payments for the first two years and she wasn't considered destitute enough to qualify for much public assistance so the rest of the payments came down to me.

I owe $60,000 in school loans. While I'm slowly paying that off, I won't lie; the assisted living facility is a big burden. Nana knows some of the extent of my financial issues, but not all. She does receive her social security check and is very frugal with money, paying what she can toward the monthly rent. But the rest comes down to me and honestly, I don't know how much longer I can keep up with the payments.

Despite the fact that we talk about everything, this is one thing I can't discuss with her. I know how much she wants to stay here and how much she wants me to lead my own life without worrying about her. So, for now, we just remain at this standstill, treading water. Something has to change.

CHAPTER FIVE

CHARLIE

I head to work right after visiting Nana, Julie's disappearance still heavy on my mind. If she told my grandmother that before she disappeared, maybe she did leave on her own. Maybe while the whole state of Alaska is looking for her, she's just sitting on a white beach someplace, drinking margaritas without a care in the world. I don't know her personally – I had only seen her a handful of times – but from what I'd heard, she wasn't the most selfless person on the planet. Her mom died when she was a teen, and she had a troubling relationship with her sister, the extent of which I only found out from the journal. Sex with their roommate? Maybe even a pregnancy? On the other hand, she was nineteen and her sister is married. It's not like she slept with her husband. With all of these thoughts swirling around in my head, I arrive at work. The sun is nowhere to be found, as usual, and darkness blankets the parking lot with familiar blackness. Climbing out of my car, I regret not scraping the snow off a little better because the car door is hard to close. Shit. I slam the door over and over until it finally locks. Even if it's not locked all the way, who the hell is going to steal a car from the police station?

I run through the parking lot to get out of the bone-chilling wind as quickly as possible. I've been working here for what feels like forever. The same nondescript office building. Second floor. Beige walls. Low ceilings. Fluorescent lighting. A typical office – kind of like the one made famous by that show, *The Office*. I never meant to become a 911 operator, and on slow mornings like this one, I wonder how I ended up one. I ended up here the way people end up doing all sorts of jobs they never imagined doing as little kids. My five-year-old niece wants to be a mermaid when she grows up. As far as I can tell, there are currently no openings for mermaids in the greater Wasilla area. But there was an opening for a 911 operator.

When I first started nine months ago, it seemed like it would be a fun job with just enough level of excitement to make the time fly. But within a week, I knew why there were so many openings. The pay is shit. There's no union. The hours are long. The work is exhausting. People don't call 911 just to talk. They don't call to tell you how awesome you are or to share something good that has happened in their life. They only call when they have something bad happen. And that makes for a skewed view of life.

For twelve hours a day, I talk to people going through a crisis. Some are small crises: a kid is missing but fifteen minutes later, the mom finds him at the neighbors' playing Xbox with his friends. Some are average size: a car skidded off the road into a ditch with a whole family inside. Some are big: a husband is threatening his wife with a gun.

I have no idea how today is going to turn out except that it looks like it's going to be a pretty boring day. I sit down at my console and stare at my phone. Melissa, the other operator, winks at me and sends me a video on Facebook of dogs kissing cats. In this line of work, you grab on to any positivity you can. I send her a smiley face and scroll through my emails. I delete the spam and start looking at things to brighten up my room at home.

'Isn't it nice like this?' Melissa asks, taking a sip of her coffee. We're the only ones in the office today. I shrug.

'I sort of prefer when it's a little bit busier.'

'Oh, really?' Melissa's eyes widen in disbelief. 'But now we can chat or just waste time online. Or play *World of Warcraft*.'

Melissa will use any opportunity to play that game. I don't like video games myself, but I appreciate the sentiment. The problem is that I like to stay busy. I don't really have a hobby I can easily do in my spare time. Besides, I'm here to help others. Answering calls from people with problems actually makes time go by much faster.

Suddenly, the phone rings. Melissa sighs. That's my cue.

'Nine-one-one. What's your emergency?'

'Um… my dad,' a faint voice says on the other side. 'My dad killed my mom.'

My heart sinks and my mind starts to race. I introduce myself and ask him for his name, age, and location. I dispatch the officers.

'Tommy, listen,' I keep my voice calm, 'everything's going to be okay. Police officers are on their way. Now, can you tell me where you are? Are you in the front or the back of your house?'

'I'm in the back.'

'Tommy, can your dad see you?'

'I don't know. I can see him.'

A lump forms in the back of my throat. If he can see his dad, his dad can see him.

'What is he doing, Tommy?'

'He's standing over my mom. He shot her. He was mad about her filing for divorce, and he came here and shot her.'

He's fifteen years old, but he sounds like he's five. His voice is shaking in fear.

'Tommy, I want you to do something for me. I want you to get yourself to a safe place. Where are you now?'

'I'm on the back deck.'

'Is there any way you can quietly get down from it and go to one of your neighbors' houses?'

'I guess,' he says quietly. 'But I can't leave my mom.'

'Tommy, your mom is going to be okay,' I lie. In reality, I can't possibly know that. 'But you might still get hurt. I want you to get away from your house. As long as you feel like you can do it safely.'

Tommy doesn't say anything for a few moments.

'Tommy? Tommy?'

My hands turn to ice. Why isn't he responding? Tommy, come back. Come back now!

'He's calling my name,' Tommy says quietly. My mind goes blank. I don't know what to do. I've never felt so helpless before.

'Tommy,' I say his name to collect my thoughts. 'I want you to go. Go now. Whatever you do, don't respond to him. Can he see you? If you feel like he will hear you, don't answer.'

'He's walking around the house. He's walking from room to room,' he whispers. 'But I don't think he can see me.'

'Tommy, you have to go.'

'No, I can't.'

'Why?'

'My legs… they're just not moving,' he whispers. 'Maybe I should just hide in the shed.'

A plausible option. But what if he keeps looking? There's a big possibility that he'll find him there. And then what? No, Tommy has to be okay. Oh, please, let him be okay, I say to myself over and over.

'No, don't hide in the shed, Tommy. He might find you there. Just run. Run!'

I yell at the top of my lungs. Melissa jumps out of her chair.

'Please, Tommy, please run,' I plead.

He doesn't reply. I listen closely. Just out of earshot, I hear someone running. One step. Another step. A deep inhale. A deeper exhale. And then suddenly, the unmistakable sound of a gunshot.

Startled, I jump back and hit my hands on the table. The tops of my fingers throb in pain while the rest of my body goes numb. Melissa kneels over me. I can feel her minty breath on my cheek.

He can't be dead. No, no, no, I say over and over to myself.

'Tommy? Tommy?' I yell into the receiver. 'Tommy, please come back. Please!'

Hot tears run down my face. Still, I don't get a response. The line is dead, but no one hung up.

'Charlie?' A faint voice comes from somewhere far away.

'Tommy!' I explode out of my chair. 'Tommy! Are you okay?'

'He… blah… blah,' he says. Tommy's mumbling through his sobs. I can't make out what he's saying.

'What? He shot you?' I ask.

Tommy gathers his strength. 'He shot himself in the head.'

CHAPTER SIX

NOAH

I sit down at my desk at the usual time this morning with a coffee. According to writers who write a lot, nothing beats word output like butt-in-seat time, meaning that there's just a certain amount of time that you have to spend sitting at your desk if you want to get word output. I have not found this to be the case thus far. As soon as I position myself in front of that white text document on my computer, my mind goes blank. After a few moments of trying to think of something, anything, I can write down, my attention quickly turns to other things.

Out of the corner of my eye, I glance at the picture that Emily made of us for my desk. It's an old one, back from our graduation from the University of Alaska Anchorage. We are both smiling, grasping our diplomas, and embracing one another. At the time, we had been together for more than three years already, but we were as in love as ever. I met Emily during my freshman year. I was in the middle of pledging a fraternity because I wanted to make friends and didn't know how to go about it. Well, a big part of fraternities is alcohol and after an afternoon of drinking way too much, the brothers told all new pledges to climb to the top of the fraternity house and jump off into the snow bank below. The three guys who did it before me did so successfully and without any injuries. Yet, when it was my turn, I managed to slip on some ice and fell awkwardly to the ground, spraining my ankle.

Colton Hays, the big man on campus and the leader of the house, was luckily not too wasted to drive quite yet, so he managed to get me to the local hospital in one piece. While we waited in the emergency room, he saw a cute volunteer who was working the night shift. Her name was Emily Green and no matter how much Colton came onto her, and what moves he put on, she was only interested in the shy guy with the sprained ankle who could do good *Saturday Night Live* impressions of Chris Farley. Luckily, Colton didn't take it too personally because Emily was just another pretty face, but I ended up asking her out.

I took Emily to a local college coffee shop for our first date. We got there around six that evening and stayed until they closed around midnight. We talked about our parents, our siblings, our dreams, and ambitions. We even found out that we actually had a class together. Introduction to Anthropology, a required course, was taught in front of a few hundred students in an auditorium. We both found it insufferable because the professor was a complete bore, though images of the Amazon were quite alluring and we both wanted to travel there one day. Emily was studying pre-med and it had been her dream to become a pediatrician. I laughed and told her that I had barely passed biology in high school, was studying English literature instead and I was going to be a famous writer one day.

After that date, Emily and I were inseparable. We started spending all of our time together, meeting up in the library to do our homework and hanging out in each other's dorm rooms. I never did end up joining the fraternity, mainly because I had realized that I wasn't cut out for that level of partying and drinking. Instead, fueled by gallons of coffee, I'd spend evenings keeping Emily company during her night shifts in the hospital. She was never much of a night person and those shifts were the hardest part of her job. In the end, Emily never did become a doctor because she failed organic chemistry twice. But she did get her nursing license after getting her bachelor's degree and working nights is still the hardest part of the job for her.

I pick up the photograph and look at it more closely. The two smiling kids looking back at me had no idea what they were getting into when they got married and started their lives together. Yet, somehow it was okay. Throughout all of these years, they continued to love one another and have fun with each other. Not everyone can say that about their marriage. There were the summers spent on the water with friends and family and cookouts with Emily's sister, Sarah, and her then-husband Colton Hays. I had the misfortune of introducing the two to each other. Like many women before her, Sarah fell for Colton's charms immediately. And like many other women, she was eventually disappointed that it all ended up being nothing but a façade.

I can't write a word for close to an hour. I try and try. And nothing comes. Managing to squeeze out a paragraph, I then read it and delete it. This is getting pathetic. My mind is on everything and nothing at once. Emily and Ava are downstairs 'letting me work'. Little do they know exactly how unproductive I'm being. I turn on my phone, scrolling through useless Facebook posts from people I haven't talked to in ages. Why do I care if they had another kid? Or went diving in Cabo? I don't know, but for some reason I do and I click on the pictures for a better look. When Facebook gets boring and the posts start to look familiar, I turn my attention to BuzzFeed, *New York Times,* and *Washington Post.* The usual suspects. Not that I really care about the news. I'm hardly a news junkie. I'm just an addict, a consumer of headlines, especially when I have a pressing word count to meet. When I first started my sabbatical, I had lofty goals. Five thousand words a day and two days off for weekends.

Then I'll be done in no time, I told myself. But as hours turned into days and days into weeks, I'm now happy with even a thousand words. Today, I doubt I'll even get that many. Maybe I should be content with two hundred?

I glance out of the window. No one's home. In fact, there's no one home on the entire street. This place is the epitome of a bedroom community. That's why Emily loves it so much. The only problem is that she works all the time and I'm the one who's stuck living in this place of the living dead.

But then, Charlie walks into her bedroom. I immediately perk up and sit up in my chair. She sits down in front of her makeup vanity and lets her hair out of its messy bun. She tosses her head from side to side and I watch as her hair cascades down her back in slow, mesmerizing waves. She picks up an eyeliner pencil and carefully outlines her eyes, adding a dose of mascara for good measure. She then presses out a little bit of liquid foundation onto the back of her hand and uses an egg-like sponge to dab it onto her face and under her eyes. I can only see her in profile and a little bit of her image in the vanity mirror, but she looks beautiful.

I don't really know what it is that I find so enchanting about her. I mean, I know that I shouldn't be spying on her. I know that I need to respect her privacy. And I do not make a habit of this. This is the first time I've ever even looked at a woman in this way besides my wife. Still, I can't force myself to pull away.

I continue to watch as Charlie opens her closet door and rifles through the mess inside. Some clothes are hanging on hangers and some are neatly folded on the various shelves of the fabric hanging closet organizer. But the majority are thrown about inside the closet. The floor is littered with jeans and long sleeve shirts and even dresses. And other pieces are haphazardly flung on top of the hangers. Charlie stands in front of the closet with her arms crossed over her chest, trying to decide what to wear. Eventually, she pulls out a long-sleeve yellow shirt with a v-neck and a pair of skinny jeans.

She takes off her gray pajama pants. The oversized T-shirt that she wears on top hangs so low, I can't quite see if she's wearing panties at all. It looks like maybe she might not be, which makes me even more aroused than I already am. Slowly, my right hand makes its way toward my crotch and over the visible erection that is creating a tent inside my sweat pants.

Before putting on her jeans, Charlie takes off her T-shirt. Now, I can clearly see that she's wearing a pair of very small black lacy panties that are not exactly a thong, but are cut very high, exposing her pert and incredibly toned ass. Unfortunately, Charlie faces away from me so her breasts elude me. Instead, I focus on the way the tight muscles in her back stretch and contract as she leans over to put on her jeans.

With a raging hard-on, it's all I can do to stop me from touching myself. But something in the back of my mind is preventing me from doing it. That will definitely be crossing the line. I will no longer just be watching and observing. No, then I will be doing something that would make this whole situation a lot more real. I adjust my position in my chair, trying to make myself more comfortable. My dick continues to press against the top of my sweat pants and my fingers are practically itching to make the move. I imagine how wonderful it would feel to just pull down my pants and get going, but I hesitate.

Just at that moment, someone clears their throat and my whole world starts to move in slow motion. I know that it's her even before I turn around. My stomach drops and I feel like I'm suspended in mid-air without a hint of gravity in sight. When I finally summon enough courage to turn around, I see Emily standing in the doorway with her arms by her sides and a bewildered look on her face. She doesn't look mad, not yet, just lost.

CHAPTER SEVEN

NOAH

'What are you doing?' Emily asks after a moment. Her brows tighten and her mouth curls up. I can see her processing the situation and the anger and disgust is finally showing up in her expression.

'Nothing,' I say quietly, pressing down on my erection, hoping against hope that it will miraculously go down at a moment's notice. No such luck.

'Are you staring at our neighbor? Are you spying on her?'

'No,' I say.

Of course, it's a lie. I know that. But I don't know what else to say. I have no idea how long she has been standing there, but probably long enough to know that Charlie was topless and had stripped down to her panties. Still, I can't stop myself from denying it. The truth is too awful and painful to admit.

'What the hell, Noah?' Emily asks. Her voice is deeper now, more adamant and demanding. The shocked look on her face is all but gone, replaced by contempt. She crosses her hands over her chest and sticks out one leg in front of the other, as if she's about to tap it on the floor. She's holding a letter in her hand. It has Final Notice in big red letters at the top.

'I mean, is this what you do up here all this time? Instead of writing?'

'No, she just came in. And I happened to look over and then she was changing.'

'And that erection? That just happened?' she asks, placing her arms on the inside of the doorway as if to brace herself for impact.

'This is all biological,' I say. 'It doesn't mean anything.'

Well, that's the first true thing that I've said to her. The erection wasn't planned. It just sort of happened, the way all do. I know that I need to get out of my chair and stop talking back to her in such a defensive manner. I should walk up to her and put my arms around her and tell her that she's the most important woman in my life. I should tell her that she's beautiful and that I don't want anyone else but her. That I don't love and will never love anyone else like I love her. And if I say these things they will be true. Because in reality, Charlie doesn't really mean anything. And it's not that I'm just afraid of losing Emily; it's because I love Emily. Yet still, I can't force myself out of the chair. I can't force myself out of this defensive and completely indefensible position.

'You're such an asshole, Noah, you know that?' Emily says, turning to walk away. 'I mean, whenever Sarah would go on one of her rants about men and how you all suck because you're all cheaters, I always stood up for you. I always brought you up as this example of a man who is committed to me and loves me, no matter what. So, what am I supposed to do now?'

'I do love you, Em. I love you very much. This doesn't mean anything,' I say. 'It's just something stupid… like looking at porn.'

Shit. I should not have said that. Emily does not approve of porn and to liken this situation to that is a terrible mistake.

'Seriously? Are you seriously bringing that up again?'

'No, I didn't mean anything by it. I mean, I didn't do anything, Em. None of this means anything.'

'And yet, here you are doing it. Why are you spying on her if it means so little? And how long has this been going on? I mean, do you think of her when we make love? And how far would this have gone if I hadn't walked in on you?'

I don't know how to begin to answer any of these questions. My mind is going a million miles a minute and one thought is quickly replaced by another, only making the situation even more convoluted. I shake my head, trying to organize my thoughts into some sort of position. But instead of coming up with a valid argument, I collapse into myself, completely overwhelmed by my inability to find the right words to convey what I'm trying to say.

The thing is, I don't know why I'm spying on her except that I've never seen anyone change in front of me before. At first, it was something of a curiosity but then it became more of a habit.

But I don't say this to Emily. Instead, I stand up and try to put my arms around her and tell her that I love her.

'Please, you have to trust me,' I say. 'I didn't mean anything by this. It doesn't have any overarching meaning or anything like that. And you know me, I'm not Colton. He is a womanizer who will stick his dick into anything with breasts. I've never cheated on you, Emily, and I never will. I was just… looking. That's all.'

I watch as Emily takes her time processing all of this. It feels like I'm finally getting through.

'Okay, well, if all of that is true, let me ask you another question,' Emily says. 'Is this the first time you have ever watched her?'

I am not expecting that question. I should say no, that I've watched her before. That I've even seen her with her boyfriend. But instead, I hesitate and hedge my bets.

'You know what, Noah? You can just go and fuck yourself!' Emily says adamantly, turning around and walking away from me. Whatever goodwill I had built up earlier is all but gone.

'Okay, fine,' I explode. 'I've watched her before a few times. She never closes her blinds. Is that what you want to hear? Will that make you feel better?'

Emily walks out. I follow her there. I want to make this right, but as soon as I enter, I realize that I have just made everything worse.

'The reason I came to see you is that we got a final notice on that credit card bill we haven't paid in months. We are more than fifty grand in debt and we can't even make the minimum payments anymore. I've been taking on as much overtime as I can, but I'm getting sick of it, Noah. It feels like I'm the only one who is trying around here.'

'We went on sabbatical before you had to have that gall bladder surgery,' I say. 'I can't really get my job back for this semester anymore, you know that.'

'Yes, I do. But I want to see you doing something.'

'I'm writing.'

'Yeah, not enough.'

She goes into the master bedroom and shuts the door.

We were never in debt as much as we were after Emily's surgery in November. It came out of the blue while we were on a trip near Haines and she had to be airlifted on an air ambulance back to Anchorage. The ride and all the medical expenses cost nearly thirty-five thousand, all of which the insurance refused to cover. Plus, they refused to cover some of the surgery as well because, as luck would have it, we forgot to make a payment the month before.

I pound on the door. 'I'm sorry, okay. I'm really sorry,' I say. But I don't get a response. Emily isn't big on silent treatments and I've never been locked out of our room before. I decide to give it one last shot.

'I know you can still hear me,' I say through the door. 'I've never cheated on you, Emily. I love you. This whole spying thing… it doesn't mean anything. I was just… intrigued. But it's stupid. And I know that, okay? Please come out so we can talk about this.'

I wait outside for some time, but she doesn't make a move to open the door.

*

The air outside hits me like a ton of bricks. The wind is loud and unforgiving. It whistles through my ears, making it nearly impossible to hear the old U2 album I'm playing on my phone. I try to remember the last time I actually went on a run. Was it really October? I turn up the sound and power through. My mind keeps spinning back to what happened upstairs, but I try to focus on the music and the heaviness of my footsteps.

Ten minutes later, I reach the end of the development. The builder bought and cleared a certain number of acres, and the rest of the land stands untouched by civilization. Usually, at least in the summer, when I run on a more regular basis, I just keep going in circles around the development. The paved road is easy on the shins and the calves of a poorly trained runner. But something about today puts me in the mood for an adventure. Maybe it's because it's a rare day when the sun is shining without a cloud in the sky. Maybe it's because I know that it will go down in only a few short hours, with who knows what kind of weather coming tomorrow, and I need to take advantage. Either way, at the edge of the development, I turn from the road toward the wilderness. A small snow-covered meadow stretches out in front of me, and my legs immediately fall deep into the snow. Obviously, it hasn't been plowed, and the snow goes past my calves. Still, I keep going. I can't turn back now. I'm going to go at least as far as the trees.

When I finally reach the trees, my pants are soaked and my whole body is shivering. But I keep on going. Nobody ever comes here in the winter. I don't know where I'm running to except that I have to see what's on the other side. If there's another side. More houses? More trees? The latter is much more likely. This whole state is something like ninety percent wilderness if not more; I'm not exactly up on my US Geological Survey statistics. I check my phone. I'm more than half a mile into the trees and more than two miles away from home. Shocked that I made it this far through the snowdrift, I stop to catch my breath. Looking up at the sky, all I see are the tops of the enormous pine trees coming together in a circle. My head feels dizzy. I lean on a tree to get my bearing straight. Then out of the corner of my eye, I see something red. Metal perhaps? A big part of me doesn't even want to bother walking the fifty feet to check it out. The snow is up to my thighs here, and whatever distance I walk is the distance that I then have to trek back. I extend my neck and narrow my eyes for a closer look.

Is that a car? With each step, I'm more and more certain of the fact that the thing in front of me is a car. An old Dodge Neon, actually. Red. Peeling on parts of it. Almost entirely covered in snow. How the hell did it get here? I follow the faint outline of what must've been the road that it took to get here. From the looks of it, it has been here for quite some time. At least through this winter. There are at least five inches of undisturbed snow on the windows and who knows how many on the top of the windshield. I run my hand over the glass on the driver's side. That's when I see her. The dead girl.

CHAPTER EIGHT

NOAH

The sight of her startles me. I jump back and fall into the snowdrift. My heart races a mile a minute. Did I really see what I think I saw? What the hell is she doing out here? I climb out and wipe the rest of the snow off the driver's window.

Her eyes are staring straight ahead. Her skin is blue from the cold. Her small hands with long fingernails are laying on her lap. There's a big bloody gash on the side of her head. It matches the dried blood on the steering wheel. It must've been an accident. Just a stupid car accident. I pull my cell phone out of my coat pocket and start to dial 911. But what is she doing here in the first place? Why did she drive all the way out here?

Putting the phone back in my pocket, I knock off the rest of the snow from the driver's side. What am I trying to find out? I have no idea. How am I going to explain this to the cops when I do call them? I have no idea. I manage to clear just enough snow off the door to tug on the handle. It doesn't move. I don't know whether it's locked or just stuck. Iced over. After pulling on it over and over, I get to work on scraping off the ice from the doorjamb with a sharp rock that I find on the ground. Finally, I scrape enough ice off so that the door opens.

I take a step back. I've seen dead bodies before, but only in funeral home settings. They were laying down, wearing pounds of makeup, all in an effort to make them look as alive as possible. The girl before me is clearly dead. And not just dead. Frozen. Her skin looks like the flesh of a chicken in the frozen aisle of a supermarket. It's no longer delicate or soft. It's hard and brittle. I'm sure that were I to touch it, it would flake off. But from the looks of it, she was definitely beautiful once. Actually, she still is. Despite the big bloody gash on her forehead, she doesn't exactly look dead. More like she's in a trance. Her skin is so white, it's practically blue. And the dark eye makeup is perfectly preserved. Her eyelashes are quite long as well. Suddenly, I remember that hair and nails keep growing after death. That must explain the really long nails with grown out nail polish.

She mesmerizes me, holding me captive. Despite the cold, her cheeks have retained the fleshiness of youth. She doesn't look like she's a day older than twenty. She could even be as young as sixteen – who knows?

Okay, I've looked enough. I should not have disturbed the scene by opening the car door. I should not be here staring at this poor dead girl. What I should be doing is reporting this to the police. I have to call 911. Maybe Charlie will answer. Maybe this is something that can bring us together. Not like that. More like give me a chance to talk to her about something that's not the weather. Maybe it'll give us a topic of conversation. Excited by this thought, I reach for my phone again. That's when I see it. The bag.

It's a large black duffel bag in the bottom of the passenger seat. How did I miss it before? I shouldn't disturb it. But then I see something sticking out of the top. No, that can't be right. I lean over closer. This time, I'm sure of it. The zipper is slightly ajar and I can just make out a corner of a $100 bill sticking out of the top. Suddenly, the bag no longer looks like something that would carry her clothes and personal belongings. Maybe that's the only money that's in there, maybe not. Either way, I have to find out.

I know that I shouldn't disturb it. But the bag no longer seems like something that's filled with just her belongings. I should call the police. But my phone remains in my pocket. Instead, I debate the pros and cons of reaching over the dead girl and retrieving the bag or digging out the other side of the car and getting it that way. Digging out the passenger side of the car would be a lot of extra work, of course. Tedious hard work. The same work I just did to get to this side. But it does have one particular advantage: I wouldn't have to reach over the dead girl. There would be absolutely no chance that I would touch the dead girl.

I open the driver's door wider and take a deep breath. I plant my feet firmly on the ground. With one hand, I grab on to the steering wheel, careful to keep away from the bloody section. I extend my other arm over the dead girl. My fingers are just a few inches away from grabbing the handle of the duffel bag. My fingers brush against the top, but I can't actually get it. I take one of my feet off the ground and place it inside the doorframe. This gives me a little more space. It doesn't look it, but this car is actually quite spacious inside, especially if you're trying to reach for something in the passenger seat without disturbing the driver. Suddenly, my foot slips, and I land directly in the girl's lap. Her frozen body collapses around me. Her right hand smacks me in the face, and her head hits the steering wheel. Without further ceremony, I grab the duffel bag and push her away from me.

'Holy shit!' I yell as I emerge from the car. 'Holy shit!'

Did that just happen? Did that really just happen? I grab a handful of snow and rub it against the part where I touched her. I've never thought of myself as a particularly squeamish person, but I've never had a dead body collapse on me before. Adrenaline surges through me and I take deep breaths trying to calm myself down. It's going to be okay. It's fine. Nothing really happened, I say to myself over and over.

Finally, when my heart no longer feels like it's going to break out of my chest and go on a run, I reach for the duffel bag. There's no way any of this was worth it. It's probably just her clothes and makeup. Maybe she was moving in with her boyfriend. Maybe she was going on a trip and got into a car accident. I've disturbed the accident scene for nothing, and the cops are definitely going to be upset when they get here. I open the bag.

Oh. My. God.

I stare at the contents. These are definitely not clothes. Or makeup. Or anything that any teenage girl should have in her car. Actually, it's not anything any normal person should have in their Dodge Neon. A Bentley, maybe. But even then.

I run my fingers over the thick stacks of crisp dollar bills. The ribbons around the stacks state that each stack holds $10,000. And there are hundreds of stacks. What the fuck?

What is this little girl doing with this amount of cash in her crappy car? Is this why she's dead? And if so, what the hell is the money still doing here?

I count out ten stacks before I stop. I have nowhere to put them except on the snow, and that's not the best thing to do to cash. So, what do I do now? The right thing to do would be to call the police and report this whole thing. Tell them how I found the body. How I disturbed the body and then show them the money. That would be the sensible thing to do. Or would it?

Maybe I should just take the money. I don't know exactly how much is in here, but I know that it's more than enough to pay off our debts and start a new life somewhere. Or at least, live a proper life here. Emily could stop working all those crazy hours. This money would be enough for me to quit my job and focus on writing full time. We could pay off the mortgage, the cars, student debts. We'd never be in debt again. We could live the life we have always dreamed of. We can put a bunch of it into Ava's college fund; she would be all set up for in the future. This money would change our lives completely. And it's not like the girl needs it anymore. It's not like anyone is looking for it. From the looks of it, she has been here for weeks, if not months, without anyone noticing a thing. I need the money. My family needs the money.

Before I can talk myself out of it, I slam the driver's side door shut, grab the bag, and head home.

I take the long way home. Nothing makes sense anymore and I run lost in a trance. Before I fully realize it, I've run almost a mile out of the way. Even if someone were to decide to look, there isn't a straight line leading to the car in the woods. In a few months, the snow will melt anyway and there won't be any trace of me ever being there in the first place.

In the time I've been gone, darkness has descended. It's even way past the twilight hour. When I reach my house, I open the front door very quietly. We live in such a safe town that we rarely lock it during the day. Before opening it completely, I peek in. Music is coming from the living room, and Ava is dancing in front of the television screen. Emily is nowhere in sight. This is my chance. I open the door, close it lightly behind me so that it doesn't slam. Just as I'm about to make a run for it up the stairs, Emily comes out of the kitchen. My heart drops when I see her. Soaked through to the skin and holding the bag in my arm, which suddenly feels like it weighs triple what it weighed a moment ago, my mind goes blank.

CHAPTER NINE

NOAH

'How was your run?' she asks. There's a detached coldness in her voice. I know that she's still pissed over what happened upstairs, but for now, I just hope she doesn't notice the bag in my hand.

'Fine.' I nod. 'Good.'

I wipe sweat off my forehead. At least, I actually look like I went on a run.

'You look exhausted,' Emily says. My ears start to buzz. I want to extricate myself from this moment as quickly as possible, but I can't think of a single thing to say to do that. So, I just stand here staring at her.

'Yes, it was a hard run,' I say. 'I'm going to go take a shower.'

I step up onto the staircase to head upstairs when Emily says, 'Aren't you going to take off your coat and shoes?'

I look down at my wet coat and soaking shoes. 'Yes, of course,' I say awkwardly. The stairs are carpeted, and we never walk in shoes upstairs to avoid getting everything muddy and dirty. I quickly toss the bag next to the bench and take off my sneakers without untying the shoe laces. My socks get soaked from stepping on the slush that I brought in, but my thoughts stay focused entirely on the bag. She hasn't asked me about it yet. Why? Did she not notice it or is she just waiting for a better time?

I glance over at Emily as I unzip my coat. She's still standing in the hallway, wearing an apron and holding a rolling pin in one hand.

I flash her a forced smile, but she doesn't reciprocate. Instead, she just continues to watch me like a suspect. She's waiting for something. But, what?

'Well, I'm going to go upstairs now,' I announce, pushing my sneakers under the bench. I hope that she turns around and goes back to the kitchen, so I can take the bag upstairs, but she doesn't. I stand at the bottom of the stairs for a moment, trying to decide what to do next. I can't leave it here in case she looks inside. And if I take it with me, then she'll definitely notice it, if she hasn't seen it already.

'What's with that bag?' Emily asks.

'Oh, this?' I grab it by the handles and press it close to my body. 'Um, nothing. Just something I found in the garage.'

'Really? I've never seen it before.'

I search my mind for a possible explanation. And then it hits me.

'Actually, I got it from school. I just have some school papers in it.'

'Uh-huh,' Emily says, clearly not convinced.

I don't want to over-sell it. I've said what it was and if I keep talking I will just make it seem even more suspicious.

'When were you in the garage?' she asks. 'I didn't hear the door.'

Shit. My heart sinks. My fingers grow numb, and I feel like I'm just about to drop the bag.

'Oh, I don't know. Why?' I say as confidently as I can. I'm about to take a step upstairs when Ava comes out of the kitchen.

'Hey, Daddy!' she says. 'You're back.'

'Yes, I am,' I say. 'Let me just take a quick shower and I'll be right down.'

'Your bag is wet, Daddy,' she announces, pointing her index finger at me. 'It's dripping.'

My hand tightens up and I suddenly feel like I can't take in a single breath.

'Oh, yes, you're right.' I lift the bag higher and wrap my arms around it. 'I'm sorry about that.'

I stare at Emily and wait for her to ask me why the bag is soaking wet if I just got it out of the garage. But she doesn't say a word. I take a deep breath and head up the stairs.

I know that she doesn't believe me. I hardly believe myself. But I don't really have any other options. I'm just relieved that she hasn't pressed me further about it.

When I get upstairs, I hide the duffel bag under the couch in my office. It's a place that Emily would never look. Then I go to our master bedroom, undress, and jump into the shower. I hope that she doesn't bother looking through it, but I rush through the shower in less than three minutes just in case.

Luckily, when I emerge, dressed in sweats, there is no sign of Emily upstairs. I close the door to my office on the way back down and turn off the lights just in case. Emily hands me a slice of pizza and I occupy myself with Ava and try to avoid eye contact with Emily while we chat. I can feel her judging me, scrutinizing me. I have never lied to Emily before and, frankly, I'm not very good at it. After eating two slices and playing with Ava for a bit, I make the excuse that I still have some writing to do.

I do have writing to finish up, or rather, start, but I have one more important thing to do. Count the money.

I try to lock the door to my office and then remember that I had forgotten to fix the lock. After making sure that it's closed tightly, I dump the contents of the bag onto the floor. Each stack is made up of nearly perfect bills. Not a single wrinkle. Not a single bent corner. I've never seen money straight from the printer, but this is probably what it would look like. I run my fingers along the ribbon with the numbers $10,000. I make $42,000 a year plus benefits. Let's call it an even $50k. Emily makes $53,000 without overtime. With overtime and benefits, it's probably close to $77,000. Our total take-home salary is around $127,000. Not bad, actually. Lots of people live on a lot less. But somehow the $4500 mortgage and the payments for two new cars make it a tight budget.

I count up thirteen stacks. Our annual salary. Right here in my hands. From the looks of what is leftover, it's a drop in the ocean.

I count the rest of the stacks, piling them in blocks of ten. When I only have a few left, I see the blood. Smudges of dark red, almost brown, around the edges of some of the stacks. The blood made its way from the top bill all the way to the bottom, marking each one. My heart skips a beat. And then another beat. I should call the police. Tell them about the body and the money. I should hand it over to the cops, but even as I'm thinking it, I continue to count it, knowing I'm not going to call the cops anytime soon.

When I'm done, I look around the room. Almost the entire floor is covered with little towers of cash. There are twenty-two of them in total. I do the math in my head. Not believing the answer, I do it again. And again.

No, this can't be.

Two point two million dollars? Is that right? There is over two million dollars lying on the floor of my office. No wonder that stupid bag was so fucking heavy.

'Hey, Noah, I just wanted to—' Before I get the chance to answer, the door bursts open.

CHAPTER TEN

NOAH

'What. The. Fuck?' Colton's eyes widen to the point that they practically pop out of their sockets. His mouth drops open.

'Close the door,' I say, but Colton just stays put as if he's bolted to the floor. I run to the door and close it behind him.

'What are you doing here?'

'What the hell is all this, Noah?'

I try to think of even one possible explanation that I can offer. Unfortunately, there isn't really any good reason to have £2.2 million in cash piled up in stacks in your office.

'Is that blood?' He leans down, picking up one of the stacks.

'Um… yes,' I mumble.

'Noah, you better start talking.'

Of all the people to walk in on me with this cash, why did it have to be my brother-in-law? Or rather ex-brother-in-law since he and Emily's sister, Sarah, just recently got divorced. Colton and I aren't really friends. We don't have very much in common. He likes football, getting drunk at barbecues, and hunting. He loves to say shocking and inappropriate things and then laugh when someone gets offended. He calls his garage his man-cave and has appointed it with a large television screen, a black sectional leather couch, and two micro fridges at either side filled with beer, as if it's too much of a trek to walk a few feet to the real refrigerator. I have little interest in any of those things. Unlike Colton, I consider reading a hobby and don't particularly care for sports.

'Noah?' Colton crosses his hands across his chest. His large broad shoulders disguise the fact that he often skips leg day at the gym. Unlike me, Colton is a big guy who can even be described as fat were it not for the muscled physique he had developed in his high school days.

'I don't know what you want me to say.' I stall for more time.

'What the hell is all this? Where did you get it?'

There is no good explanation for any of it, except for the truth. I take a deep breath and lay it on him.

'So you just found a dead body? In the woods?' Colton repeats what I'm saying. It's one of his many annoying tendencies.

'And the dead girl…?' he asks.

'She didn't mind.'

'But you didn't know what was in the bag before you pulled it out?'

'How the hell would I know that, Colton? I just saw it after I saw her. But when I found the money, I didn't really know what to do.'

'So, you kept it?'

'Yes, I kept it. What's the big deal?'

With Colton, it's always better to be on the offensive. I've learned that from my five years of being his brother-in-law.

'No, that's a good point, of course. I mean, this is a shitload of money, Noah.' Colton starts to laugh. His voice is low and bellowing. He's so loud that I get scared that it'll attract Ava and Emily upstairs.

'Keep your voice down.'

'Aren't you going to tell Emily?' Colton asks. His eyes are judging me. Analyzing me. Emily and Sarah are sisters so I know of every fight that Colton and Sarah went through in their turbulent marriage. And I'm fairly certain that he's pretty familiar with all of our issues as well.

'Of course I will. I just have to figure some things out first.'

Colton crouches down next to one of the stacks. His phone is in a holster at his hip as if it were a gun. Construction workers at least have a good reason to wear it like that. But, Colton? He's a solar salesman.

Kneeling over one of the stacks, he points to the blood. I shrug. I don't have a good answer or solution to that. Yet. So far, my plan is to just wash it off.

'Two point two million,' he says, standing up. 'That's a lot of money, buddy.'

I hate the way he calls me 'buddy'. It's meant as a joke, of course, so I have no right to get offended. But Colton's the type of guy whose jokes are really kernels of truth. He tells you what he really thinks of you and then is too much of a coward to admit it so he disguises it as a joke. I'm a high school teacher. I'm very familiar with this line of defense.

'I can't imagine that no one's going to miss it.'

'No one has missed it yet.'

'Really?'

'That girl has been in that car for a long time, and no one has come looking for her. I'm not sure anyone knows that it's out there.'

'Well, this is fucking exciting, man.' Colton's eyes light up as he slaps me on the back. 'Have you thought about what you're going to do with it?'

'Honestly, I don't know. I've just been too busy worried about hiding it so far.'

'Well, here, I'll help you.'

I'm surprised by Colton's helpfulness. He's not the type to even assist the girls in carrying a plate out for the barbecue, let alone lifting a finger to mow the lawn. Colton's kind of a lazy bastard, and if he's helping with this, he must think there's something in it for him.

Of course, there has to be. He knows exactly how much money I have. He knows exactly where I got it. If I want him to stay quiet about this, I have to pay him. A kind of thank you disguised as a bribe. But if I'm going to pay him then I'm going to make him earn it.

'So, I was thinking…' I say, making sure that the uncertainty in my voice comes through loud and clear. 'Maybe I shouldn't have taken all of it. Maybe that would be too suspicious if the cops find her body and they expect her to have the money. Plus, I left a big mess in the snow around the car.'

'What are you getting at, Noah?' Colton asks when we get the last of the bills back into the bag.

'Um, maybe, I should put the money back.'

'What? Are you crazy?' Colton jumps back. 'You can't do that!'

'Well, no, not all of it. Just some of it. Just in case someone does come looking for it.'

'You mean, in case someone knows that she's supposed to have money on her and she doesn't?'

'Exactly.'

CHAPTER ELEVEN

NOAH

While Colton and I continue to argue about how much money we should take back, I think of the dead girl and the blank expression she had on her face. She was so young when she died, just starting out in life. She was just on the verge of becoming someone. She may have made some bad decisions along the way, but I have no idea what kind of things she struggled with that led to those bad decisions. Besides, despite whatever kind of business she was involved with, she didn't deserve to die the way she did. And she definitely doesn't deserve to continue to lay frozen in a car while her loved ones search for what happened to their little girl.

My mind goes to Ava and how I would feel if she were that age and found herself in a similar situation. The dead girl was someone's little girl once and I'm sure that person is still out there somewhere wondering what happened to her. What would I want if that were Ava? I'd want the person who randomly found her to not be so greedy and just take the money and keep quiet about the dead body that came with it, but to call the police and tell them everything.

I hadn't done anything wrong yet. I mean, it was wrong to take the money, but I can still return it. I can still turn back the clock. I can still make it okay. I have a good job. I don't need the money. Yes, I want it, but that didn't make it right to take it. I shake my head at my own impulsive decisions. Besides, who knows? Maybe the money is cursed. Not by some supernatural force, but maybe it's just plain old bad luck. I mean, I took the money and Emily caught me with the bag. And then Colton showed up out of the blue. He's the last person I'd want to share this news with, and if it were up to me, he would be the last person to know. And yet, here he is, intertwined in something he has no business being involved in.

I pace around the room, trying to decide what to do as Colton sits comfortably on the couch at the far end. He has spread out, taking up a lot more room than he should. How can he be so unfazed by this? How can he just accept this as if it's a completely normal thing to come to your brother-in-law's house and find him with a bag of stolen cash? He is either supremely confident or a complete idiot and at this moment I'm not sure which one he really is.

'Can you stop doing that?' he asks after a moment. 'You're making my head hurt walking back and forth like that.'

I sink into my office chair and try to gather my thoughts. Pacing around the room like a caged animal is making them rush around in my head a mile a minute, jumping from one thought to another. I take a deep breath and try to calm down.

'What's wrong?' Colton asks.

'I'm not sure if I can keep the money,' I say after a moment. The expression on Colton's face falls for a moment as he probably considers what this means for him. But his eyes remain fixed on me. Suddenly, I see it. There's a deadness in them, something that is unwavering.

'What are you talking about?' Colton asks carefully. He isn't rushing to change my mind. He's taking his time, maybe trying to figure out what approach would work best. But I don't have time for his games.

'I just keep thinking about the girl. I mean, she's so young. And she has been stuck, frozen, in the car, for God knows how long. I'm sure she has a family. And I'm sure that they're looking for her.'

'And if she doesn't?' Colton asks.

I ignore his question. 'I mean, what if this were Ava? Twenty-year-olds do lots of stupid things. She probably had no idea that her decisions would lead to her death. And if my daughter were dead and someone found her, I'd like for them to come forward. To notify the police. So I could put her at rest.'

Even imagining a hypothetical situation that involves Ava being in the place of the dead girl sends chills through my whole body.

'But the thing is, it's not Ava, Noah. Besides, if you found her, then maybe someone else will as well. Why do we have to be the ones to report her missing?'

I stare at him dumbfounded.

'Because I'm the one who found her. And, no, I'm not sure that she's so easy to find because she has been there for some time and so far, no one has found her. I was the first person to come along.'

I can see that I'm getting nowhere with this. But I don't need his permission. I just need to decide once and for all if I'm actually going to keep the money. Keeping the money, even a part of it, would probably mean that we can't contact anyone about her whereabouts.

'What about an anonymous tip?' I ask. 'Can't we just call the cops from a pay phone and tell them about her?'

Colton considers this option for a moment.

There's a knock on the door and before I can answer, it swings open. My heart skips a beat as I frantically look around the room to try to make sure that the money is out of sight.

'Just wondering if you want to have something to drink? Coffee? Tea? A beer?' Emily asks. I can't tell if she's spying on us or genuinely being hospitable because my mind is going a mile a minute.

'I'm good,' I say way too quickly.

'Yeah, I'm fine too,' Colton says after a moment of hesitation.

'Suit yourselves,' Emily says with a shrug, looking at us both a little longer than I find comfortable. 'If you change your mind, we have fresh baked cookies downstairs.'

'That sounds delicious,' Colton says.

My heartbeat doesn't slow down one bit until Emily closes the door and I hear her go back down the stairs. Only then do I let out a sigh of relief.

'You okay?' Colton asks. 'You look like you've seen a ghost.'

I can't believe he's so calm about this. I nod and steer the conversation back to what we were originally talking about.

'I guess we could do an anonymous tip,' Colton says. 'They can still track calls that come from pay phones. We'd have to be very careful to make sure that there are no cameras around and wipe down the phone.'

I nod.

'But the thing is,' Colton says after a moment, 'I haven't seen a pay phone in ages. Have you? I mean, we can try to find one, but it's not the nineties anymore.'

Dammit. He has a point there. Come to think about it, I haven't seen a pay phone myself anywhere for who knows how long.

'Burner phone?' I ask, as if I know anything more about burner phones besides what I've seen in crime movies on television.

'Maybe.' Colton shrugs.

We sit in silence for a while. Besides reporting the whereabouts of the girl, there is a more pressing issue at hand. What to do with the money?

'I still don't feel right taking the money,' I say after a moment. I don't have a good solution, but it feels good just to voice this concern.

'Why?' Colton asks.

'It doesn't belong to us. It's probably dirty. Actually, it's most likely dirty,' I say.

'Of course, it's dirty,' Colton says with a shrug. 'No regular person has that much cash just laying around.'

'So? Isn't that a bad thing?'

'Perhaps. But isn't the fact that it's dirty also make it a good thing?'

'How?' I shake my head at his backward reasoning.

'Well, it's probably drug money, right? Well, that means that the people who it belongs to don't actually have any real ownership to it, right? I mean, what they're doing is illegal. So, taking it isn't a big deal. It's not like you're stealing it from some orphans or something.'

I think about that for a moment. In his own twisted way, Colton definitely has a point. The bad guys don't have any real ownership of the money since they shouldn't have it in the first place. So why not take it?

'Doesn't that make sense?' Colton asks.

I shrug. 'Yes, I guess. But the thing is that I don't know how I feel about living my life on drug money in the first place. Plus, I just have a bad feeling about it.'

'What do you mean?'

'Maybe the money is bad luck. I mean, look, the girl took the money from whomever it belonged to – I doubt that she was some large drug lord at her young age – and then she ended up dead. Doesn't that mean something?'

Colton starts to laugh. It begins as a low-lying chuckle originating somewhere in his stomach and quickly morphs into a deep bellowing laugh that consumes the whole room.

'Why are you laughing?'

'The thing is, people are always trying to find reason or rationality or order in the world. That's just what we do as a species. Something bad happens to us over and over, it must be because of this person or phenomenon or something you did in the past. But that's all bullshit, Noah. Things just fucking happen. There's no rhyme or reason. People make their own luck. The reason why successful people are successful is not because they're luckier than other people, but because they aren't fazed by failure. They believe they're entitled to whatever the world has to offer and they go out and get it.'

'I don't see what that has to do with this,' I say after a moment.

'This money isn't cursed. The girl may have taken it and then she drove down the wrong road, got into an accident, and died. Or maybe someone who she crossed followed her and killed her. But that has nothing to do with the money being bad luck. It just happens the way everything else in the world happens.

'I mean, look at what happened today. You found the money, brought it home, and then I just happen to come by,' Colton says, as if he's able to read my mind. 'I wouldn't call that good luck, just something that happened. In my favor.'

I look away, shaking my head and glancing out of the window. Or my bad luck, I want to add. I hate to admit it, but he does have a point. I'm not a big believer in luck or superstitions anyway, but I've never been in this situation before either. Maybe it comes more into play when you start making decisions that lead you further to the edge than the normal person.

'Look, putting the money back isn't going to solve anything, right?' Colton asks after a moment.

'We could put the money back and report the missing girl.'

'And where do you think all the money is going to go then?'

I shrug. I have no idea.

'The police are going to take it. They take everything into evidence that they find at crime scenes. If it's money, then they just keep it.'

'So?' I ask.

'So? Why do they need more money? This is a pretty wealthy town and they get paid six figures a year. This isn't some cash-strapped place in the lower forty-eight with too much crime and not enough cops. But you… you could really use the money. It could change your whole life.'

I hate to admit it, but he's right again.

'I mean, look at all the hours that Emily works. I mean, I know she enjoys her job, but I also know that she hates working nights. And with this money, she wouldn't have to. She could stay home and spend more time with Ava. That little girl is growing up way too fast, and you know it.'

Dammit, Colton is one hell of a salesman. I know he's bullshitting me, manipulating me, but he's also telling the truth.

'And what about you? I know that you aren't the biggest fan of being a teacher. You just do it for the money, right? And what kind of money exactly? The pay is total shit and the kids you teach couldn't care less about anything that you have to say.'

Fuck you, Colton, I want to say. But in the back of my head, I know that he's right.

'How much would this money change your life, Noah? Imagine what you can do for your family with it. You could pay off your house and put money away for Ava's college education. You can finally take a vacation. When was the last time you went away anywhere? You could even stop working, or at least cut back. Maybe spend all of your time writing, like you want.'

I shake my head. Somewhere deep inside of me anger is starting to build. Of course, I want those things. And Colton knows it. But that doesn't make it right. Does it?

'Listen, why don't we just go back to the original plan?' Colton asks.

'What's that?'

'Why don't we just return some of the money? That way if, no, when the girl is found, she has it with her. And we just take some of it. Who will ever know how much money was supposed to be there, right?'

CHAPTER TWELVE

CHARLIE

I arrive back at work a hero. Everyone congratulates me for saving Tommy's life. In addition to being mad at his wife filing for divorce, Tommy's dad just lost his job and he couldn't bear the thought of having his kid grow up poor. To some people, being poor is a fate worse than death. I tend to think that having your dad kill your mom and then go on a hunt for you would be a lot worse. As I sit down at my console, I feel jittery. I don't want to take the first call. But I suck it up and answer. It turns out fine. Just some gunshots heard in the area that the cops are sent to investigate. Turns out to be nothing at all. The second call is for an accident out on Highland Avenue. A car skidded on the ice and hit a chain-link fence. Again, no big deal. No major trauma. The driver just hit his head on the steering wheel. But didn't even request that an ambulance be sent.

On my break, I buy myself a can of Sprite. I try not to drink too much soda, but sometimes I just have to have one. The clear liquid with cold bubbles feels refreshing running down my throat. I decide to splurge and get myself a bag of salt and vinegar chips. I have a salad waiting for me in the refrigerator, but adrenaline is still coursing through my body from the first two calls. That's the thing about this job. Sometimes, it's a simple accident. And sometimes, it's Tommy. The worst thing is that you never know what you're going to get when you sit at the console. I crunch on a few chips to calm myself down. Food isn't supposed to be a thing you turn to for comfort, but it certainly does its job, doesn't it? Halfway through devouring the bag, I feel a sudden wave of relief sweep over me. Everything's going to be okay. I haven't had a Tommy call for months. So, common sense would say that a Tommy isn't going to call again for a long time. I sit back down at the console and wait for the ring.

'Nine-one-one. What's your emergency?'

'Um… I need the police to come to my house,' a calm female voice says. She doesn't sound like a smoker, no heavy breathing, or rushed breaths here. Her voice is high. I doubt that she's older than thirty.

I ask for her name and location. But before I dispatch the officers, I need more information.

'What is your emergency, Nancy?'

Using first names is supposed to create better contact between the callers and us. It's one of the few training instructions that I got before I started answering the phone.

'I just need someone to come,' she says very calmly. 'It's hard to explain.'

Her words are very deliberate and quiet. It's like she's talking in slow motion.

'Are you okay, Nancy? What happened?'

A lump is forming in the back of my throat. Usually, I can't get callers to calm down enough for me to get what they're trying to tell me. But not Nancy.

'I did something bad.'

My hands go numb. My fingers are slamming on the keyboard, but I can't feel them pressing even one letter.

'Okay, Nancy. I'm going to dispatch the officers to your location right now. But you have to tell me a little more about what happened.'

'They were just being so loud,' she says quietly. 'Why did they have to be so loud?'

'Who?'

'My children.'

My heart sinks and my mind immediately flashes back to that hospital room a few years ago, when they laid my stillborn baby into my arms. I was in college. I barely knew the guy who got me pregnant. The whole thing was an accident, but deciding to keep her wasn't. I didn't have any money or much in the way of support except my grandmother, but I knew that I could do it. I knew that I wanted her. But life had other plans.

'Hello?' The woman's voice brings me back to reality.

What the hell did you do, Nancy? I want to scream into the phone. But I have to remain calm. I need her to talk to me.

'The officers are coming, Nancy. Where are your children?'

She doesn't respond. A part of me thinks that this might be a prank. All 911 operators have been there. We've had people call us with no emergencies whatsoever. Someone taps someone's bumper. They know they need to exchange insurance information and call the cops to document the scene, but they don't know that they need to call the non-emergency line. And then there are those who call about nothing at all. They've smoked too much weed and who knows what else, start tripping and then call to chat. Or complain.

'My husband should not have said that,' Nancy says. Her voice is dead calm. Absent. It's like she's there, but not there.

'What did he say, Nancy?'

She takes forever to respond. I repeat the question.

'He said that I was a bad mother. But I'm not a bad mother. I love them.' I've never talked to someone like this before. My hands tremble. The calmer she is, the more anxious I become. I tap my foot on the floor, but it doesn't do much.

'I'm sure you're a wonderful mother, Nancy.'

'Don't patronize me,' she says quietly.

She isn't my typical caller. I don't talk to very many people who know the meaning of that word.

'I'm sorry, I didn't mean anything by that, Nancy. Where are your children now? Are they okay?'

'It's okay, I know you didn't mean it. It's just your job,' she says in the same deadpan way. 'My kids are here. In the house.'

'Are they okay?'

'They're great. They're the best they've ever been.'

Something about that statement is not reassuring in the least. I'm not getting anywhere with this line of questioning. Police officers should be there soon. I need to give them more info.

'Do you have any guns in the house, Nancy?'

'None, except the one in my hand.'

My heart sinks even lower.

'Why do you have a gun, Nancy?'

'Because I needed it.'

'You're going to have to put it away when the cops arrive.'

'Or what?'

Or what? They'll blow your head off, that's what, I want to scream. But I need to remain calm. I need to take whatever the hell Nancy's on. Then it hits me!

'Nancy, have you taken any medication today?'

'About a bottle of Xanax. I'm feeling very tired right now.'

'Yes, I can imagine.'

'I think I'm going to go to sleep now.'

'No, Nancy. Please stay on the line.'

'Why?'

I don't have a good answer to that. I'm at a loss for words.

'Will you put the gun away, Nancy?' I pivot instead. 'The cops should be there soon and your gun will frighten them.'

More like scare them into shooting you, but I don't go that far into the explanation. I hear footsteps on the other line.

'My mom's here,' Nancy says.

'How do you know that?'

'I can see her from my window.'

Oh my God. Her mom's going to walk into an ambush, and I have no way of warning her. Stopping her.

'Nancy, did you put the gun down?' I ask, trembling with my whole body.

'What's wrong, Nancy?' I hear a deep, frightened female voice through the phone. 'What did you do?'

'Alex wouldn't stop, Mom. He just kept saying what a bad mom I was,' Nancy says. Her voice goes up a bit in tempo, gets a little rushed, but not by much. The Xanax makes it impossible for her to exhibit any emotions.

'Where's Peter, Nancy? Where's Olivia?' I hear her mom push past her and disappear somewhere into the house.

'He wanted to take them away, Mom. You know how much I love them. I can't have them go live with him,' Nancy says. She's no longer holding the phone to her face, but I can still hear her slow diction and her struggle to get out each word. The deliberateness of her speech is the scariest thing I've ever heard.

'And her. He left me for her,' Nancy continues. 'And now he wants her to raise our kids.'

Somewhere in the distance, I hear police sirens. I've warned them about the gun in her hand and told them what I know, which isn't much.

'He said I was a drunk and an addict,' I hear Nancy say. 'He said all these horrible things today in court, Mom. They aren't true. But no one believed me, Mom. Not even my own lawyer.'

A loud, piercing scream startles me, making me knock my can of Sprite from the table. This scream is quickly followed by another and another followed by a cacophony of sobs. Somewhere in between the devastating cries, I hear Nancy's mother say the kids' names over and over.

'I'm going to go to sleep now,' Nancy says and hangs up.

I sit back in my chair. I don't know the details of what happened to Peter and Olivia, and yet I do. Every atom in my body tells me that they're dead. I grab the trashcan under my desk and throw up.

CHAPTER THIRTEEN

NOAH

It takes us a while to decide on the amount that we should return to the car with the dead girl. Two hundred thousand seems like a lot to give away and ten thousand is too little. After going back and forth for a while, Colton and I finally settle on fifty grand. Fifty thousand dollars doesn't sound like much out of over two million, but it's a big enough amount in case someone comes looking for her and the money. Hell, that's my annual salary.

I insist on keeping the money in the same bag. It came from the car and I don't have any desire to keep part of that scene anywhere near me or my family. So, this decision to return the money will also serve two purposes. Get rid of the bag in the best way possible by returning it to where it came from and filling it with its original contents. Who cares if it's not the full amount? No one is going to be any the wiser.

'What about fingerprints?' Colton asks, bursting my newly inflated bubble of self-assuredness and competence. Fingerprints. Of course. I touched practically every stack with my bare hands, to say nothing of the bag itself. How could I be so stupid?

'How can we get rid of them?' I ask. Watching all those episodes of *CSI* and *Law and Order: SVU* should've better prepared me for this, but frankly I'm at a loss. Googling the problem is the only way I can think of to get the answer, though that brings up other issues: how do I get rid of that question from my computer? A question for another time.

'Apparently, the ability to lift prints in the first place depends on the type of surface they're on,' Colton announces with authority. He knows even less than I do about all this, but that doesn't stop him from marching forward with an arrogant air.

'Glass, tile, lacquered furniture, and smooth metal are pretty easy to get prints off. Organic surfaces like tree leaves and feathers are more difficult. Human skin and rough or textured surfaces are even harder. Oily, rusty, or dirty surfaces are virtually impossible.'

'Tree leaves, got it. Now, what about money?' I say.

'There's no need to get testy,' he says, scrolling. 'It just says that paper, drywall, leather, and dashboards are more involved.'

'More involved, but not impossible,' I mutter to myself. Well, that was really helpful. I push him out of my chair and scroll back to the first page of Google results. Somewhere, down at the bottom, I find a link to a forum where someone is asking about getting rid of fingerprints on some cash being sent through the mail. There's a long string of answers, most of which suggest to simply take a T-shirt or some sort of rag and smudge the fingerprints. There's something about them being smudged that makes it impossible for the investigators to lift prints.

Colton reads through the advice as I run off to the bathroom, grab a pair of Emily's yellow toilet cleaning gloves and a towel.

'What are you doing?' Ava says, startling me. Her high, innocent voice scares me so much that I nearly drop everything. I glance down at my hands.

'I just spilled something in the office.'

'Mom! Dad spilled something in the office,' she announces happily. She's not tattle-telling, just reporting the latest news. It's not that I don't help Emily clean the house, it's that I don't really know how to use the millions of cleaning products that lurk in our cabinets. If it were up to me, I'd just clean off water stains from the bathroom mirror with some water and a paper towel.

'I'm fine,' I yell over the stairs, hoping that she won't come up here. 'It's nothing.'

'Are you sure?' Emily asks. 'You don't want to leave a stain on the carpet.'

'No, just some water,' I yell. 'It's fine.'

I turn to Ava.

'Go have fun with Mommy, honey. Me and uncle Colton will be down in just a minute.'

After giving her a warm hug, I watch her descend the stairs and disappear around the corner.

'What took you so long?' Colton asks. The money is back out on the floor, laid out in neat little stacks.

'Ava. It's fine,' I mutter. 'Go stand by the door, just in case.'

I pull on the gloves and get to work. I count out fifty thousand and carefully wipe the outside of the ten-thousand-dollar stack.

'You think I need to wipe the individual bills?' I ask.

'I have no idea.'

I think about it for a second. I haven't removed the wrap before. So, I don't have any of my fingerprints on the inside of the stack. After going back and forth, I decide to only wipe the stack on the outside and a little bit around the edges.

Once the fifty grand is ready to go and the duffel bag is wiped clean, we put the rest of the money back under the couch.

'Colton, do you want to stay for a late lunch or an early dinner?' Emily asks as soon as she sees us on the stairs.

'Am I that pathetic, Em? Just because I'm divorced, you know that my phone still works, right? That I'm still capable of ordering takeout?'

Emily smiles.

'Nah, actually, I'm meaning to steal your husband away for a few,' Colton says, grabbing the duffel bag away from me. He has a plan. Colton's the constant salesman. 'I'm borrowing some of Noah's rarely used weights here, and we're actually heading out to the gym.'

'To the gym?' Emily laughs.

I shrug. Colton's got us into this, so he'll have to get us out.

'Didn't you just get back from a run?' she asks. Apparently, Colton was not aware of this little tidbit of information. But that doesn't faze him one bit. The lies just keep flowing as easily as they had before.

'Well, he's not going to work out. I just joined and I've been meaning to show him the steam room.'

'Oh, that's nice. You did say you were really sore from the run,' Emily says.

'Yep.' I nod, giving her a kiss on the forehead. 'See you two later.'

I hug Ava, inhaling that magical aroma that she emanates from the top of her head. She's not a baby anymore, but she still smells just as sweet.

'Don't eat too much sugar,' I say to Ava as I put on my boots.

'Sugar!' she yells at the top of her lungs and sprints back to the kitchen island for another cookie.

'No!' Emily catches her in time. 'Dinner first.'

'Can I have one for the road?' Colton asks, grabbing a big yellow cookie and jamming it into his mouth.

'You mean right before you head to the gym?' she jokes.

'Well, you know, a guy's gotta live, right? These are delicious!'

'I really shouldn't bake so much, but when it's dark and cold, all I crave is sweets,' Emily says. 'Noah, don't take too long. Remember, we've got Ava's recital at seven.'

Their casual banter would've continued for another two hours if I hadn't rushed Colton out of there. Hell, he probably would've even stayed for dinner. How he can just act like there's nothing wrong? I have no idea.

CHAPTER FOURTEEN

NOAH

'So, why did you stop by to see me?' I ask Colton as I drive my SUV out of the development. I think there's a way to get to the dead girl by driving at least most of the distance.

'Oh, I actually needed to borrow a saw. I watched a YouTube video about building your own end table and I wanted to try it.'

'A saw?' I ask, uncertain if I had heard him right. The thing about Colton is that he is the last person on earth to do anything with his hands. He sells solar for a living. I've met salesmen who liked to work with their hands, but he isn't the handy type.

'Don't look so shocked,' Colton says. 'Hey, I'm recently divorced. I'm supposed to go out there and try new things, right?'

'Yeah, I guess. I just thought that in your situation that would mean meeting new women.'

'Well, that wouldn't necessarily be a new thing, would it?' he jokes. Unfortunately, his tendencies toward infidelity are not something that he has ever kept quiet about. Much to Sarah's disappointment, I'm sure.

'I don't know, I just watched the video and thought, what the hell? You know? If that guy can do it, and he probably lives in his mom's basement, why can't I?'

'I'm sure that's true,' I say unenthusiastically.

'Did Emily tell you? We've sold the house.'

'Yeah, she mentioned it. How do you feel about it?'

Colton's four thousand square foot house in one of the fanciest subdivisions around has been his pride and joy. It's not just a house, but a smart home, as he had explained it to me on a number of occasions. He has wired that place up so much that he could have his choice of entrance music playing when he came in, as if he's some sort of character on TV.

'We got a good deal for it. Made a pretty penny. Still, it's a shame to sell it, you know?'

'And there was no way you could hold onto it? Pay the mortgage yourself? Maybe with a roommate?'

Colton stares at me as if I have lost my mind. 'Roommate? Aren't we a little too old for roommates?'

'Yeah, maybe. But people in the lower forty-eight do it all the time. Even guys our age. Or you could Airbnb some of the rooms.'

'Eh, I don't have time for that. Besides, Sarah was pretty adamant about getting her share of the profits now, just in case the market crashes again. We did overpay for it, you know.'

I know. They haven't stopped talking about that since they married. As I remember how the story goes, both he and Sarah fell in love with the place at first sight. But the way he likes to tell it is that it was all Sarah's idea.

A few minutes later, I pull over to the side of the empty road. There are no lights out here, a common occurrence in Alaska, even so close to developments, and it's pitch black.

'We have to hike in a bit,' I say. 'You think the car's going to be okay?'

'Yeah, what's going to happen? If someone does pull over to help, they'll just think we ran out of gas and started walking.'

We get out of the car. I zip up my parka and pull my hat closer around my ears. The wind is whistling all around, and the drop in temperature from this afternoon is definitely significant. Wasilla is over the mountain range away from Anchorage, in the dry part. While Anchorage can be wet and even humid, it rarely gets as cold as it does over here. In the summers, it's always warmer and sunnier, but we pay for that luxury in the winters. I wrap my scarf around my neck again to keep out some of the wind. But a gust quickly pulls it open again, mocking me.

Colton is walking right next to me. The wind makes it almost impossible to talk until we reach the trees. There, we finally have a little bit of respite.

'Hey, look what I brought.' Colton lifts up his parka just a bit, showing the Glock on his hip.

'A gun! What the hell are you doing with a gun?'

'Hey, man, calm down. I just got my permit to carry.'

'You brought it to my house? With my wife and child?'

'It's all legal. I don't need a reason. Besides, this is Alaska. Everyone's got a gun here.'

Clearly, Colton is not understanding the direness of the situation.

'The thing is that we have no business being here. I shouldn't have been here even once. We should not be returning now. And to bring a gun… I mean, what if something happens? This will just escalate this whole thing beyond…'

I don't know how to explain something so simple to him. Unlike most people around here, I'm not a big fan of guns. I think they make any argument worse. But I'm definitely against bringing a gun to a crime scene with a dead girl and over two million in cash. Fuck. Accident scene, not crime scene.

Colton rambles on about the importance of having it just in case. I listen, regretting telling him about this whole thing in the first place. Not like I had a choice though. Eventually, we agree to disagree and he promises to keep the gun locked away.

I walk a few feet ahead of Colton steaming. He's a guy who lives in a ridiculously large house, which is wired up the ass with all sorts of gadgets. He has never chopped a piece of wood, not even for one of his four fireplaces – they always had cords of wood ordered and delivered. He calls professionals to deal with every aspect of that house, never lifting a finger to do anything himself. And now, he's walking around pretending to be a real Alaskan with a gun on his hip?

As my feet sink deep into the snow, I feel the weight of the world on my shoulders. Something bad is going to happen, I can just feel it. But I have no way of stopping it. Shit.

We finally get closer to the car. We approach it from a different direction than from which I came earlier. At first, I don't see it. For a moment, I question whether I imagined the whole thing. Maybe there is no dead girl at all. Maybe there is no car. Maybe the whole thing is some sort of cold weather induced hallucination. But as we get closer, I see the car hidden behind an outcrop of trees and piled under feet of snow.

My heart skips a beat. Do I dare to see her again? I hate being here. I know that I shouldn't take her money and I should report her missing. Her family is looking for her. And even if that money is dirty, so what? I'm no more entitled to it than anyone else. I can still put a stop to this. I can still do the right thing. We can just put the money back and call the police. But that will just leave me back at square one with all of my debts.

I walk over to the driver's side. Colton flips on his phone.

'Hold it out here, so I can see,' I say. He turns the flash toward the girl.

She has the same lost and forgotten look on her face, but something seems different. Familiar even. Maybe it's the way her hair is framing her face or the way her head is tilted slightly to the side. But she's no longer the stranger that I had seen earlier.

Again, the thought of returning all of the money runs through my mind. Or maybe just keeping some of the money and reporting her to the police. Before my sense of guilt and responsibility completely overwhelms me, I push these thoughts aside. I take a deep breath and open the driver's door. I sneak the duffel bag past the girl back into its place, careful not to disturb her. Touching her would somehow make all of this even worse.

After closing the door, I nearly bump into Colton who is standing right behind me.

'What the hell?' I ask, pushing him away. For a second, I'm blinded by his phone's flashlight. For a few moments, all I see are little black spots as my eyes adjust back to the darkness.

'That's her,' he whispers.

'What?'

'That's the missing girl from the news.'

I stare at him. It never occurred to me that he would recognize her.

'She went missing a while ago. Five months or so, I think. I remember because Sarah likes to watch the local news, and she was following the case for a while on Facebook. I think her name's Julie something.'

'Oh,' I say callously. Frankly, I don't really know what else to say except that I hate that he recognizes her. As much as I want to know who she is, I don't want to know anything about her. Not her name or age. All those things, those little details that make people unique, those are all the things that would make it harder for me to keep the money.

I turn on the engine of my SUV as soon as I get inside. The warmth of the heat blowing straight into my face feels nice. Slowly, I start to warm up. The freezing gusts continue to whistle outside, but it's no longer penetrating me to the bone. Next to me, Colton rubs his hands to warm up. Suddenly, I see headlights in my rearview mirror. They're somewhere far away, but getting closer to us with every second.

'It's just a car,' Colton says to reassure both of us. 'It's not necessarily going to stop.'

I start the car and pull out. If we get off the shoulder, then there will be no reason for the car to stop. But the headlights catch up with me, and the bright lights of a police cruiser come on.

'Oh, shit,' Colton whispers.

I pull back over to the shoulder and watch the cop take his time getting out of his vehicle. His headlights are blinding, but I've seen enough movies to know that he's likely taking down my license plate number. Eventually, he walks over and knocks on my window.

'What seems to be the problem, Officer?' I ask in the most cheerful voice possible. He's a pudgy, middle-aged man who does not seem to be enjoying the cold one bit. His nametag says his name is Officer Teaghan.

'You are aware that you just pulled out into traffic without using your turn signal, Mr. Kendall?' Teaghan says, reading off my license.

'Well, there was no one coming,' Colton pipes in. I glare at him.

'I'm sorry about that, Officer. And I apologize for my brother-in-law here. His divorce just came through and he's having a rough time.'

My voice is rushed, too eager to please.

The cop eyes us suspiciously. My heart skips a beat.

'You two aren't drinking, are you?' Officer Teaghan asks. My chest seizes up. For a moment, I can't take in a full breath.

'Oh, no, sir. Not at all.' I manage to force a weak smile. The cop takes a step away and shines his flashlight around the car. I grab onto the steering wheel so tightly, my knuckles turn white. I let go just as his flashlight blinds me.

After a few moments, after he's satisfied that we aren't drunk, he gives me back my license and lets us off with a warning.

As soon as I'm free to go, I drive off. My heart is beating a mile a minute. I can barely catch my breath. Suddenly, I feel sick to my stomach. I turn on my blinker and pull over. I barely have enough time to open the car door before I throw up.

'Oh, gross, man!' Colton pushes me out of the car.

The cold air feels good. It calms down my nerves a little, but not enough to stop me from kneeling over again and depositing the rest of my stomach contents onto the highway. When I'm about to get back into the car, Colton takes my keys.

'C'mon, I'll drive. Just let me know if you need to throw up again.'

That sounds like a good idea. I pull myself into the passenger seat and exhale.

Instead of pulling back onto the highway and heading back home, Colton swerves the car around.

'What the hell are you doing?'

'I just want to see that the cop actually left.'

A few moments later, we drive past the cop car, which is parked in the exact same place where we had left it. But the cop is nowhere to be found.

'Shit, he's following our footsteps into the woods,' Colton says. I peer into the darkness, but don't see a thing.

'If he follows them all of the way to the end, he'll find the dead girl. And he wrote down your license plate.'

He doesn't finish his sentence. But I know where it's going. If he finds the dead girl, we're fucked. He'll think we did it.

'C'mon,' Colton says, hopping out of the car and racing across the street. I follow closely behind him. Powered by adrenaline, we make it to the trees in no time. In between the hanging branches,

I see Officer Teaghan walk around the car. He shines his flashlight into the driver's seat.

'Why didn't you believe us, man?' Colton shouts out, holding the gun in his right hand. 'Now, look what we have to do.'

'Put that down!' I yell and try to grab it out of his hand. But Colton just pushes me away.

Startled, Teaghan reaches for the gun on his hip. But he's too slow. Colton empties two bullets into his chest and the cop slumps into the snow.

My body seizes up. Everything starts to move in slow motion. I watch as blood seeps out of the cop's chest onto the white snow.

CHAPTER FIFTEEN

NOAH

'Why the hell did you shoot him?' I yell out. The word *him* echoes all around us.

'He wrote down your plate number. Then he followed our footsteps into the woods and found the dead girl.'

'So what? We didn't kill her,' I say. 'We just found her. And found fifty thousand dollars. We took it and then decided to return it. You could've even told them that you convinced me that I couldn't keep the money and had to return it back to her and call the police to report her body.'

'What if they thought that we killed her?'

'I don't know why they would. She looks like she has been dead for weeks. And besides, she wasn't murdered. She had an accident. We didn't do anything wrong.'

I keep trying to convince myself of this fact. Though everything that happened today feels very, very wrong.

'What the fuck are you saying, Noah?' Colton walks up to me with his arms crossed over his chest.

Watch out now, Noah, I say to myself. Colton has never killed anyone before, not that I know of. Now there's a dead body lying right in front of us and he still has the gun.

'Nothing,' I say. 'I guess I'm just trying to say, you need to be careful. We need to be careful.'

'If I hadn't shot him, then he would've shot us,' Colton says.

That much I do agree with.

'So what do we do now? What should we do with the body?' I ask, changing the subject.

Colton's a hot head and the last person who should be walking around with a gun. He acts before he thinks. But it's useless to play Monday night quarterback now. We have a dead cop on our hands, and we have to decide what to do with him. We consider leaving him here. Right next to the dead girl. But after a few minutes, that seems like a bad idea. What if they find him when they find her? Or vice versa. No, it would be much better to keep these two separated with as little of a connection as possible.

'If we take the body and someone finds his car out there, they are likely to find the dead girl,' I say. 'Is that something we want?'

That's not a rhetorical question. I actually don't know. My phone vibrates. When I fish it out, I see two texts from Emily.

'Shit. The recital. I completely forgot,' I say.

'You can't miss that. That would be suspicious.'

'So, what do you want to do?'

We decide to move both the body *and* the cop car. It's quite a feat, but if we don't then they'll find the dead girl as a result of the cop car and then go looking for the cop. We want to keep both hidden for as long as possible.

I grab his legs and Colton takes his shoulders.

'Oh wow,' I say, dropping his boots into the snow after taking just one step. Not only is he much heavier than I thought, but the limpness of the body makes it nearly impossible to carry.

Drenched in sweat after just a few more steps, we see headlights somewhere in the distance. Colton immediately crouches down and I follow quickly after him.

Once the car passes, I pick him up again. But after a few steps, a loud piercing sound sends shivers up my spine and I drop him once more.

'What was that?' I whisper.

'I think that was a screeching owl,' Colton says. 'But I don't know.'

When we pick up and go again, we keep looking over our shoulders. Every unusual sound throws my body in a cold sweat, but we eventually make it to the car.

'I'll drive his car and you follow me behind,' Colton says as we struggle the last couple of feet to the car. 'I'm going to try to find a good spot to leave it where it won't be found for a bit.'

'And then?' I ask. 'I can't have him in my trunk.'

'No, of course, not. When we get to your house, we'll transfer him to my trunk and I'll take care of it.'

I'm pleasantly surprised. That's actually quite a generous thing for Colton to say. I guess, he does feel bad over causing this whole thing.

When we finally get to my car, we wrap the body in a blanket I have in the backseat and place it in the trunk.

Colton hops into the cop car and follows closely behind me. We drive about half an hour away down the highway and he parks the car on an empty, snow-swept road. The road is unpaved and, from the looks of it, it hasn't been plowed in months. This appears to be as good a spot as any.

Colton climbs into my car and we drive the rest of the way in silence. The dead body in the trunk makes the whole car feel heavy.

'Okay, so we have to be careful in transferring him to your car in case Emily or anyone else looks out of the window,' I say when we get close to my house. 'I'll just pull right up to your car and if she says something, I'll just say—'

'Listen, about that, I don't know. The housekeeper's coming over tomorrow. I don't want her finding him,' Colton says.

'What are you talking about? We're putting him into your car, that was *your* plan. That's what you said.'

'Well, now I don't want to. I mean, why do I have to do all the dirty work? Why don't you do something?' he says getting out of the car.

I stare at him. Is he really saying all this?

'Colton, I can't take him. Emily and Ava are home. My house isn't even as big as yours. Where am I going to put him?'

'Listen, the housekeeper snoops around all the time. Besides, you always take Emily's car everywhere anyway. Just leave him in your trunk.'

I look at the time. I'm running late.

'Colton, I'm putting him in your car whether you help me or not,' I say, popping the trunk. Colton slams it shut, nearly jamming my fingers inside.

'What the fuck?' I yell out.

'Listen to me, you asshole. I shot the guy. I drove his damn car away from the scene. I'm through with helping with this shit. You are *not* putting his dead body in my garage.'

The tone of his voice sends chills through my body.

'I can't take him with me. What are you thinking?'

'That's not my problem,' Colton says. His voice drops another octave. He's not kidding. And I'm out of time.

I'm steaming, but starting a loud fight will only make things worse. It will draw attention to us and that's the last thing we need. And who knows what else Colton is capable of doing? He shot an innocent man, a police officer, in cold blood. All because he didn't want to get caught. Who the hell knows what he will do to me if I were to cross him.

I pull away from his house, with a feeling of utter dread weighing heavily on every molecule in my body. I know in the very pit of my stomach that the cop did not have to die. Colton killed him for the same reason that Colton does everything – he acts before he thinks. I'm so sick of his brash demeanor and his action before thought mentality. If we had taken a few moments to figure out what to do, we could've gotten away with the money and no one would have to die.

Yes, he was curious, but so what? That's what cops are. Curious. If he had followed our footsteps to the car, he would've found the girl and the money. But that doesn't mean anything. We still have the rest of the money back home. Besides, I want her found. We didn't kill her and this way her family would be notified and she would've been identified. But instead of all that, I'm now driving in a car with a dead cop in my trunk. How the hell did this happen?

I watch as the snow flurries burst open on impact with my windshield and I wonder if this will be me one day if I keep playing these games with Colton. Maybe the best thing to do right now is to just call the police. There is still time to explain everything. There's still time to make things right. Maybe I can't turn back the clock, maybe I can't bring Officer Teaghan back, but I can still make some sort of peace. I imagine myself picking up my phone and consider what I could say. Where would I even start? Would I still keep some of the money? Or should I make a deal first before telling them anything? That would be the smart thing to do, but that would also be the calculating thing to do. In that case, I would need a lawyer.

I take a deep breath as my heart starts to feel like it's going to jump out of my chest. Suddenly, my thoughts turn to Ava and Emily. Things between Emily and me aren't great right now, but I know that I can get back into her good graces again. And I know that, no matter what she thinks about me now, she still loves me. We have been together for a very long time and we have built a life together. And not just a life, but a happy life. What would become of them if I went to prison? Emily would become a single mother and would have to carry the burden of the mortgage and caring for Ava all by herself. We can barely make the payments now on two salaries. How will she manage? She would have to work even more hours, even more double shifts. Maybe she'll have to take another job. And Ava? She'll have to spend all of her time with a babysitter or at a daycare while her mom works all those hours to support her.

That's not fair. Not at all. That's not what I want for either of them. No, I want to be the provider. I want to take care of them. I don't want them to worry about anything. And if I go away to prison, their lives will be nothing but worries. The whole foundation of everything they know will be shattered. Forever.

And outside all of these mundane, financial repercussions, there's something else as well. I will miss them. Terribly. Emily and Ava are my life. Without them, I don't have anything. And I can't even imagine what life would be like in prison. I know that no one is really cut out for prison, but I'm a man who is particularly ill-suited for prison life. How many years would I have to spend there? How much of Officer Teaghan's death is on my hands? I feel responsible, of course, but I had no idea that Colton was going to do what he was going to do. I never wanted anyone to die. There was just nothing I could do to stop it. But would anyone care in delving that deep into my justifications, however poor they are? Does justice work that way? Not really. Teaghan's family would want everyone who was involved to pay for what they had done. As they should. As I would if someone were to take Emily or Ava from me. And they won't give a rat's ass how sorry I was or how much I tried to stop Colton from doing what he did. It wasn't done and Teaghan is dead and that is all they would care about.

As I pull onto my street, I notice that my knuckles are white because I'm grasping the steering wheel so hard. I relax my hands, but that doesn't appease the anxiety that's pounding through my body. I'm covered in cold sweat. Again, my thoughts return to the money. Even though I had doubts about it when Colton caught me with it and wanted to return it all, I now know for sure that it was a bad idea to take it. Any of it. I should've never done it. It was just a stupid impulsive moment in which all I thought about was how much my life would be improved if I just had all that money. But now, look at me. My life is so much worse than it was before. Not only is the girl not reported and her family continues to worry, but now there's another dead body in the mix. Someone whose death I'm responsible for. Yes, Colton was actually the killer, but if it weren't for me, he would never have been there in the first place. This is the problem with taking action before thinking things through. You end up doing something that you regret, something that you can't change no matter how much you try.

I take a deep breath and try to calm my nerves, but nothing is working. Driving over an ice patch, Teaghan's dead body in the trunk jolts and my heart sinks. Okay, enough with what you should've done or would've done, I say silently to myself. It's too late for second guesses. It's too late for assigning blame, or maybe it's too early. There's nothing I can really say or do that will probably not result in me going away to prison for a very long time at this point. And if I do end up in prison, there will be plenty of time to think of all the possible other ways I could've dealt with this situation. The only thing that I have to do now is to accept reality as it is and deal with it the best I can.

CHAPTER SIXTEEN

NOAH

Emily and Ava are outside the house when I pull in. The garage door opens and Emily's getting something from her car.

'I know, I know.' I wave my hand. 'I'm late. I'm sorry.'

I jump out, ready to help with whatever's needed.

'Help me move this car seat to your car,' Emily says.

I take a step back in shock.

'No, we should take your car.'

'Yes, I know, your car is a total mess. And we're already late. But the brakes were making that weird noise again this afternoon, and I really don't feel good about taking it out.'

My blood sugar drops in an instant. I feel sick to my stomach. My head starts to swim.

'What's wrong?' Emily asks when I fold in two, putting my head between my knees.

'I'm okay,' I say, slowly standing up.

I have to take control of this situation. Under no circumstance can she open the trunk. Fighting back the sick feeling in the pit of my stomach, I rush over to help Emily with the car seat. After Ava is safely plugged in, I walk around the car.

'I just have to get the bag.' Emily runs back inside the garage. 'Start the car.'

I'm about to jump into the driver's seat when something gives me pause. Just at that moment, I see Emily running past the passenger door and heading toward the trunk. Shit. She was supposed to carry the bag on her lap. Or toss it into the backseat with Ava.

'I'll take that for you.' I meet her on the other side of the car. Tripping over my feet, I collide into her.

Startled, Emily jumps back, but doesn't give it much thought beyond that.

'Hurry up. It's so fucking cold out here,' she hisses, relinquishing the bag. I feel the drops of sweat that have just formed on my forehead freeze with the plummeting temperatures. I toss the bag under Ava's feet in the backseat and get behind the wheel, finally letting out a sigh of relief.

The drive over is frosty, and not just because it's so cold outside. The tension that exists between Emily and me can be cut through with a knife. I want to apologize and make amends, but whenever I try to say anything, she glares in my direction and points to Ava in the backseat. We both grew up in households where our parents fought in front of the kids and called each other vile names. We both know how painful those words are for kids to hear, so we decided a long time ago that we would never fight in front of her. Keeping my promise to Emily is the least I can do right now.

We arrive at Ava's dance studio ten minutes later. Luckily, underneath her parka, Ava is already dressed in her leotard and tights, so we're not as late as we could be. I help her climb out of her car seat, hand Emily the bag, and rush inside after them after checking on the dead body in my trunk. Tightly rolled up in a blanket, it makes a Z-shape. Luckily, there's not one limb sticking out. There is nothing suspicious about this whole thing, right? Yeah, except that I don't have a single good explanation for what it could be except for a dead body.

As the recital starts, all the proud parents in the room stand up and cheer. Phones and cameras have been prohibited at The Little

Dance Company recitals ever since two dads got into a fist fight over a blocked shot and both ended up in the emergency room. Emily thinks it's just an excuse for them to sell their own videos and photos at a high mark up. As the lights dim and the curtain goes up, all the eyes around me focus on the stage, frantically looking for their kids.

'There she is!' Emily whispers. 'She's the third one from the left.'

I nod, count, and focus my attention on where Emily has pointed. We're sitting all the way in the back and I can't tell the difference between one jumping tutu and the next. Emily continues to complain about our seats even though she knows very well that unless you get here a full hour and a half early, there's no way of getting any seats up front.

For the next five dances, I run my fingers along the spine of the phone in my pocket and debate in my head whether or not I should call or text Colton. Intermission finally comes. Decision time. I excuse myself and sneak outside. I don't bring my coat because I'm just supposed to be heading to the bathroom, and the blast of cold air coming straight from the mountains on the horizon wakes me up. I have to make this quick if I want to hold on to any feeling in my fingertips.

'We have to do it tonight,' I say when Colton finally answers on the fourth ring.

'I can't tonight. Besides aren't you at your daughter's recital?' By the sound of his voice, I know that he has already had a couple of drinks.

'I mean after that. To*night*.'

'I have a date.'

'Cancel it.'

'I can't. She's hot, newly single. I've been asking her out for weeks and this is the first time she has given me the time of day.'

We go back and forth for a while without much luck. Hey, I get it. There's no urgency for him. He's already unwinding from our shitty day. He's not the one with a dead body in his trunk. He's not the one who drove the dead body to his daughter's ballet recital. Shit. Now, I need a drink. It takes me the rest of the show to warm up from standing outside, but it's not enough time to come up with a good plan to get rid of the cop.

On the drive home, Emily and I praise Ava about her performance. We tell her how proud we are and how amazing she was. I go through the motions, but my heart isn't in it. Luckily, Ava doesn't seem to notice. I can see her beaming from ear to ear in the rearview mirror and all I can think is that there's a dead cop in the trunk of the car.

CHAPTER SEVENTEEN

NOAH

After I put Ava to bed, I come into the master bedroom. Emily is sitting at the edge of the bed with her head in her hands, a familiar sight.

'There were just too many kids in there. And the bright lights,' Emily says even though she doesn't need to explain. I already know that one of her migraines is coming on.

She pops a pill, dims the lights, and climbs into bed.

'I'll be up in a bit,' I say, kissing her on her forehead.

'Hey, wait,' Emily says. 'Are you okay?'

'Yes, of course.' I nod.

'I know that you must be worried about money, but you know that things are going to work out, right? Something will happen for us.'

'You think so?'

'They have to. I mean bad luck has to run out at some point, right? We can't always be in this position.'

I wish with all of my heart that I could believe that, but the truth is that some people just have bad luck all of their lives. They struggle and struggle and nothing ever gets any better.

'We'll make it through this. You just have to be honest with me.'

'I will. I promise,' I say after a moment.

'No secrets.'

'No secrets,' I say and give her another peck. If only it were that easy. No, I'm in too deep now. And the only way out is to keep going.

I head downstairs with an unexpected spring in my step. I hate to say it but usually Emily's migraines are a big pain in the ass. They tend to come on at large gatherings and in bright lights, and we have left more than one fun party in an effort to avoid her getting one, usually without much luck. But this time, it seemed to have come on at just the right time. This is my chance.

I head to the garage and put a shovel in my car. The ground is frozen over and buried under feet of snow, but I want to have one just in case. Who knows what might happen? Just as I'm about to climb into the driver's seat, I hear a whimper. Someone's crying. When I turn around, I see a silhouette across the street. She's sitting on their poorly shoveled porch. It doesn't matter, I say to myself. This doesn't concern me. But the whimpers get louder. When she lifts her head up, I wave. She waves back.

'Are you okay?' I yell across the street. Charlie forces a smile. Her blonde hair hangs down uncombed around her face. She's wearing a white ski cap, which brings out the sparkle in her waterlogged eyes.

'Yeah, I'm fine.' She nods.

'Yeah, I can see that,' I joke, walking over to her porch. Charlie and I don't know each other very well. Hardly at all. I think we've spoken to each other barely a couple of times. I want to get to know her better. But why does it have to be tonight of all nights?

'So, are you going to tell me what's wrong or do we both have to freeze to death out here?'

'Nobody asked you to be here. If you're cold, you can leave,' she says with a shrug. I nod. She's right of course. And I have better things to do anyway. But I linger nevertheless. Just sitting here next to her feels like a gift. I inhale and exhale deeply, watching my breath make little clouds in front of me.

Just as I'm about to leave, she finally says, 'I can't go to work anymore.'

I wait for her to continue.

'I'm a 911 operator. It has always been kind of a tedious and stressful job. But the last call I took, it really fucked me up.'

'What happened?'

'This woman called in. With this really dead voice. Like she was absent or something. There, but not really there. It didn't sound like she had an emergency at all. Most people call in freaking out, you know? Well, after talking to me for a bit, she informs me that she just killed her kids. She fuckin' killed them and acted like it wasn't a big deal at all.'

As Charlie fills me in on the chilling details, I start to shudder. I can only imagine what it would be like to get that kind of phone call.

'Why don't you call in sick for a bit? Do you have any sick days?'

'I can take days off, but I don't have any official sick days. I just don't get paid.'

'Well, that might be worth it, nevertheless.'

She nods. We sit in silence for a while, staring at the stars above. There isn't a cloud in sight, and the sky is peppered with stars. Somewhere in the distance, the lights of aurora borealis are dancing in a sea of green.

'How do you feel about breakfast at night?' I ask.

As soon as the words escape my lips, I immediately regret them. Why did I say that? Yes, she does look sad and broken up sitting all alone on that cold porch. But I can't make her feel better. Not tonight of all nights. I have things to do. Very important things, such as getting rid of that body in my trunk. She'll say no, right? She has to. Of course, she will. We are barely acquaintances, basically strangers.

Why would she want to go to breakfast with someone she barely knows this late at night?

'Um, sure.' Charlie shrugs. 'Let me just get my wallet.'

Fuck. There's no getting out of this now. I climb into the driver's seat with a sense of utter dread. Charlie leaps into the passenger seat with a little hop in her step.

'Thank you so much for asking me,' she says when I pull out of the development. 'I was just sitting there wallowing and that never makes anything better, does it? It's nice to go out.'

Go out. Is that what we're doing? Oh my God. Could this night get any worse? And this is right after Emily caught me spying on her. How would I ever explain this outing? No, she can't ever find out. No one can.

I feel my heartbeat rising as I get on the highway and head to the furthest Denny's that I know of. It's all the way across town. There are plenty of diners which are much closer to us, but I can't risk running into anyone I know. I tell Charlie we have to go to this Denny's because they have the best Grand Slam around, but I can tell that she isn't exactly buying it.

'What do you want to listen to?' I ask, hoping I can drown out my thoughts in a familiar tune.

'Oh, I don't care,' Charlie says, shrugging.

'Feel free to put on whatever.'

It takes Charlie a solid five minutes to find anything that she wants to listen to. She listens to each station for a total of two seconds before realizing that it's not the right one. But I enjoy the distraction. My thoughts aren't running in circles after a while, and I finally believe that it might all turn out okay in the end.

A few miles away from Denny's, a police cruiser pulls onto the empty highway behind. Immediately, my heart jumps into my throat and my head starts to buzz.

It's going to be fine, I say to myself silently, as if it were my mantra. It's going to be fine. Don't worry.

But then the lights come on. And a few seconds later, the siren pierces through the upbeat Taylor Swift song that Charlie eventually settled on.

Charlie whips her head around to look at the cop behind us.

'Are you speeding?' she asks. I press down on the brakes and turn on my blinker to pull over to the side of the road.

'No, not at all,' I say, unable to make my voice go any louder than a whisper. At least, I don't think so. Frankly, I have no idea what the speed limit is here.

After parking the car, I watch through my rearview mirror as the police officer takes his time getting out of his vehicle and coming over to us. My fingers are ice cold at this point and my heart is beating so hard, I feel like it's about to burst out of my chest at any moment.

'Are you hot?' Charlie asks. I shake my head and quickly wipe my forehead, which is drenched in sweat. Shit. I'm not going to get away with this. He's going to ask to see what's in my trunk and then it will all be over.

'License and registration,' the police officer says when I roll down my window. I already have them ready for him. When I hand them over, I try not to look at him. Making eye contact seems like a dangerous thing to do at this particular juncture.

'What seems to be the problem, Officer?' Charlie asks. That's supposed to be my line, but I can't bear to engage with him on any level.

'Well, your back left taillight is out.'

'Oh, okay,' I mumble. 'I'm sorry about that. I had no idea.'

'Mmm-mmm,' the officer says, scribbling something on his notepad. No one says anything for a few minutes, which feels like a century. I let the cold blasts of Arctic air burst in through the open window and wash over me as I pray that the cop lets me drive away without checking the car.

'Okay, have a safe night.' He hands me the ticket. 'And make sure to get that light fixed asap. You're on notice now.'

'Yes, I will,' I say quickly. I close the window and turn on the engine, but don't dare move quite yet. Instead, I watch as the cop walks back to his vehicle and drives away. Only then do I let out a long sigh of relief.

CHAPTER EIGHTEEN
CHARLIE

We drive all the way to the Denny's across town. There are plenty of diners which are closer, but Noah insists that we need to go to Denny's. I'm pretty sure it's not just because he is in love with their Grand Slam, but rather that he wants to go to a place where we are least likely to be seen.

A tired waitress working the night shift shows us to our booth. The worn faux leather is soft and welcoming. I'm not a big fan of fluorescent lights, but somehow in this place they aren't that offensive. They give a warm glow to the place, complementing the delicious smells of fried food coming from the kitchen.

I open the large menu in front of me and examine the options. I'm not a big breakfast eater, but I occasionally enjoy one. It feels so illicit to have eggs and pancakes with maple syrup at night that it makes even mediocre food delicious. After narrowing down my choice to the Double Berry Banana Pancake breakfast without the bacon or sausage links, I close the menu and look at Noah.

He's tall and slim. He looks to be in his mid to late-thirties, and his dark hair is just getting a few sprinkles of salt and pepper around the temples. Crow's feet surround his eyes, and his skin looks like he has been outside too long without proper hydration. Dry and a little sallow. Or maybe he's just tired.

I've never really talked to Noah before. I have lived across the street from him since the fall, but people in our neighborhood tend to keep to themselves, especially in the winter. Everyone has garages and no one really spends much time outside unless they're actually going hunting, fishing, or snowmobiling. But Noah isn't really the type. He's more of an inside guy.

'So, you said you were a teacher?' I ask.

'Yep. English. Tenth grade.'

'Wow, what's that like?'

Noah puts down the menu and takes a sip of his coffee.

'It's okay, I guess. It pays the bills. But it's not really for me. The kids frustrate me when they don't do their assignments. They keep making the same mistakes on their essays over and over. It's kind of tedious, actually.'

I stare at him.

'Yeah, that must be hard. But they're kids, you know. I mean, did you care about every single class you took in high school?'

'No, I guess not,' he says as if the thought had never occurred to him before.

'So, if you don't want to be a teacher, what is it that you do want to do?'

The waitress comes to take our orders.

After she leaves, he says, 'I want to be a writer. Well, I am a writer.'

'You are?'

'I've written a lot of short stories. Not many have been published. Do you know that some of these self-published writers write a book in two months? Some in even less time? Well, I can barely squeeze out two hundred words in a day.'

'Maybe you just need to focus more.'

'That's what I thought. That's why I took a sabbatical, that we can't really afford, to write. I thought I would get a series going. Publish it. And the money would roll in.'

'But it hasn't happened?'

'Well, I can't even finish the first novella. It has been a month and a half. And that's ridiculous.'

I shrug. 'I don't really know anything about writing. Though I do enjoy a good thriller.'

He nods.

'What kind of series are you writing?'

'I have no idea.' He shrugs. 'At first, I was thinking of a detective novel. Then some sort of action adventure. Now fantasy. I'm just all over the place. I keep changing my mind.'

'Well, you're probably not going to get anywhere doing that. You have to pick a topic and stick to it. Maybe an outline will help. Then there's the actual butt-in-seat time. Just lock yourself in the room with your outline and no Internet or phone and write until you're done.'

Our food comes. My mouth waters as I realize for the first time today, just how hungry I am. My stomach growls as I look at the juicy hash browns surrounding two fluffy buttermilk pancakes with juicy blueberries cooked on the inside. They are generously topped with strawberries, bananas, and whipped cream. I lift up one of the eggs with my fork and inhale the sunny side.

'So, how did you get so smart?' Noah asks as he pours maple syrup into every square of his waffle.

'I don't know.' I shrug. 'I just always try to look for the simple way out. People tend to make everything too complicated. They think too much. Especially about artistic endeavors. Maybe that's good. Maybe that makes you an artist. But you said that you want to write a lot. And if other writers are publishing a book every two, three months, you have to as well to compete, right? Well, then you don't have too much time to navel gaze.'

Noah bursts out laughing.

'I've never really thought of it that way. Maybe that is my problem. Too much thinking.'

'Think about it,' I say, taking a sip of my tea.

'So, what about you? Have you always wanted to be a 911 operator?'

'No, actually. I didn't know what I wanted to do. I got my degree in communications at UAF, and I thought I would try to go down to the lower forty-eight to find a job. But then my grandmother got sick, so I moved in to help take care of her. I needed a job. I didn't want to work in retail or be a waitress. But around here, other types of jobs are hard to come by, as you know.'

'But she doesn't live with you anymore,' Noah says. 'You have your roommates.'

'Yeah, she lives in an assisted living home now.'

'Oh, I'm sorry about that.'

'It's okay. I visit all the time. And she's got a lot of friends there. Anyway, one of her friends, the one who's actually her next-door neighbor now, introduced me to her son, who's the chief of police here.'

Noah chokes on his coffee. As he struggles to clear his windpipes, I hand him a glass of cold water. But he just waves me away.

'I'm okay, I'm okay,' he whispers, wiping away tears. After a few minutes, he finally composes himself.

'Are you sure?'

'Yeah, I don't know what happened.' He shrugs. 'I guess it just went down the wrong way.'

I nod sympathetically. But the fact that he choked right when I mentioned the chief of police isn't lost on me.

'So, how did you end up getting the job?' he asks, taking another bite of his hash browns.

'Well, that's actually a funny story.' I smile and tell him what happened.

'When I met with Chief Walters for the interview, he asked me if I had ever committed a crime.'

'The chief of police interviewed you?'

'Well, he's the one who knew my grandmother so he wanted to meet with me.'

'Okay, go on.'

'When I met with the chief, he asked me if I'd ever committed a crime, right? This should've been a simple yes or no question. I knew immediately that I should've answered no. That would've been the end of it. But for some reason, I didn't. The thing is that I have stolen a car. My car. The guy who was my boyfriend at the time took it. We had a big fight and he just drove off with it. I wasn't sure if we were together at that time, but I knew that I needed it back. So, in the middle of the night, I took a cab to his house. In the morning, he reported the car stolen and the cops got involved.'

'So, did you get in trouble?' Noah asks.

'No, not really. I showed them my registration and they let me go on my way. But the truth was that I did steal a car.'

'And Chief Walters gave you the job on the spot?'

'Ha. I wish.' I shake my head, pouring a lavish serving of maple syrup over the blueberries and the rest of the pancakes.

'No, he listened carefully and said that someone from the office would be in touch. I didn't hear from anyone for two months. I pretty much gave up on the whole thing, but then I ran into him at Costco and he asked if I could start the following Monday. It was Saturday. And I did.'

I don't love talking about my job, but Noah seems to be very interested in the whole thing so I indulge him.

'There isn't really any training at all. I sat with Pete, the other 911 operator, and watched him take a call on my first day. Then he set me up at my own console and told me to pick up the phone when they called. The only real responsibilities of my job are to take the caller's name, the nature of their emergency, and then dispatch cops if necessary.'

'What happened on your first call?' Noah asks, wiping his plate clean.

'A fire. Someone lit two acres around their house. When the firemen got there, they discovered a bunch of marijuana plants in the house. It turned out to be the competitor of the guy. He didn't like that he was growing too much weed and took matters into his own hands. The thing is, you never know what is going on in people's lives. In my job, you learn that even the most normal of people are hiding something.'

Noah nods and looks away. It feels like I've struck a chord.

'You know, you don't seem to be the type to live around here,' I say when he grabs for the check. I offer to pay, of course, but he waves me off.

'What do you mean?'

'I don't know.' I shrug. 'Just that guys around here are sort of the rugged type. They like to fish, hunt, and build their own cabins. You don't seem to be like that at all.'

'So, you're saying I'm not a real guy?' he says with a smile. 'And that after I paid for your meal.'

'Hey, I offered. But no, I don't mean it like an insult. You're just different. I never see you snowmobiling. I never see you do anything outdoors. Talking to you now, it doesn't even seem like you're really into nature.'

'Well, to tell you the truth, I'm not. I don't really like the cold. And I'd rather stay home with a good book anyway over hunting or going out there and suffering through the cold and the snow.'

'So, why do you still live here?' I ask.

'Because that's what I do. I came here a while ago and met my wife. She has family here. And I sort of got used to being around here. And it's not like I don't like nature. I love running. I love looking at those tall majestic mountains and glaciers from the comforts of my SUV.'

I nod as if I understand. But in reality, I don't. Not really. Alaska isn't like other places in the lower forty-eight. This isn't like some place in upstate New York where people get stuck and end up spending generations. Everyone who lives here thrives on the place. Perhaps, it's because it's such a hard place to live. Beautiful, breathtaking, and difficult. Everything's expensive. The houses, the boats, the fishing, even the hunting. And there's a ton of weather. Wind. Snow. Ice. Rain. All depending on the location. So the people who end up making this place home tend to be the ones that love the place. You either fall in love or you leave. This isn't a place that's too easy to get stuck in.

After Noah pulls up to my house, I thank him again for breakfast.

'Thanks again for… everything,' I say, turning to face him. I hope that the word expresses what I really mean, though I have my doubts. I don't have the courage to really thank him for what I mean. A few hours ago, on the porch, I was in a really dark place. I never wanted to go back to work again. And I had no idea if I wanted to do anything else.

'You're welcome. Hope it cheered you up a bit.'

'It did. I'm still not sure what I'm going to do about work, but at least I don't feel so horrible about what happened.'

'That's good,' he says, leaning back in his seat. Suddenly, something feels strange. Just getting out of the car and waving goodbye doesn't seem like it's enough. So I lean closer to him and give him a peck on the cheek. I mean it only as a thank you, but suddenly, he turns his head toward me and my lips collide with his. A moment later, I pull away from him, but it's already too late.

CHAPTER NINETEEN

NOAH

In a daze, I run through a stop sign. I only notice it when I'm through the intersection. My heart jumps into my chest. The sudden stop and start jolts my memory, reminding me of the fact I have a dead cop in my car. Shit. I really need to be more careful. Luckily, there was no cop here, but what if there were?

She kissed me. She actually kissed me. Oh, fuck. My feelings oscillate between excitement, fear, and guilt. I promised myself that nothing would happen. I don't like her that way. Besides, I'm married. Happily, I might add. But when she leaned over to me in the car, there was nothing I could do to stop her. I had imagined this moment for a long time, ever since I started spying on her. I want her lips on mine. I want to kiss her neck. I want to taste every bit of her.

I drive northeast on Wasilla-Fishhook Road as far as it takes me. This road merges into North Palmer-Fishhook Road and I follow it along as it meets Little Susitna River. I consider dumping the body here. But then reconsider. The river is popular with fishermen, white water rafters, and kayakers. It's full of large boulders, which make it particularly enticing to those looking for a challenge. For all of these reasons, Little Su is not a good option for me. I'd love nothing more than to drop the body in the river and let it carry it away from here. But what if it gets stuck on one of the boulders? What if it doesn't sink? Or comes back up after sinking? No, I can't risk any of these eventualities. I need to bury it somewhere where no one would ever find it.

I drive on. I drive north past the Hatcher Pass Public Use Area and continue on until the road curves left and becomes Fishhook-Willow Road. This is far enough. There are acres of wilderness on both sides, tall, powerful pine trees standing proud in the frozen ground challenging my endurance. There's nothing in particular that makes this area better or worse than any of the others I've passed except that I finally reached the end. I have to get rid of this thing once and for all or just drive home and ask Colton for help. The second option is not really an option at all. I can't risk Emily waking up tomorrow and driving Ava to school in this car. With the body in the back.

The road in front of me splits in two. One smaller route goes off to the right, and the large one goes off to the left. I choose the one less traveled. Immediately, I'm reminded of Robert Frost's poem 'The Road Not Taken'. '*Two roads diverged in a wood, and I – I took the one less traveled by, And that has made all the difference.*' I assign this poem every spring to my students. I ask them to read it, think about it, and write an essay about how it applies to their own lives. Most of them submit long expositional stories about the one time that they hiked or fished in one or another place that they found by accident. Some don't take the poem so literally and instead write about the one time they didn't drink or smoke a cigarette with all of their friends. Unfortunately, these submissions typically come from students who are most likely to offend. The popular ones. The ones whose parents spoil them a little too much with too many toys and too little attention.

As I follow this road, taking the one less traveled by, the situational irony is not lost on me. Tonight, I'm driving down the road looking for a place to unload the dead body of an Alaska State Trooper. It's the last thing that a boring suburban father and a high school English teacher should be doing in the middle of the night.

In these parts, there are hardly any pine trees at all. The land is hilly and uneven, full of round shrubs and tall bushes. They kneel down under the snow, as if they are suffering under their own weight. A few miles past the last cabin, I pull over to the side of the road. By the looks of the starry sky, the night is in full swing. I have to work faster. When I open the trunk and pull the body forward, a weapon tucked into his arms falls out. It makes a loud clink sound when it hits the ground. I jump back. What the hell is this doing here? I pick up the gun and hold it up to the light. It's Colton's gun. What a fuckin' son-of-a-bitch. He actually stuck the gun here instead of taking it back with him, like he had promised. Fuck. What the hell am I supposed to do with it now? I have no idea. But I need to get this body and the gun off the road in case anyone comes by.

Making sure that the safety is on, I tuck the gun into the back of my pants and pull my parka over it. With great effort, I swing the body over my shoulder. It would be best not to leave evidence that something weighty was dragged up over the hill. My footsteps will still be visible for some time, but only until the next snowfall. Then, it will be as if no one was here at all.

I grunt under the weight of the cop. It takes almost everything out of me to walk even a hundred yards. When I'm finally far enough up the hill that the road is completely out of sight, I walk up to a bush near a cluster of pine trees and drop the body to the ground. It makes a loud thump sound that echoes a little in the distance. I pick up the shovel and tap the edge at the ground. Under the five or so feet of fluffy dry snow, the ground is as hard as stone. I shovel off a few clumps and feel the ground with my feet. This ground needs a jackhammer to get through.

Now that burying the body underground seems like a lost cause, I fall back on plan B. Looking around, I see that one of the pine trees in the patch has fallen over. I walk over and shovel out all of the snow from the north side. Then I take the pick ax and use it to loosen the ground. It's not exactly a jackhammer, but it makes a dent. After digging at it for some time, I place the trooper's body there and cover it with earth and snow.

By the time I'm finished, I'm drenched in sweat. I wipe my brow and catch my breath. Okay, this should work until spring. Then I can come back and actually bury it six feet under. I walk over to another bush at the far end of the trees. I unzip my parka and wipe the gun with my shirt just in case. Then, I use the shovel and pick ax to make a small hole in the ground, just big enough for the gun and drop it inside. The hole is about a foot deep. That should be deep enough that I won't need to re-hide the gun in the spring. Now, all I need to do now is cover up my footprints. It would be nice if I had a broom, but a shovel will have to do. Holding it lightly over, I drag it behind me everywhere I have walked and all the way back to the car. It smooths the snow, removing almost all evidence of my presence.

When I get back into the car, my thoughts return to Colton. How could he do this to me? Why would he do this to me? First, he left me with this goddamn dead body. And then the murder weapon on top of it? Doesn't he know how close I got to being found out today?

It's early morning by the time I pull back onto my street. Despite the stress, the anxiety, and the sheer physical exhaustion of the day, a feeling of relief sweeps over me. The body is no longer in my car. It's safe to drive around again. I park the car in the driveway, fearing that Emily will wake up with the sound of the garage door opening, which can be heard throughout the house. When I get out, I hear a door slam shut. My heart sinks all the way into the pit of my stomach. I stop dead in my tracks.

'Hey!' Charlie says, waving to me as she runs by. Dressed in workout clothes, she's about to break into a run. I watch helplessly as the expression on her face changes from a casual hello to bewilderment. I feel her trying to process my being there. I'm drenched in sweat and covered in dirt. I'm wearing the same clothes I wore to breakfast last night. At a loss as to what to say, I simply stand here dumbfounded. She stares at me for a moment and then takes off, quickly disappearing around the corner.

CHAPTER TWENTY

NOAH

I sit in front of my computer screen again, with the cursor flashing. A paragraph comes out smoothly, the words flow faster than my fingers can keep up with. And then, suddenly, nothing else comes. My mind goes blank. I stare into space. No, my mind isn't blank. Instead, it keeps circling back to what happened, sending me into a tailspin. Charlie saw me covered in dirt and sweat and wearing the same clothes as from the night before. On the surface, this doesn't necessarily have to mean anything, but of course it does. She was going on a run and here I was just pulling into my driveway looking like I had just committed a crime.

But is that what she thought? The thing about being guilty of something is that you assume that other people see you and know immediately what crime you have committed. But in reality, that may not be what she's thinking or feeling at all. I try to think of all the possible variations of truth that Charlie could think of seeing me like that. She could think I just went on a drive after I had dropped her off. While that's plausible, perhaps it's not very realistic. And beyond that, my mind goes blank. I can't think of one possible reason why I would look like I was dressed in the same clothes that early in the morning.

The tips of my fingers turn ice cold as I tap them anxiously on my table. I try to turn my attention to my computer screen and distract myself with something else. But writing at this moment is out of the question. I lick my lips and suddenly another image pops into my head. Our kiss. It was just a stupid, spontaneous thing that I should have never done. It's something I never had any plans to do. But alone in my office with my thoughts, I can't lie to myself. It felt nice. Still, it's something that should've never happened.

Charlie and I kissed. A part of me has hoped and imagined this moment for a very long time, ever since I first saw her walk around her room in only a bra and panties. But another part of me, the reasonable and logical one, knew that going down this path would lead nowhere good. I'm not a cheater and I love my wife. What Emily and I have is so much more than just a physical attraction. We have a life together and I would never want to do anything to hurt her. And yet, I already have. She caught me looking at Charlie, lusting at her. That's not something any wife wants to see.

But to be more precise, Charlie and I didn't really kiss. Even though I hate to see the truth for what it is, I know that Charlie had leaned over to give me a kiss on my cheek in a platonic way. She may have opened up to me, but she does not seem to have any feelings toward me at all. No matter how much I would like her to. She leaned over to kiss me and I turned my head. Our lips collided and made the moment a lot more complicated than it ever needed to be.

I take a deep breath, trying to calm my heartbeat. No, all of this has become a lot more complicated than I ever wanted it to. We kissed and then she saw me come back home after burying a body. My only hope is that she doesn't know exactly what it is that she saw. And even though I can't think of a possible explanation for my actions, maybe she can. There's no way she would suspect me of driving around to a diner with her with a body in my trunk. Nor would she think that after we went out for breakfast, I drove straight out and buried a body. How do I know this? Because that's a crazy thing to do. No, she would have to explain the situation to herself in a much more reasonable way.

Pursuing anything further with Charlie will just make the mess that I've already made a lot more complicated. I just have too much to lose. Charlie doesn't mean anything to me in comparison to my family. She is just a pretty girl who lives next door. Emily and Ava are the most important people in my life and I'm not going to do anything to hurt them anymore. I need to try to patch things up with Emily. The whole reason I started down this path in the first place was to give us a chance at a new life. And starting a new life somewhere else isn't going to work out if I don't have Emily by my side. I don't want the money if I don't have her.

My breath quickens and my hands get sweaty. My heart feels like it's about to jump out of my chest. When I first took the money, I thought that it would be an easy fix. With all the bills piling up, I was suffocating. Drowning. Desperate, I made a silly, snap decision. And now? Now, I'm too far in to turn back. Everything has gone to shit and there's no way out but through. I now know that I shouldn't have taken the money; it's not worth all of this. But it's too late to think like that now. What has happened has already happened. And if I want to get away with this, I need to stop making mistakes. If I want this to have any sort of happy ending, I need to be smarter than everyone else.

CHAPTER TWENTY-ONE
CHARLIE

I meet with Stephen for lunch at Chepo's Mexican Restaurant. I love this place for the good service, fresh ceviche, and awesome margaritas. I order a blackberry habanero margarita as soon as we are seated. Stephen Silko has been an Alaska State Trooper for three and a half years. He has previously served with the North Pole Police department. He moved to the area about a year ago after his pregnant fiancée killed herself. Stephen is tall, broad-shouldered, with a square jaw and a typical cop haircut, which actually looks really good on him. He's a friend of mine. More than friend, really, but not quite a boyfriend.

As Stephen peruses the menu, my mind wanders back to Noah. Where was he this morning? Why did he stay up so late? Where did he go after he dropped me home? And then there was the sweat and the crazy-eyed expression on his face. And the dirt all over his parka and pants. He had been digging around in the dirt. But why would he do that in the middle of the night with the temperatures below zero? And why did he do that all night long? I know he's up to something.

'Oh, man, I'm so tired.' Stephen stretches his arms out, gulping down his coffee. After working a twelve-hour shift, they got a call about a dead body. Everyone available had to go in, so he ended up working another shift. At least there's overtime.

'So, what happened last night?' I ask.

The waitress comes back with our super nachos and drinks. My mouth salivates as I grab a tortilla chip covered in melted jack and cheddar cheese, beans, tomatoes, black olives, and jalapeños. I scoop up a generous portion of sour cream and wait for him to answer.

'We found Steven Dossey shot dead sitting in his office. Point blank. He was doing the books and someone came in and shot him right in the forehead.'

Steven Dossey. That name sounds familiar, but I can't quite place it.

'He's the owner of one of the biggest salvage yards in the state. He's a real shady character. We suspect him in about half a dozen disappearances of business associates, but could never pin anything on him. We're pretty sure he's running the biggest meth operation in the state.'

'Like making meth?'

'No, his strength is in distribution. In addition to the salvage yard, he also has a bunch of trucks working for him. Delivering all sorts of supplies to the North Slope. We always thought he used those trucks to distribute meth and cocaine all over the state. We got a few warrants, searched the trucks a few times, but someone always must've tipped him off. The trucks we searched were always clean.'

'And now he's dead?' I ask.

Stephen hangs his head and nods. We don't say anything for a few minutes, enjoying the nachos. I look around the place. With its dark carpet, low lighting, and large wooden booths, it resembles something of a dive bar. It isn't much to look at, but the food never disappoints. After I'm almost filled to the brim, our main course arrives. I ordered Chepo's exclusive ceviche, a light fish marinated in lemon juice, mixed with onions, tomatoes, green and black olives, cilantro, and mild green chilis. It's served chilled with sliced avocados atop a bed of lettuce. Looking at the size of the portion, I know immediately that there's no way I'm going to finish this off in one sitting. A doggy bag is definitely in my future. Stephen, on the other hand, doesn't seem daunted at all.

'It's not that I'm upset that that son-of-a-bitch is dead. I'm just angry that someone else did it. And now, I'm not sure we'll ever find out the extent of all of his business dealings. Whoever did this also cleaned out the contents of his safe. We don't really know what was in it, but probably cash. The door to the safe was swinging open when we arrived,' Stephen says. He digs into his chicken fajita quesadilla served with guacamole, sour cream, and pico de gallo with ferociousness.

'There was one funny thing at the crime scene. Dossey's fucking brains were all over Pamela Anderson's tits. You should've seen it, Charlie.'

I don't really understand what he's saying.

'He had this huge Pamela Anderson poster in his office behind his desk. She's all bronze and oiled up, posing in an itty-bitty bikini. It looked like a fucking work of art.'

Suddenly, Stephen's phone goes off. I ask for a doggy bag while he takes the call. By the tone of his voice, I know that whatever happened isn't good. Stephen's already pale skin turns almost translucent as all the blood drains away from his face.

'What do you mean he's missing?' Stephen asks whomever is on the other end. 'Where was the car found? Did they get a license plate for the other car?' Stephen pulls out his notepad.

After hanging up, he pulls out his wallet.

'No, it's fine. I'll get it,' I say. 'What happened?'

'No need,' Stephen says, putting two twenties on the table. 'Sorry, I have to go. Tim Teaghan's missing and his car has been found abandoned a few miles out of town.'

After putting on his coat, he grabs the notepad facing me: *AK. Standard Gold plate. KJC?*

I've never met Tim, but I've heard of him often. He's one of Stephen's closest friends in the department. They went to the academy together.

The words from the notepad run over and over in my head as I drive home. While waiting for the light to turn, I look up Standard Gold AK on Google. Of course! Standard Gold refers to the standard yellow license plate, the most common plate around here. So, KJC must be the beginning of the license plate.

Pulling in my driveway, I glance in my rearview mirror at Noah's house across the street. My heart skips a beat. All blood drains from my face. The bright yellow license plate on his SUV reads KJC5HS.

CHAPTER TWENTY-TWO

CHARLIE

I can't relax for the rest of the afternoon. I pace around the living room. That's Noah's car, right? Well, not necessarily. Noah's car has three additional characters. What is the likelihood of having the first three letters in that combination on a license plate anyway? I have no idea. I don't even know how many characters most license plates in Alaska have. But what was Noah doing all last night? He was definitely up to something.

Thoughts swirl around in my head until I feel dizzy. Instead of coming up with a solution, my mind just comes up with more possibilities. What if Noah did it? He was acting funny after the diner. I did see him come home all covered in dirt. What was he doing out after our time at the diner? What if he had something to do with Teaghan's death? Why would he kill a police officer? Thoughts continue to swirl around until I convince myself Noah couldn't have anything to do with Teaghan's disappearance. He's just a normal guy, right? I'm becoming one of those nosy know-it-all judgmental neighbors from an old sitcom. It's a fucking cliché.

I flip on the television and drown my thoughts in the mindless chatter of some reality show, which one I'm not entirely sure. Then, just right out of earshot, I hear a door slam behind me. Without turning around, I know it's Noah's front door. *Don't look*, I say to myself. It doesn't matter. It's probably not even him. Maybe it's his wife and daughter. And even if it were him, who cares? He has the right to go wherever he pleases. There's nothing suspicious about sharing the first three characters of a license plate with someone else. It doesn't mean anything.

Despite all of my best efforts, I'm unable to stop myself from turning around. It's Noah, walking around his SUV to the driver's side. Without a second thought, I grab my coat, wallet, and keys. Hopping into my car, I follow him.

Noah pulls into The Moose Hut, a small hole in the wall a few blocks away.

As he disappears inside, I stay outside, at the far end of the parking lot, debating whether or not I should follow him. I've been there on only one occasion, during a bar hop. It's a place where people come not to be seen. All I remember is that the place reeks of old fried food buns and has two entrances.

I walk through the back, position myself by the bathroom, and look around at the room. It's a dark place with low ceilings and poor ventilation. About half of the booths have customers. I scan the room for Noah and find him in the far left corner sitting across from another guy about his own age with a thick beard.

'Can I help you?' A waitress comes up to me. Startled, I jump back a foot. 'Oh my gosh, I didn't mean to scare you.'

We laugh it off and I ask her for a table. Glancing behind her, I can see that if she leads me counterclockwise around the room, I can slip into the booth right next to Noah's without him noticing me.

'Can I sit in that booth by the clock?'

'Sure thing, girlie.' The waitress smiles at me. She's an older, friendly woman who seems to genuinely enjoy her job – a dying breed.

I sit on the opposite side of Noah in my booth and hide behind the large menu for good measure. They are talking in low voices. Most words come out jumbled, but one thing comes through: money.

'What if the money is marked, Colton?' I hear Noah ask.

'Marked how?' the other guy asks.

'So, what would you like, miss?' The waitress comes back. I glance at the menu for a second.

'I'd like a beer,' I say, my voice is so quiet it's barely a whisper.

'What was that, honey?' the waitress asks. 'I didn't quite catch that.'

I clear my throat and try again.

'An IPA and the French onion soup,' I say a little louder. I'm not very hungry after the huge lunch I had with Stephen, but I can't very well order nothing.

'Shh, what was that?' Noah asks. I crouch down in my seat.

'What?'

'I just heard someone. It sounded like someone I know.' I drop my napkin and reach under the table to get it. I hear him breathing somewhere above me. He's looking straight at the table. I hold my breath until I can't hold it any longer. I pray that he doesn't look any further.

'No, no one's there. I think I'm going mad,' Noah says from somewhere high above me. My throat closes up. My hands start to shake. I remain firmly on the floor until I hear him flop on the bench in the other booth.

'I read online that there's a number of ways they can mark the money,' Noah says as I climb back up into the booth. The house music dies down, and their voices start to come in crystal clear.

'They can mark it with invisible ink, which is visible with UV rays only. And they can also track it using serial numbers,' Noah says.

'But that's only if they knew the money would go missing. Like at the bank. We don't know where the money came from,' the other guy says.

'True. But we need to think about this,' Noah says. 'We can't spend a dollar until we're completely sure. And we need to monitor the situation with the cop.'

The house music comes back on again with a vengeance, and I can't make out another word they say. I rush through my meal and get back in my car just as they exit the restaurant.

CHAPTER TWENTY-THREE

NOAH

I try to put my meeting with Colton out of my mind as I sit down at my computer the next day. Suddenly, writing has become something of an escape. Life has become so crazy and surreal that sitting down with my characters has become a way for me to disengage and take my mind somewhere else.

When writing is going well, there's a flow to it. There's nothing more natural. I put my hands on the keyboard and words come out of me at a rate that my hands have a difficult time keeping up with. I lose all sense of time and place. Nothing else exists except for the world on the page. And that world becomes all encompassing – all consuming. My characters suffer and I suffer along with them. My characters rejoice and I rejoice along with them. When writing is going well, the life that I create becomes so much more meaningful and real than my own world. In real life, I don't really know what Emily and Ava are thinking or feeling. They can tell me and I listen, but I don't know it the way I know my own feelings. There's a separation between us that doesn't exist between me and my characters on the page. I've always wondered about why that was and I think it's because I, like all writers, create my characters out of whole cloth. I give them certain characteristics in the beginning of the process – age, gender, basic physical and emotional attributes – and then I let them go. A better way of saying it would be that I follow them along their journey. I put them through hoops. I test them. I make up scenarios for them to endure and either overcome or be crushed by. The most exciting thing about this process is that somewhere in the middle, or sometimes in the beginning or the end, the characters break free of me. They start to live and act on their own terms. I make all of these plans for them – the basic outline of the story. But somewhere in the middle, they rebel. They stand up to me. They challenge me. They show me that this is not what they want to do, and I have to abide. I can't force them to act against their nature. I can't force them to be who they're not. At some point in my creative process, I have to let go. It's kind of like being a father. You create this person. You do everything for her. In the beginning, she follows you around. She worships you. She wants to be just like you. But as she starts to find out who she is, what feels right and wrong for her, she pulls away. She needs that space to become her true self. Ava isn't there yet. But I know it's coming. That's the ebb and flow of life, I guess.

I knew that this morning would be different by the way it smelled when I woke up. Instead of dragging my feet out of bed, procrastinating with making coffee and then dragging myself against my will to my office, I spring out of bed and run straight in. I don't bother changing out of my pajamas or even throwing on a robe. The room is icy cold and I wrap myself up in a blanket from the couch and grab a pen. Sometime in the middle of the night, I had an idea, an idea I'm desperate to jot down before it leaves me completely.

I see an old man who has lived the life of a bank manager in a land-locked state like Ohio. He had never wanted much and was always happy with the life he has led, raising two girls with his wife, who stayed home with them. And then one day, he reads a magazine article about a young man who built himself a sailboat and sailed around the world. The young man is in his twenties, without much money or security, and he lives in California. He also has long unkempt hair and ripped jeans. On the surface, the young man is the exact opposite of the old man. But something about the young man strikes him and he isn't able to get him out of his mind. He thinks about him and his sailboat while golfing with his friends, going to early bird dinners with his wife, and visiting his grandkids in the neighboring town. Then he decides to do something about it.

He buys some plans and the wood and starts to build a sailboat in his garage. At first, his wife thinks it's just an impulse project – something that he'll soon get sick of. But as days turn into weeks and then into months, she realizes she was wrong. The old man's interest in building the boat is only getting more and more intense and now he's talking about sailing to California around Cape Horn. His wife isn't keen on it. Even sailing the Caribbean scares her, because she's afraid of the third world. That's why she has never even been on a cruise.

But the old man's dream only picks up steam. The more he works on his boat, the more he has to work on it. He becomes obsessed. He hardly eats and sleeps and when he does it's always in the garage. Six months later, he is finally done. When he comes back inside the house to tell his wife, he discovers that she has moved out to live with their eldest daughter. The old man knows that he can persuade her to come back just by going over there, but he doesn't. Instead, he gets piss drunk on beer and champagne and considers lighting the damn thing on fire.

In the morning, he wakes up with a clearer head and makes a plan to move the boat to Chesapeake Bay and sail off from there. A bad storm pushes him back to shore and he lands somewhere in North Carolina. While riding out the storm, he goes into town and meets a woman. To say he falls in love with her would be an understatement. He doesn't fall for her like a man his age. He falls for her like an eighteen-year-old. He loves her as much as he loved his seventeen-year-old girlfriend all those years ago, his first love.

That's all I have so far about the old man and his sailboat. I'm not sure how I want it to end. What happens to his new love and his old marriage? What happens to his dream of sailing to California? One thing's for sure, he isn't getting stuck in that little North Carolina town. No, he's forging on. But does he actually go all the way around Cape Horn or does he die trying?

He could die at sea, and the ending could be either tragic or triumphant. In one version, we can see him dying without reaching his ultimate goal. In another, we can see him dying doing what he loves most in the world. I'm still not sure. One thing that I'm sure about is that I can't wait to get started on the story. I open my computer and start to write. The words pour out of me like water. I barely stop to take a break when my hands cramp up from typing so fast. I barely acknowledge Ava who comes into the room to play with her toys. I am completely immersed in the process, and I've never felt so alive.

Three hours later, I stop and look at the pages that I've written. There's nothing perfect about this draft, as if a draft can ever be perfect. But it's perfect for what it is – a first draft. The story isn't complete, not even close; it's a novel, after all. But I need a break.

I stretch my arms around behind me, cracking my back. Wow, I am sore. I haven't worked this hard in, I don't know how long and it's both daunting and exhilarating. Excitement is pushing through my veins, and I have a smile on my face. I swivel around in my chair. The sun is barely up outside, just a sliver of yellow over the horizon. A part of me wants to rush downstairs and tell Emily what I just did, but I'm afraid of breaking the spell. What if talking about it makes the muse go away? No, I can't do that. Not yet. I need to keep this under wraps for now. I sit down on the couch on the other side of the room and take in the moment. Why now? Why, after all those weeks and months of writer's block, is this finally happening? What's different? And then it hits me. I look over at the closet, where under a pile of empty Amazon boxes, which Emily has asked me to break down a million times, sits a suitcase full of cash.

It's the money. It has to be.

Despite all the shit that came with it, the money has set me free. There are piles and piles of cash sitting in my closet. But its value goes way beyond $2.2 million. It represents freedom. I don't have to go back to working as a teacher this summer to scrape together enough money to make the mortgage every month. I get the suitcase out of the closet and open it on my lap. Just holding the money in my hands is a breath of fresh air. It's a relief. Now, I can actually write for a living and still support my family.

I close the bag, hide it under a pile of boxes and some jeans for good measure, and head downstairs. Emily is already wearing her work clothes and is not pleased with the fact that I'm late.

'What were you doing up there all morning?' she asks.

'Writing,' I say. I consider telling her how much I've written and how excited I am, but I don't want to curse myself. No, some things I have to keep private – like the muse and the money.

Ava barely looks up when Emily kisses her goodbye because she's so engrossed in her coloring book. Some kids don't have much of an attention span, but growing up in this household, Ava was forced to develop the ability to entertain herself. I like that. She can occupy herself for hours with her books, drawings, and stories. She doesn't need other kids or parents to tell her what to do. She's rarely bored. I ask her if she wants a grilled cheese sandwich and she nods okay.

I get the bread out, American cheese, and butter. Ava prefers my grilled cheese to Emily's because I butter both sides of the bread and fry them on the skillet first. Then I add the cheese and grill the rest.

Just as we dig into our sandwiches, there's a knock at the door. It's Colton. I'm expecting him. We have some work to do. I turn on *Beauty and the Beast* for Ava so she can watch it as she's coloring and we head upstairs.

'Where did you get the UV light?' I ask, as he unpacks the box.

'Ordered it on Amazon, one day shipping.'

We put on latex gloves, take out the money, and lay it out on the floor. First, he carefully checks the top and back of each neatly sealed bundle. Nothing. We exchange smiles, but agree that we need to check each individual bill just to make sure. The process is rather labor-intensive, but eventually we get through the whole thing without finding any UV markings of any kind.

'Okay, good,' Colton says. 'I guess it isn't marked. So, I guess it's only fair for me to take a portion.'

'What?' I gasp.

Colton leans back on the couch, resting his leg on the opposite knee.

'Well, I've been thinking,' he says in his most salesman-y voice. 'I think it's only fair, Noah.'

They're taught to use people's names to make and solidify a connection. Apparently, if you use a person's name enough then they are more likely to cave and buy whatever it is you're trying to sell them. I know all this because I worked as a solar salesman myself once. I was off for the summer and Emily and Colton thought it would be a great way for me to make some extra cash while I wasn't teaching. First, I had to complete a one-week training session, which I graduated at the top of my class. Little did I know that despite that, I still couldn't make a sale to save my life.

'What's only fair, Colton?' I ask. Two can play the name game.

'Well, I wouldn't ask, Noah, except that I went through a lot. I mean, I was the one who shot that cop,' Colton says, whispering the word cop.

'And no one asked you to.'

'Oh, c'mon.' He rolls his eyes. 'You knew that I didn't have a choice.'

'And then you were supposed to take the body. And you didn't. You stuck me with it. Did you know that Emily insisted on taking my car to the recital? So, I was basically driving all around town with my family and that dead fucking cop in the trunk.'

'Listen…'

'No, you listen. You aren't taking any money. It's all my money. I did you a favor by getting rid of the body. You don't have to deal with it. I also got rid of the gun, which you conveniently didn't mention. What the hell was that about, Colton?'

Colton drops his leg. My aggressiveness seems to take him aback. For a few moments, he's at a loss for words. I'm actually shocked. I don't think I've ever seen him in this state before.

'I reported my gun missing a couple of days ago,' Colton says when he gathers his thoughts. 'And as for the rest of all that, I have no idea what you're talking about.'

We stare into each other's eyes. Neither of us blinks.

'What I do know is that you need to give me some of that money,' he finally says. 'If you want to keep this whole thing under wraps. From Emily. And the cops.'

'What are you going to do? Report me? And I'll report you back.'

'You may, but I don't have any money, Noah. Why would anyone think that I had anything to do with any of this?'

He has a good point there. Son-of-a bitch. I bite down on the inside of my lip.

'You're an asshole,' I say.

'I know. But so are you.'

'So you want hush money?'

'I think I'm entitled to it.'

'How much?'

'I want fifty percent.'

My jaw actually drops open. The audacity. What a prick!

'No, I don't think so. I can give you… ten. Tops.'

'Fine, thirty. That's my last offer.' Colton stares straight into my eyes.

I don't blink. He's toying with me. This isn't his final offer, not even close.

'Fifteen.'

'Twenty-five.'

'Twenty. Final offer,' I say. He nods. I'm pleasantly surprised. I thought I'd have to pay more, but I keep the angry smirk on my face for good measure. There's no need to explore my true feelings.

Colton picks up his phone and does the math. Then he heads straight into the bag and starts to count the money – $440,000. I look over his shoulder to make sure that he doesn't make a mistake in his favor.

'Listen, there's no hard feelings, right? We're still friends. Just think of it this way. You'll feel a lot better about this whole situation if I have some teeth in the game. I have something to lose now, too. Now, you know that I won't go to the police. I have no reason to.'

Luckily, Colton doesn't stick around after stealing my money. He heads straight out, without even bothering to saying bye to Ava. It's all for the best. I can't stand his face right now. Watching him pull out of my driveway, I make a promise to myself. One way or another, I'm going to get that money back.

CHAPTER TWENTY-FOUR

NOAH

With the wind blowing loudly behind me, I hustle from my car so that I spend the least amount of time outside possible. It's still pitch black and the sun won't be up until after ten this morning. Even then, it is likely that the cloud cover will make the few hours of sunlight gray and lackluster. It is days like these that I do not miss my work as a teacher and dread the thought of having to come back here. I walk into the classroom just as the rest of the kids start to shuffle in.

This is the only class I'm substitute teaching today, and that's enough for me. I walk into the room, take off my coat, and hang it on the back of my chair. My boots are covered in wet heavy snow and I stomp my feet hard to knock some of it off. Kids are starting to pile in, laughing and talking, without a worry in the world. Once they see that I'm the one who will be teaching their class instead of their regular teacher, their eyes light up. Most kids know that no substitute is as difficult or demanding as the primary teacher because we basically lack all authority. We don't have any power to assign any additional work other than what their teacher told us to do and we have little control over the lesson plan. In fact, most substitute teachers don't teach at all. They simply put on a video and zone out for fifty minutes.

I won't lie. Last night when I got the call, I was hoping that this would be an easy hour and I could pass the time with a video as well.

Unfortunately, Mrs. Rice is one of the oldest teachers at the school and isn't one to take shortcuts in her lesson plans. So, even if she can't be here, her kids are going to learn what they're supposed to today.

Once the kids settle in and get quiet, I pick up my notes and start to write on the board. They are reading *Romeo and Juliet*, not a favorite of kids this age, but definitely not as difficult and foreign a work as *The Scarlet Letter*. Why we still make kids read Hawthorne's historical fiction with its obscure language and customs, I have no idea. I've always believed that the way you reach kids is to get down on their level and make them read and analyze works of fiction that relate to their everyday life. And even if the writers aren't completely contemporary, a book like *The Catcher in the Rye* will get a lot further in making them connect to the literary world than anything by Hawthorne. Oh, well, unfortunately, I'm not the one in charge of the curriculum so I pretty much have no say in anything.

'Okay, so according to Mrs. Rice, you all should've read the second act of *Romeo and Juliet* for today,' I start, facing the class after writing my name and the topic at hand on the board.

A couple of kids text furiously on their phones and I debate whether I should interrupt what I'm saying to make them stop. For now, I let it go.

'What I would like to discuss now is the scene where Friar Laurence is advising Romeo against marrying Juliet so soon after meeting each other. In this scene, he's trying to warn Romeo of the dangers of moving too fast and rushing things. What were your thoughts about this scene?' I ask.

I wait, but no one responds. A few people have their books open, feverishly trying to find the scene that I'm talking about. Others are scribbling away in their notebooks, doodling, or working on something that has nothing to do with what we're discussing. Three other people pick up their phones, hiding them poorly behind their desks. I haven't been in the classroom for some time, so for a moment I am surprised by the fact that all of these students think that I don't know exactly what's going on and the fact that they're not doing what they're supposed to.

I ask the question another way, trying to relate to them on their level. 'Have any of your parents ever said that to you? That you were moving too fast in a relationship?'

Again, no one responds, and even more students look like they are losing interest. I repress the desire to shout at the top of my lungs for them to answer me, and instead let it go. I'm not their teacher and no amount of effort on my part is going to make them wake up.

'Okay, if you don't want to talk about that, let's talk about a very important line from the second act. The part where Friar Laurence tells Romeo, *these violent delights have violent ends.* What does that mean to you?'

Someone in the back raises his hand. I smile as I become overjoyed by the fact that a student actually wants to engage with me.

'Yes, you in the back,' I say.

'Can I get the hall pass?' the guy with a crew cut and a cocky grin on his face says. 'I need to use the bathroom.'

'Um, yes,' I stutter, feeling myself caught off guard. He walks up to the front and I hand him the hall pass. He stares at me, dumbfounded.

'Um, you have to fill it out.'

'What?'

'You have to fill out all the lines there, otherwise the hall pass monitor won't accept it.'

Now it's my turn to stare at him. Another stupid idea that the school administration came up with to waste the teachers' time. I mean, I have to interrupt the flow and momentum of my lecture, however little, to fill out half a page with useless information just for one person to go to the bathroom. There are lines for my name, class, time, the student's name, and my signature. What a fucking waste.

It takes me a few minutes to collect my thoughts and remember what the hell I was talking about in the first place. Instead of asking any more questions, I decide to just tell them what they need to know and hope that a few will write it down in their notes.

'Now, this line plays a very important role not just in this book, but in the whole body of literature. It's now even spilling over to pop culture with shows like *Westworld* mentioning it a number of times throughout the first season. What Shakespeare is trying to say is that violent delights are the pleasure that people take in violence. The history of humanity is filled with violence and we are known for taking great pleasure in revenge, war, and other violent endeavors. But all of these pleasures or delights are also what's going to lead to the downfall of our characters. That by taking in the pleasure of violence we are doomed to lose our lives to this violence.'

I'm not sure how much of that makes it into their heads, but I do spot a few people taking notes, and for now that's enough for me. A girl in the front row raises her hand. She is one of the scribblers and she looks like she's about to add something to this conversation.

'Yes, you, right there,' I say.

'Um, is this going to be on the test?' she asks, shattering my hopes of a stimulating critical thinking dialogue with a single question.

The rest of the class period proceeds pretty much in the same fashion. I talk until my throat is parched, hoping that one of my statements will encourage them to participate, but it's all to no avail. By the end of the period, I'm exhausted and bored. Instead of heading straight home, I decide to visit the teachers' lounge and decompress a little.

I get a pack of peanut M&Ms from the vending machine and sit down on the couch, letting the sugar dissolve on my tongue.

'You look exhausted,' Mrs. Biddle says, sitting down next to me. She's in her early forties, mother of two, and a dedicated teacher ever since she got her teaching license right after college. She teaches US history and her enthusiasm seems to be never ending. When I first started teaching, I found her and her well-organized room with color-coded binders and typed lesson plans to be incredibly annoying. But now, I'm just thankful that people like her exist. She was born to be a teacher and she would do this job no matter what – whether she got paid ten thousand dollars a year or two hundred thousand.

'I am,' I say, popping another M&M into my mouth. 'That's why I'm having candy and it's not even ten in the morning.'

Mrs. Biddle laughs, opening her notebook and getting out a ruler from her bag. Who the hell carries around rulers in their bags? I wonder, but don't mention it.

'I'm just subbing for Mrs. Rice and those kids are really hard to engage.'

'Really?' Mrs. Biddle asks.

With Mrs. Rice suffering with a recurrence of breast cancer, almost everyone at the school has been asked to sub for her.

'I've never really found that to be the case,' Mrs. Biddle adds, drawing perfect lines down the center of her notebook. It sounds like she's showing me up, but I know her well enough to not take her seriously. She doesn't mean it in a bad way.

'Maybe I'm just not cut out for this. I really hope that I can finish my book soon,' I say.

Everyone in the school knows that I'm working on a novel. Besides an illness, there is no other explanation for taking such a long sabbatical. And before I got started, I thought that it would be nice to tell everyone, even those people who I didn't particularly like, as a way of keeping myself accountable. Isn't that what they're always saying? You should put your goals out there, tell everyone you know about them, just to keep yourself honest.

'Oh, yes, of course. How's that going?'

'Really good actually,' I say. 'Much better than I thought.'

Up until today, I've always said that and it has always been a lie. It was too hard to admit the truth. It would be like admitting failure and with failure it would mean that I would have to come back here next semester and teach again.

'Really? That's wonderful,' Mrs. Biddle says in her usual upbeat and encouraging tone. 'Well, whatever it is that's helping you write, keep doing more of it.'

'Yes, I sure will.'

'What's it about?'

'I'd rather not say. You know, hoping that the muse doesn't go away. I mean, I struggled with writer's block for quite some time so I don't want to do anything to jinx it.'

'I understand,' Mrs. Biddle says and returns to making lines in her notebook. I watch her work for a bit and then realize that she's making a calendar. She carefully writes the dates in the upper right-hand corner of each box. And even though the calendar is homemade, I'm actually impressed by her workmanship.

I recline into the couch and lose myself in my own thoughts. I need a moment to process the fact that I'm actually telling the truth about my writing. Up until now, I've lied so much about the progress of my work – always being a little bit embarrassed at the fact that it wasn't going as well as I thought it should be. Telling the truth now feels rather odd. I pop another M&M in my mouth and smile. At last I think the future is looking good for me.

CHAPTER TWENTY-FIVE

CHARLIE

Nana and I have a standing date for lunch that I generally look forward to every week. But today, my mind is elsewhere. I keep going back to what happened at the diner yesterday. I can't stop thinking about the fact that they almost caught me spying on them and what I overheard. They were talking about ways that money could be marked. They mentioned a cop. Is Noah involved in Teaghan's disappearance? What exactly did I overhear?

'Can I help you?' the front desk receptionist in the lobby asks me as I wander in, lost in my own thoughts. I nod absentmindedly and sign in.

Nana isn't like my mom at all. Even though she likes to dress up and get made up, she never makes a fuss about my own appearance the way my mom did. She's a lot easier to deal with than Mom was, too. It's like she actually listens to me, rather than just waiting for her turn to speak.

When I get to Nana's two-room suite, I hear sobbing through the crack in the door. I've never seen my grandmother cry except at Papa's funeral. And even then, it wasn't these big sloppy sobs like the ones coming from her room now.

'Nana, are you okay?' I burst through the door. She presses her index finger to her lips to hush me and wraps her arms tighter around the crying woman who has her head on Nana's chest.

'Oh, my, I'm so sorry.' The woman turns around. Her honey-blonde shoulder-length hair is a frizzy mess. Her round face is covered in large red spots. Her eyes are puffy and barely visible.

'No, I'm sorry, I can come back.'

'No, there's no need,' Nana says. The woman wipes her eyes and blows her nose into the tissue that Nana hands her.

'Hi, I'm Holly Donaldson,' the woman says, extending her hand. I introduce myself and apologize again for interrupting them. 'I'm the one who's sorry. Your grandmother is just so kind. And after she moved here, I just miss our talks so much. She was the best neighbor, you know?'

I smile and nod.

'Help yourself, Charlie.' Nana offers me some tea and cookies.

I help myself to a round gingerbread cookie and pour myself a cup of Earl Grey.

'You work in the police department, don't you?' Holly asks. 'I'm sure your grandmother told you that my sister, Julie, has gone missing.'

'Yes, of course. I'm so sorry,' I say. 'I used to babysit her, remember?'

'Oh yes, of course,' Holly says absentmindedly.

'Is there any news about her? Have they found anything?' I ask as my mind wanders back to the journal I read. I feel guilty for reading it, but I also wish that she didn't come back for it so soon.

Tears well up in her eyes, and she buries her head in her nana's lap. I'm about to say something, but Nana raises her hand to stop me. We sit here in silence as Holly cries.

'I just feel so lost,' Holly says after composing herself somewhat. 'The police don't know anything. They think she ran away to Florida and is just not getting back to me for whatever reason. But they don't know what teenagers are like. It's like they don't know how normal it is for them to say all sorts of crazy things and then still love you and still come home.'

'The thing is that there's this guy, Kevin. He's my roommate's friend. Jonathan's friend,' Holly says.

Oh, yeah, Jonathan. I remember the journal entry I read the last time I was here. He's the guy Holly has been falling for. He's the guy who has slept with Julie.

'We went out a couple of nights ago. Jonathan was supposed to go, too, but he couldn't because his baby's mom threw a fit and wanted him to come over. So, it was Kevin and me. I only knew of him through Jonathan so I sort of enjoyed getting to know him a little better. Well, he got really drunk. I drank a little, too, but I didn't want James to get mad at me when I got home. Anyway, he got drunk and then he mentioned that Julie did work for him.'

Tears run down Holly's face. She can't wipe them away quickly enough. I wait for her to continue.

'As far I knew, Julie didn't have a job. She was allergic to work. I asked her to get a job as a waitress a million times. She's pretty and the out-of-towners love to tip big. But she just never seemed interested. And she always seemed to have money. Well, now, Kevin mentions that apparently she delivered packages for him. And he, or rather his boss, paid her good money to do that.'

'What kind of packages?' I ask.

'I have no idea. But I'm not stupid. Of course, it has to be something illegal. Otherwise, why wouldn't they just use the Post Office?'

'So, you think she was delivering drugs for this Kevin guy?' I ask with anticipation.

'I think so. Or guns. Or both. Who the hell knows?'

'Did he say anything else?'

She shakes her head.

'He just said that and then immediately regretted it and asked me to promise to never tell anyone. Especially the cops. Otherwise, he can't guarantee my safety.'

Nana and I exchange looks. Wow, this is big.

'Are you going to tell them?' Nana asks.

'I don't know.' She shrugs. 'If I tell the detectives in charge of her case, then they'll definitely reach out to Kevin and ask him questions about it. And he'll definitely know that I spilled the beans.'

'Are you afraid of him?' I ask.

Holly stares at me with her large doe-like eyes. She blinks once before answering.

'I'm not really afraid of him. But maybe I should be. I mean, I had no idea that he was into anything like that. I thought he was a pharmacy technician at Rite Aid just like Jonathan.'

'This is a tough one,' Nana says. 'On the one hand, you don't want any trouble. But on the other, this is the first good lead you've had in a while. What if the cops can get something out of him? It could lead to finding Julie once and for all.'

Holly nods. A few minutes later, the debate is over. It's decided. Holly will go to the cops. Whether this is indeed the best idea, none of us really know.

As I pull into my driveway, I see a strange car parked across the street. I search my bag for a piece of gum and when I finally find it, a guy comes out of Noah's house. Looking closer, he looks familiar. Where have I see him before? Oh, yeah, it finally hits me. He's the same guy that Noah had dinner with at that diner. What did Noah call him? Colton? The guy looks to be about Noah's age, but more confident, cocky even. He has broad shoulders and is clearly not a stranger to the gym. As he gets into his car and pulls out of the driveway, I decide to follow him. I don't have a good reason to follow him except that I want to know more. The conversation at the diner left me with more questions than answers.

I stay a few cars away, the way that Stephen showed me when I went on a drive-by with him. I follow him in his BMW SUV for about twenty minutes. Then we pull into Eklunta Historical Park. I haven't been here since my sixth grade field trip. Located at the head of Knik Arm of Cook Inlet and the mouth of the Eklunta River, it's about twenty-five miles outside of Anchorage.

I watch as he parks and gets out of his car, carrying a shoe box, and walks to the last row of the spirit houses. He's gone for a few minutes. While I wait, I get out of my car and head to the other side of the church to read the historic plaque. Apparently, this was a place where people would cremate their dead.

I duck behind the other side of the church when I see the guy heading back to his car. He no longer has the shoe box. I wait for him to drive away before following his footsteps to the back of the cemetery. At first, I don't see anything. Just a bunch of colorful burial boxes and stomped footsteps behind each one. There's snow on the ground, and the guy was definitely being careful. I walk back and forth behind the last row of the spirit houses, kicking myself for not following him further.

I should've just followed him back to his house and then come back here. What was the rush? At least that way, I could find out his name.

And then, just as I'm about to give up, I spot something out of the corner of my eye. A small bug sneaks out from the back panel of the white and green spirit house at the end of the row. There's a crack! I kneel down and press on the panel. Much to my surprise, it just falls back, but not all the way. What is going on? I grab the panel and wiggle it out of place. It's a false wall. The real wall of the spirit house is just on the other side of the shoe box! Crouching down to make sure that no one from the church sees me, I carefully open the lid.

CHAPTER TWENTY-SIX

NOAH

I want to make it up to Emily so I invite her out to dinner. She's reluctant at first, but I insist. I tell her I want to make amends and that the place that I want to take her will not disappoint her. When I call to make reservations, I get the feeling that Emily isn't taking my offer very seriously. Lounging on the couch with her face buried in her Kindle, she has probably decided that I'm going to take her to some chain place with a predicable menu and unlimited breadsticks. There's nothing wrong with places like that, of course, and I'm known to enjoy their soups and cookie-cutter Italian cuisine. But I know that in order to make an impact on Emily, this place needs to be a lot more special.

I find the number of the babysitter in the drawer next to the refrigerator. When we first found her, we promised each other to go out every week for a date night, but as weeks blended into months and our financial situation got worse and worse, we'd ended up only using her services twice in two years. Luckily, she's free tonight.

'The babysitter is all set up,' I say, heading upstairs to change into a suit and tie. 'She'll be here in an hour if you want to start getting ready.'

Emily looks up at me from the couch with a perplexed look on her face. 'Where are we going?'

'The Grape Tap,' I say and wait for her reaction. This has been the place Emily has begged me to take her for ages, but I always used money as an excuse. It is quite expensive, of course, but the reason I have avoided it was that I hated the idea of putting on a tie and dress shoes.

'Seriously?' Emily's eyes light up. I nod.

'I really think we deserve a fun night out. We haven't been there before. And I want to have a special night.'

Emily nods. 'Well, in that case, I better had start getting ready.'

An hour later, we both meet downstairs in our Sunday best, so to speak. I'm wearing the most expensive suit that I have complete with dress shoes, socks, and a thin black tie. Emily looks stunning in her little black dress. It's sleeveless and hugs her in just the right places. She's also wearing black closed-toe heels and is carrying a bright red shawl.

'Wow,' I say, shaking my head. I don't remember the last time I saw my wife look like this. My mouth drops open a bit because she looks so gorgeous. Large loose curls fall softly around her face and her lips are outlined with succulent deep red lipstick. It's all I can do to not reach over and kiss her.

'You look so beautiful,' I say.

'Thank you.' She nods.

The babysitter arrives shortly after and Ava welcomes her with both arms. As they settle down in the living room to play restaurant, I escort Emily to the car.

A gust of cold northern air hits me like a brick and suddenly, I'm keenly aware of why dressing like this isn't advised in Alaska. I can't even imagine how Emily is feeling with her bare legs exposed to the elements so I rush to get her into the car.

'Wow, it's really getting cold out there,' Emily says, turning the heat up and warming her hands in front of the vents.

'This should make things more comfortable,' I say, turning on the seat warmers and waiting for the hot air to warm me from the inside out.

'I still can't believe that you are taking me to the Grape Tap,' Emily says on the drive over. 'I've wanted to go there forever.'

'I know. And I'm sorry that I haven't taken you there before. It's supposed to be wonderful.'

We sit in silence for a moment at the red light.

'I guess you must be really sorry,' Emily says after a few moments. It's unlike her to just come out and say anything like that, but instead of denying it, I nod and agree. The point of this dinner is to make amends, so why not start now?

'Yes, I am. You have no idea. I didn't mean to do anything, but that's no excuse. I just want to apologize for everything and start over. I love you, Emily.'

It isn't my intention to say all this in the car while I'm turning left and focusing on not running into any other cars. Instead, I would've preferred to say all this staring lovingly into her eyes over dinner, but I decide to seize the moment. A bad moment is still better than nothing at all.

'Well, thank you for taking me out,' Emily says after a few moments. The coldness that has been ever-present between us ever since she walked in on me in my office is starting to thaw. It's not completely gone, of course, but we're on our way. I smile and squeeze her hand.

'My pleasure,' I say.

When we get to the restaurant, the hostess leads us past the bright and cheery upstairs sitting area toward the cozy and dark downstairs room with a rich, much more moody tone. Here, the walls are made of jagged rocks and the lights look like candles, creating an atmosphere of mystery and magic. The restaurant has a wine cellar and it's famous for unique wines and craft beers. A server in black pants, a starched white shirt, and a tie shows us to a charming table to one side.

He gives us the wine list and the menu and asks us if we have ever been here before. When we tell him that we haven't, he tells us a little bit about the history of the place. Apparently, it opened in 2009 after it was remodeled from an original homesteaded home. I glance over the menu as he explains that the food is all contemporary with items made from scratch using the freshest ingredients available. Local produce is used whenever possible.

After asking the server to recommend us some wine, we look at the menu. My mouth immediately starts to salivate at the options. There's the plump dates stuffed with chèvre cheese and wrapped in bacon and French brie encrusted with mixed nuts, served with a French baguette and orange mango marmalade.

'The sesame ahi tuna looks good,' Emily says.

'Fresh seared tuna encrusted with sesame seeds with wasabi crispy rice cake and Ponzu dipping sauce.' I read the description. 'Wow, that does sound good.'

When the server comes back, he lets us taste our wine to get our approval before pouring us our glasses. I place the order for the appetizer and my dinner and, after a few moments of hesitation, Emily finally decides on what she wants. Once the server departs, I raise my glass of wine to say a few words.

'I just want to thank you for coming out tonight. You have no idea what it means to me,' I say.

'Thank you,' Emily says, clinking her glass to mine.

Taking a sip of my wine, I look at her face and see the woman that I fell in love with all those years ago. There are a few lines around her eyes, mostly laugh lines, but otherwise she has changed very little. She has the same wicked sense of humor and a tongue full of venom and sarcasm. And her eyes light up just as brightly as before when she sees something that she wants.

Even though I'm not out of the woods yet, I still can't believe how close I got to losing it all. I take Emily's hand and run my fingers gently around her wrist. My desire for Charlie seems so far away; it's almost as if it had been someone else entirely. I don't know her well, but in this moment I'm certain that she is half the woman that my wife is. This is the person who supported me emotionally, financially, and any other way there is to be supported all these years, and helped make our family what it is. I cannot imagine my life without her. What would that even be like?

Emily smiles to herself and shakes her head.

'What?' I ask. She shakes her head again and waves me off. But I press her. Finally, she caves.

'I'm just surprised, that's all,' she says after a moment.

'By what?'

'Nothing,' she says with a shrug. 'I don't know.'

She's clearly hesitating in saying whatever she means to say.

'Okay, I'm surprised by the fact that you took me here. I know that money is a bit tight right now.'

I nod. I know exactly what she means. I hate this quality about myself, but I'm quite stingy with money. Mostly, I don't like going out to fancy dinners in general and our lack of financial resources and considerable debt are just a good excuse not to indulge in things that I don't really have any interest in in the first place.

'I've been a pretty bad husband lately,' I say after a moment. 'And I just wanted to make it up to you. We haven't been out in ages and this place seemed perfect.'

'It is,' Emily says, looking around and taking in the atmosphere. 'But still. You've been acting really weird lately.'

'Weird how?'

'Kind of absent. Sneaking around. Is something wrong?'

'No, not at all.'

'Are you sure?'

'Well, actually, there was reason I wanted to bring you here,' I say after a moment.

CHAPTER TWENTY-SEVEN

NOAH

I run my fingers over the little box in my pocket. I bought it online and it came just this morning, luckily before Emily got the chance to check the mail.

I put the box on the table and watch as her eyes light up. She opens it slowly, extending the moment as long as possible. That's her trademark move. She's never one to rush. No matter how excited she gets, she always takes a deep breath and centers herself first.

When she opens the lid, she pulls out the delicate bracelet made of white gold and tiny little emeralds. Her eyes well up with tears and she bites her lower lip to keep them at bay.

'Oh my God, Noah,' she whispers. I smile and help her put the bracelet on. 'It's beautiful, Noah. Just beautiful.'

She loves it. Adores it. She can't keep her eyes off it. I know because Emily isn't one to fake any emotions just for the sake of being polite. I let out a deep sigh of relief. I loved this bracelet the minute that I saw it on Amazon, but I wasn't sure what Emily would think of the emeralds. My wife isn't the type to wear a lot of jewelry. In fact, we rarely exchange presents at all and when we do, it's usually something practical, something we both could use around the house. That's sort of missing the whole point of presents, I know, but that was just the habit we fell into over the years.

'But, Noah, we can't afford this,' Emily says quietly after a few moments. 'I mean, I love it, don't get me wrong. But it must've cost a fortune.'

Emily has always been the practical one. Even though I can be quite stingy sometimes about stuff that I don't like – in particular, going out to fancy restaurants and going shopping – I have been known to indulge in a few toys for myself, even if we couldn't quite afford it. But Emily has always been the rock. She is the one in our relationship who has known whether we could or couldn't afford something. Except for now, of course. She doesn't know how much we have in cash back at our house.

'It's fine. You deserve it. I wanted to get it for you. Not just to say that I'm sorry, but to tell you how much I love you. And always have.'

'I love you, too,' Emily whispers. 'But still, I don't think we can afford it.'

'Okay, I got it for a discount, okay? I didn't want to tell you, but it was a big going-out-of-business sale. They were selling everything. Dirt cheap.'

Suddenly, as I look into Emily's eyes, I feel the guilt of lying to her. I get a strong urge to just come out and tell her everything. The whole truth. Well, maybe not the part about the police officer, but definitely the part about the money. I know that she worries about money a lot, and maybe if she knows about the stacks of cash, she wouldn't worry so much. But, of course, there's a risk in that. Emily is a very honest person, which I have always admired about her. But that also makes it quite difficult to tell her the truth about the cash. I mean, what if she wants me to give it back? What if she doesn't want to keep it?

As the words hover on my lips, the waiter arrives with the food.

We dig into our meal with great appetite and moans of pleasure. It's the most delicious thing I've tasted in a long time. I insist on Emily trying some of my crab cakes and feed her from my fork.

'Oh my God, these are amazing,' she concurs, taking another forkful of her prawns and offering it to me.

'Wow, I have to say this place is totally worth the price,' I say after a moment.

'I never thought I'd hear you say that,' Emily jokes, chewing. 'You realize that the entrées here are like twenty-five to thirty-five dollars, right?'

'I know, I know.' I shrug. 'But, wow, that's all I have to say.'

Emily takes another bite, shaking her head. 'Who are you, Noah? You seem like a totally new person.'

I watch her take a sip of wine and wonder if I have indeed changed that much. I don't see it myself, but perhaps I have. I don't know if it is all the cash or all the stuff that I've gone through over the past few days, but I do feel a lot different. More assertive. More certain. More confident, even. Again, I feel a pang in my chest and a strong desire to tell her about it. But again, I tell myself that this isn't the right time. Not yet.

'You know, I have been thinking about something,' I say after a moment. Emily finishes her glass of wine and waits for me to continue. After the server fills her glass back up, I say, 'Well, what would you think about starting a new life somewhere?'

She looks at me with a flat expression. I can't really read anything into it, so I continue.

'There are places in the world where the weather is much nicer.'

'That's true.'

'Ava's not in school yet. And the market is up, so we can probably make a little bit of a profit by selling the house.'

'Where would you like to go?'

'I don't know,' I say. I actually don't. Besides just the idea of going somewhere warmer, I don't really have any specific place in mind. But then again, almost everywhere is warmer than here in the deep north.

'It's so funny that you brought this up,' Emily says. 'But I was actually reading about Key West, Florida, a couple of days ago. It's a very old town, cobblestone streets, big palm trees. Lots of historic properties. They're surrounded by water and it's sunny all year round. Except for when they have hurricanes, of course.'

'Key West.' I mull over that idea. 'I don't really know anything about it except that Hemingway lived there. But I like the sound of it.'

'It's not very cheap,' Emily says.

'Well, neither is this place,' I point out. The cost of living in Alaska is quite high, actually. Given how hard it is to live here, Emily and I have often wondered why things are so expensive. Short summers make for short construction seasons and the fact that we are so far from the lower forty-eight states also doesn't help in bringing the costs of supplies down.

Emily looks up Key West on her phone and shows me images of bright-colored houses and Key Lime pie, people wearing nothing but flip-flops, shorts, and tank tops in January and men proudly standing next to their large catches of swordfish and other types of fish.

'I have to say, this place doesn't look all that bad,' I say. Emily stares wistfully at the screen.

'No, it doesn't,' she says. 'Besides, I'm pretty sure that a Hemingway lifestyle is something that you could really get used to quite easily.'

'What do you mean?' I smile.

'Well, you know, you could write in the mornings, fish in the afternoons. Or the other way around.'

'But when will I do all of my drinking?'

'Anytime. I'm pretty sure that everywhere in the Caribbean people have the same motto. "It's five p.m. somewhere," right?'

I laugh and finish my glass of wine. While the server pours me another, I try to imagine what it would actually be like to live there.

'But what would we do there?' Emily asks.

'Oh, you mean before my book becomes a bestseller? I don't know. They probably have a hospital. You can get a job there as a nurse. And I'm sure they have a school there as well.'

'So, basically, what we do here?' Emily asks. The expression on her face falls and the pain in her eyes is undeniable. I know that Emily isn't the biggest fan of her job, but I didn't realize exactly how much she doesn't like it. Perhaps she feels about nursing the exact same way that I feel about teaching.

'It's not that I hate being a nurse, except that I sort of do. I mean, I thought that going into nursing would be a good option after I couldn't get into medical school, but now I'm not so sure. I mean, everyone I work with is so unhappy. We work hours that are way too long. The patients are difficult and uncompromising and the doctors are worse. They just take advantage of us; we have to do everything. And we get paid like half of what they do.'

'If you could do anything else, what would it be?'

'You mean for money?'

'No, not exactly. I mean, if you could just spend your days doing whatever. What would that be?'

She shrugs and looks away from me.

'I'm not like you, Noah. I don't have this desire to write. I mean, you have wanted to be a writer for a very long time. Ever since we met. Probably even before college. But I just wanted to be a doctor because I thought it would be a good profession. Sort of like the reason I went into nursing. But now that we have Ava... honestly, I don't really want to do anything but be there for her. I want to have time to play with her, to take her to the park, to just spend time with her. That and maybe do a little pottery. I like working with my hands.'

'You made some beautiful plates last summer,' I say.

'I really enjoyed that class and I just wish I had more time for pottery and for Ava. But as far as my job goes, I sort of hate it, you know? I mean, I need to do it for money, but then I resent it because it takes me away from everything else that I really want to do.'

I take a deep breath. 'I hate my job, too,' I say after a moment. 'I mean, just even going back to substitute for a few days really reminded me about how much I hate it exactly. The kids don't care about anything and they barely listen to me. There are so many other people there who just love teaching, despite the kids and their attitudes, but that's just not me.'

'I know,' Emily says, putting her hand on mine. 'Man, we really got ourselves in a pickle, didn't we?'

'But the thing is that I really do love writing. Even when it's really hard sometimes, well, most of the time. Even when the words are just not coming. Even when it feels like I'm trying to squeeze water out of a stone, there's nothing else I would rather do. There's something so exhilarating about telling a story. There's nothing else like it. It makes me feel… complete.'

Emily and I talk about our dreams all through dinner and into dessert. We haven't talked like this in years, probably before Ava was born. The thing that's most disappointing about adulthood is that often you forget the things that you wanted to be as a child. And not just forget, but forcibly push away. But even though you're older now, an adult with certain responsibilities like a mortgage and a child, that doesn't mean that the person you once were is gone. Those dreams and aspirations that you had within you when you were younger are still there. They never really go away. They stay with you, buried deep inside somewhere and will continue to gnaw at you from the inside out. You can't ever get rid of them because they make you who you are.

CHAPTER TWENTY-EIGHT

NOAH

Sitting in my old classroom, I run my fingers against the grain on the desk. I try to count how many hours of my life I've spent here and I can't come up with a good number. Can I imagine spending the rest of my life here? I used to think so. Now, I'm not so sure. Colton had no right to take my money. His half? He thinks he's entitled to a half? What planet is he living on? I never asked him to kill anyone. He went out and did that all on his own. My heart skips a beat. That cop did not deserve to die. If it weren't for Colton, my gun-obsessed, trigger-happy asshole of an ex-brother-in-law, he would still be alive. The guilt is consuming me from inside out and there's not one damn thing I can do about it.

I look around the room. The kids all have their heads down, writing furiously in their blue notebooks. Most have illegible handwriting – something in between cursive and print, but luckily it's not going to be my job to grade these tests. That privilege will fall to Mrs. Bryson this semester. I'm still on sabbatical, but I'm filling in for her today since all the regular subs are busy. Supervising tests is my favorite thing about teaching. Just sitting at the front of the class and working on my novel or staring into space. Not repeating the same lecture I have given in two other classes that day. Not asking questions that no one has an answer to. Not calling on kids who are only raising their hands so that they can go to the bathroom.

I should've never been a teacher. For some reason, everyone in this profession is expected to have a big passion for it. Many do, but there are many who don't. Plumbers aren't expected to have a passion for their jobs. Neither are police officers. Or insurance claims adjustors. But teachers are somehow expected to do this job entirely for the joy of teaching. One thing is for sure, we definitely don't do this for the abysmal salary.

I glance at the clock. I haven't typed a word in fifteen minutes. Okay, focus, I say to myself. At home, I've been working nonstop on the old man and the sailboat novel, but here, I can't focus at all. The amount of momentum that I've gained ever since I started on this thing has been surprising. The words were pouring out of me. I have a few brief notes about each chapter, but I'm never at a loss as to what to write. I know that it has everything to do with the thick stash of cash in my house. Money is freedom. Its presence has taken away all of the fears and worries about paying for basic necessities. It has liberated me to do exactly what I want to do. And what I want to do right now is finish this novel. I'm still undecided about the ending, but I have decided to stop worrying about it. Maybe it will just come to me when I get there. Just like everything else.

A confident knock startles me. Through the glass window in the door, I see that it's Colton. What the hell is he doing here? I shake my head at him and point to the students. But he continues to knock. Doesn't he get the fact that I'm at work? What is he thinking?

He waves his hand at me, urging me to come out. Eventually, I give in.

'What the hell are you doing here? I'm subbing a test, can't you see that?' I ask.

'Did you think I wouldn't find out, you asshole?' Colton takes a step forward to intimidate me. 'Who do you think you are?'

I stare at him, dumbfounded. Is this the same person I saw last night? He's dressed in the same clothes. His hair is rumpled and out of control. He looks like he hasn't slept a wink. And what is the stench? It's some sort of gut wrenching combination of urine and sweat.

'I don't know what you're talking about.' I stare at him.

Colton's eyes are nearly popping out of his head in anger.

'Keep your voice down,' I add.

'You stole my money.'

His voice echoes around the hallway. Shivers run down my spine.

'No, I didn't.'

'I hid the money in a very secure place and you fucking followed me and stole it, you son-of-a-bitch.'

Colton walks in circles in between two walls of lockers. He paces like a caged lion.

'I don't know what you're talking about,' I say calmly. 'I don't even know where you put it. Was it somewhere in your house?'

'No. I hid it in Eklunta.'

Eklunta? I think to myself. I've seen the sign for that town on the highway, but I've never taken that exit.

Suddenly, Colton grabs me by my collar.

'Oh, c'mon, don't pretend that you don't know. You know! I took out fifteen grand and went to the casino. And when I went back for more, it wasn't there anymore.'

Colton slams me into the lockers. The crashing sound echoes along the long hallway, briefly transporting me to my own high school years, which had not been kind.

'Colton, listen to me. I don't know what happened to your money. I've never been to Eklunta.'

Before his fist even reaches my face, I see it in his eyes that he doesn't believe me. Acting on instinct, I duck. His fist barely grazes my cheek and slams into the locker behind me.

'And what about the cop?' he asks.

I glance around. Everyone's eyes are on us. My blood runs cold. He needs to shut the hell up.

'I have no idea what you're talking about.' I try to shush him.

'You're a fuckin' liar!' he roars. Fueled by pain and anger, Colton grabs me and throws me to the floor. He throws one punch, which lands squarely in my gut, briefly knocking out my breath. But before he's able to hit me again, I manage to slip out of his grasp and punch him in the head. Somewhere in the distance, I hear footsteps gathering around us. Someone gasps and says my name. Colton refuses to let me go. We continue to tussle around on the cold linoleum floor until a loud buzzing sound startles us. Kids start to stream into the hallway all around us. Colton finally releases his grasp on me and I rise to my feet. I'm saved by the bell.

'This isn't over,' Colton hisses before walking away.

A few kids from my classroom ask me if I'm okay as I straighten my clothes and push my hair somewhat back into place.

'Yes, I'm fine. Really. It's fine,' I say as convincingly as possible.

Walking back into the empty classroom, I collect all the blue notebooks thrown haphazardly around my desk. I gather my stuff, drop off the tests in Mrs. Bryson's mailbox, and head back to my car. I speed through the yellow lights to get home. I don't know where Colton went, but he knows where I keep my money. I need to move it as soon as possible.

CHAPTER TWENTY-NINE

NOAH

I enter the house holding my breath. I want to slip upstairs without being noticed, but I can't do that with my dirty boots on. Quickly, I unlace them and look around. My heart rate is jacked, beating so hard it feels like it's going to jump out of my chest. I try to act normal. After taking off my boots, I take off my coat.

That's when I notice it.

Shit.

The stairs and foyer have lines in the carpet. Evidence that Emily has vacuumed. I had

promised to do that earlier and I forgot.

Maybe it would be best to make my presence known before sneaking away.

'Hello?' I yell, trying to act as normal as possible.

'We're in here,' Ava squeaks over the familiar sound of *The Little Mermaid* playing in the background. It's her favorite movie of all time this month. She is watching it on loop from morning to night. Well, not so much watching as having it on the television while she's playing.

'You're home early,' Emily says.

'Yeah, they didn't need me for the other classes, apparently.'

Ava runs into my legs, holding an opened bottle of nail polish in one hand and the dripping paintbrush in the other.

'Be careful,' Emily says. 'You're going to get that everywhere.'

She almost does. I catch the bright pink drop in my palm before it falls onto the carpet.

'It's okay, I got it,' I say, giving Ava a big kiss on her head. It doesn't smell like her shampoo. No, it's so much more than that. It's the scent of love, hope, and the future, all rolled into one.

'So, what are you two doing?' I ask. Heading to the refrigerator for a bite to eat, my back muscles finally relax and uncoil. Colton isn't here. Whether he isn't here *yet* or isn't coming *at all*, I do not know.

'Well, as you can see, I'm getting a manicure,' Emily says.

'Oh, yeah, new salon?' I ask jokingly. I pull out a head of lettuce, a loaf of multi-grain bread, a tomato, a pack of sliced turkey, and a bottle of Dijon.

'It just opened up, I'm their first customer,' Emily says.

'Is it any good?' I ask.

'The best!' Ava pipes in. 'We're the best nail salon in Alaska.'

'Oh, wow. And you just opened?'

'Yep,' she says, beaming from ear to ear.

I love her confidence. Like many parents, Emily and I have a lot of doubts about our parenting decisions and conflicting parenting styles. But one thing that we do agree on is that we want to raise a girl with unwavering confidence. As a teacher, I know that belief in yourself is the key to success in anything. In order to do anything, to attempt any project, you first have to have confidence in your abilities. I've seen many a kid who failed at something just because he or she didn't believe in themselves enough to begin. It's self-esteem that gets you through the hard times as well. It's the thing that keeps you going when things quit working out in your favor.

Grabbing the plate with my sandwich, I'm about to head upstairs when Emily waves at me.

'Why don't you have lunch with us?' she asks in that familiar tone, making it more of a statement than a request.

'Eh, I really have to get back to work on my novel.'

'C'mon, please. Just while you have lunch,' Emily says.

'Yes, Daddy. Pleaaaaaase!' Ava yells at the top of her lungs. Outnumbered, I give in.

The 'Under the Sea' song comes on the television and Ava takes a brief pause in working to sing along and dance for us. Emily and I exchange looks and break out in laughter.

Despite all the distraction, my thoughts keep swirling back to Colton. What if he shows up like he did at school? I squirrel around in my seat and keep glancing at my phone.

'Why are you fidgeting so much?' Emily asks.

'Um, no reason.' I shrug, trying to appear as nonchalant as possible.

After finishing with one set of fingers, Ava moves onto Emily's other hand.

'But wait, these aren't done,' Emily says. Each one of her fingernails is painted a different color and only halfway down. 'Why did I only get half of my nail done? I'm a paying customer and I want the whole thing.'

'Oh, Mom.' Ava rolls her eyes. 'This is what's popular now. This is how it's done.'

'Oh, really?' Emily laughs. 'And what makes you an expert?'

'Um, I'm the manicurist, duh!'

Emily cracks up laughing and I follow her lead. My mind is still on Colton, but I can't let him take me out of this moment.

Taking a bite of the sandwich, it suddenly hits me. This can be our life. This can be our reality. That money sitting upstairs is enough – more than enough – for both of us to quit our jobs and just spend our days as we see fit. No more putting Emily into daycare while we're both at work. No more arguing over who can drive her where. Without Emily's crazy and ever changing hours, she could be home all the time with Ava. But this can only happen if everything else goes to plan. And if Colton doesn't ruin everything.

'I can't even tell you how much I don't want to go to work today,' Emily says, tossing her hair back.

'You don't?' Ava asks.

'No, not one bit.' She leans over and kisses her on the cheek. 'I just want to stay home with you.'

'Maybe after the manicure, I can do your feet,' Ava says. She gets a sparkle in her eye like she just came up with the most brilliant idea ever.

'I'd like that.'

'And then… then, I can do your hair!'

Emily's face drops. 'I don't think we have time for that, sweetie. I have my shift.'

Emily shrugs apologetically at me. At this moment, I want to tell her about the money more than I've ever wanted anything. It takes everything in my power to keep my mouth shut. This isn't the right time. But, oh, if I could just tell her that all of our problems are about to come to an end. No more worrying about paying the mortgage. No more clipping coupons and skipping family dinners. No more restrictions on how many times a week she can go to Starbucks.

When Ava stops painting again to watch one of her favorite scenes in *The Little Mermaid*, Emily turns to me and mouths something. I shake my head. I don't understand. She doesn't say it out loud because we don't want Ava to hear us complaining. We were both raised being a little too exposed to everything that our parents had and we agreed to shelter her a bit from reality. When she makes her gestures more pronounced, I finally get it: 'Life sucks.'

'It's going to be okay,' I say.

'Easy for you to say, you're on sabbatical,' she says, jealously.

'Listen, we're going to get out of this one way or another. I see really good things in our future.'

'Oh, yeah? Like what?'

'Like you not working any more than you have to. Like me selling this book and making a living off my writing. Maybe not being a teacher anymore.'

'Ha, in our dreams,' she whispers.

'Listen.' I get up and sit down at the coffee table next to her. 'You know me. I'm not much of an optimist. But something's different now. It's all going to be okay.'

'Wow, that must be some book you're working on,' she says, half-jokingly. 'If you think it's going to pay for this whale of a mortgage.'

'Yeah, something like that.'

The three of us sit and watch Ursula take Ariel's voice in exchange for human legs. As she dances and rants, I realize that everything comes at a sacrifice. Life is a give and take. It's not just about finding a bag of money, it's about keeping it. And spending it. Finding it was the easy part. I know that now. But to keep it and spend it will require sacrifice. How far am I willing to go for my family? I don't know that yet.

I leave Emily and Ava in the living room and head upstairs to try to decide what to do. Colton's not here, but that doesn't mean that he isn't coming. He knows where it's currently hidden so it definitely can't stay here. But where can I put it? A storage unit is an option. But I'm pretty sure that it will require identification. Pretty sure, but not certain. What about a safety deposit box in a bank? That would be a very safe place indeed. There's no way that Colton or anyone else would be able to get to it then. I've never had a safety deposit box before. But the ones I've seen in movies were all tiny. They would barely fit a few bundles. Do they even have bigger safety deposit boxes? I wonder. But besides the size, there is one other problem with this. It's through a bank and it definitely requires identification. At this point, I'm not so sure that I need the money to be tied to me so closely. The local Bank of America branch is not a numbered account in Switzerland or the Caymans. And getting a numbered account is not something I can easily execute at this time.

What if I found a good spot for the money somewhere outside? Somewhere out of the way where no one could find it? But isn't that what Colton essentially did? Look what happened to him. The spot needs to be hidden enough that it absolutely could not be found by some bored kids or bleary-eyed dog walkers.

Despite the thoughts swirling around in my head, I look at myself in the mirror and decide to take action. The only thing I know for sure is that the money cannot stay here. I have to move it. I grab the bag and peek out into the hallway. The girls are still downstairs. I creep downstairs on my tiptoes, praying that Emily doesn't come out, and put on my boots. I close the door to the garage behind me, still holding my breath. I scan our disorganized garage. There's crap along the entire perimeter. Opened Amazon boxes, bikes, various toolboxes and tools, camping gear, boxes of old clothes, boxes of summer clothes, boxes of Ava's baby stuff. And that's just the things that I can point out. This is technically my space so Emily rarely comes down here except when she takes the car in and out. When my sabbatical first started, she was on my case all the time about getting the place fixed up. But in the recent weeks, she has given up.

I place the bag behind the bikes and position a few empty suitcases in front of it for good measure. This is a temporary hiding place, just in case Emily comes in. I look around the garage for a more secure option. Unfortunately, the walls are concrete and there are no hidden trapdoors behind which I could hide this thing. I stare at the refrigerator in the corner. I bought it on Craigslist after

Emily said that one isn't enough. I didn't think we needed it at all, but within a week, it was stocked with soda and beer as well as large supplies of fish or meat from Costco. I could always move the fridge and hide the bag behind it?

My eyes slowly drift upward. Tim and Claire, our neighbors, have the most organized garage on the street. When Emily first stepped foot in it, she was amazed by the shelving and the neatly labeled boxes near the ceiling, going around the whole perimeter of the garage. I managed to only put up one metal shelf along the left side. Still, it proved very useful. We got a bunch of large plastic containers and stored… something in it. What exactly is in those red bins? I can't remember. This was a project from last August and whatever is in those bins, we haven't needed since. I reach up to pull one of them down, but I can barely budge it, it's so heavy.

I look around for the small ladder that I bought when I put up the shelves. Eventually, I find it deep behind a bunch of folded moving boxes. It's a pain in the ass to get out, but after a few minutes of struggling, while holding up the boxes with my legs, I manage to wriggle it free.

'Need any help?' A man's voice startles me. I nearly drop the ladder on my foot.

When I turn around, I see that the voice belongs to a cop.

'Sorry, didn't meant to scare you,' he says in his low, confident voice.

'Oh, no, not at all,' I mumble.

He walks into the garage and Emily follows closely behind. She introduces him as Stephen Silko with the Alaska State Troopers. I nod and shake his hand. Something about him looks familiar. It's as if I had seen him somewhere before.

'This is quite a garage,' Silko says, walking around like he owns the place.

'Yes, it's quite a mess, isn't it? Noah keeps promising to organize it,' Emily pipes up.

With his chest out, his hands on his hips, and his legs wide apart, Silko reminds of me of a posturing rooster. All that's missing is a loud pronouncement of his testosterone-driven confidence.

Oh my God, of course! I suddenly remember why he looks so familiar. He's the guy that Charlie's seeing. I've seen them in her bedroom.

As if one shock to the system isn't enough, right at that moment, one of the empty suitcases in front of the bikes falls over. My heart sinks all the way down to my feet. The duffel bag behind the bikes is exposed. I glance over at Emily and Silko – neither pays much attention.

As casually as possible, I make my way there and put the suitcases back in place.

'So, I just had a question about where you were last Wednesday.'

I stare at him and shrug.

'I was home, I think.'

'Did you leave for any reason?'

'Wasn't that the day that Colton came over?' I ask Emily. 'That's my brother-in-law.'

She nods.

I try to remember what lie I told Emily about where we went that night. Was it the gym? But didn't I just get back from a run?

'Yeah, he came over and then we went for a steam at his gym,' I say confidently. Look him straight in the eyes, I say to myself. Don't look away. That's what an honest person would do.

'I'm going to need Colton's number and address,' Silko says.

'Of course.' I shrug.

'What's this about, Officer?' Emily asks.

'Well, if you must know,' Silko says, 'your license plate is a partial match to the one found at the scene of a missing police officer.'

All blood drains from my body. My fingers and toes lose all feeling. It takes all of my strength to keep the mildly interested smile plastered on my face.

'Partial match?' I ask as nonchalantly as possible.

'Well, we only have the first characters.'

'I'm sure that we're not the only ones in the state of Alaska with those characters,' Emily says with utter confidence. I feel all those hours of crime shows are kicking her into high gear. Suddenly, I'm beyond grateful that she's here.

'Well, you're right. That's why I'm making the rounds.'

We both nod at him sympathetically. He looks around the garage again and then looks us up and down.

'Well, I guess I better be going now. Thank you for your help,' he says without even taking out a notebook to jot anything down. Is he just here to intimidate me?

'Thanks for coming by,' Emily says cheerily. 'Good luck with your investigation.'

We walk him out. I don't let out a breath of relief until he finally gets into his car and disappears around the corner.

CHAPTER THIRTY

NOAH

I feel sweat dripping down the back of my neck. I crack my knuckles. Even though the cop is gone, a million thoughts rush through my mind at the speed of light. I can't keep the money in the house. It isn't safe. The police may get a warrant at any time. And then what? My stomach churns at the thought of them raiding my house. Searching through all of our things. If they come back, they'll find the money. And what then? What possible explanation would I have for all that cash?

My mind is racing a mile a minute. If they find the money, they will arrest me and confiscate it. My whole body shudders at the thought. I'm not going down this easily.

'I'm feeling like some Starbucks,' I say, putting on my coat. 'You want anything?'

'I have to go to work soon,' Emily says.

'I know, I won't be long.'

'Okay, in that case, I'd like the usual. Vanilla latte with an extra shot of espresso.'

As I pull out of the driveway with the duffel bag in the trunk, I dial Colton's number. He's probably still pissed at me for supposedly taking his money, but I need to warn him about Silko. We need to have our stories straight about the steam. Shit. Suddenly, it hits me. It's a gym. It probably has recording equipment or at least some sort of check in process to show the cops that we weren't actually there that night. Oh, well. It's too late. Maybe it will never even come to that. They don't have my full license plate number. So, if Colton corroborates my story, it will at least buy us some time to come up with a better one.

The call goes directly to voice message. Pick up, pick up, I say as I listen to the instruction. For a brief moment, I consider leaving him a voice mail telling him about Silko. But what if someone gets a hold of his phone? No, it's too risky. I have no way of erasing it in case I need to. When I hear the beep, I hang up. I'll try him again in a bit. If the cops do call him in the meantime, hopefully he'll have enough sense to tell the same story as we told Emily. That will be enough for now.

I drive out of the development, and pull into the Starbucks drive-thru. This place always has a line, even though another one opened just a few blocks away. But today, the line is relatively short, only five cars. As I inch my way closer and closer to the order window, I once again consider my options. The bank option is out. Definitely. But what about a storage unit? That's a possibility. I look up the closest place on my phone. It's only five miles away.

Ten minutes later, I'm driving to We-Store while sipping on a Grande Caffe Americano, a tall espresso with just enough caffeine to match my anxiety and somehow cancel it out. Emily's Vanilla Latte is sitting in the cup holder next to me. I finish my coffee even before I reach the counter where a bored teenage girl with black eye makeup and a shaved head tells me that she cannot rent me a storage unit without two forms of identification and a credit card. I nod, thank her for her time, and get back into the car in need of another plan.

Okay, what about some abandoned building? There aren't too many multi-story abandoned buildings around here, but there are plenty of abandoned homesteads. They're places where people used to live and then either got foreclosed upon or just left to rot after the original owners moved out. The only problem with going with one of these places is that they tend to be very popular with local kids. They like them because they're fun places to shoot off guns and drink. Not a season goes by without one being lit on fire either accidentally or on purpose.

My phone rings, breaking my concentration.

'Hi, Em,' I answer.

'Where the hell are you?' she asks. I glance at the clock. Shit, I'm running late.

'Oh, I'm sorry, there was a huge line.'

'Get back soon. Sarah's here,' Emily says. There's a tinge to her voice that's unsettling.

'What's wrong? Did something happen to Ava?'

'No,' she says. 'Just come back.'

I don't know what to do. I don't have time to scout out any of these possible hiding spots, and I can't just leave the money knowing that's it not safe. I decide to just drive home. Pulling into the driveway, I suddenly have an idea. I glance over at Charlie's house across the street, past the lone pine tree weighed down by snow. All the houses on our street are nearly identical – gray with light blue trim. Two story. Built around the same time. The only thing that really varies is the interiors, a choice between three or four models of open space layouts.

The crawl space. That's where I will put the duffel bag. But not my crawl space. Charlie's. If the cops do get a search warrant, it won't be for Charlie's house. As for possible discovery by the present owners? That's unlikely. Charlie's roommates are all girls and girls aren't known to spend time in crawl spaces. Emily probably doesn't even know that we have one.

As I cross the street, I look both ways to make sure that no one is watching me. Being a bedroom community, the houses sit empty most of the day. Our crawl space can be accessed through the porch out front. Ducking by the side of Charlie's house, on the other side of the front door, I see that hers is in the exact same place. There are some footsteps stomped into the snow, but it's hard to tell if they're recent or not. I move the lattice to expose the tunnel underneath the porch.

Crouching down on my knees, I peek into the darkness. I turn on the flashlight on my phone for some light and shine in all corners. That's when I see it. A box, about the size of a shoe box, sitting next to the left wall. What's in it?

I grab the shoe box and open the lid. My mouth opens. It's money. Nice little bundles, a perfect match for the bundles in my duffel bag.

CHAPTER THIRTY-ONE

NOAH

'What is Colton's money doing here?' I whisper to myself. I hear footsteps somewhere inside the house and freeze. I place the lattice back into place, grab the shoe box and the duffel bag, and race back to my house. I count the money quickly in the garage. It's exactly the amount of Colton's 'share,' minus the fifteen grand he blew at the casino. Could he have hidden it there and forgot? No, he was pretty adamant that he took it to Eklunta. So, what the hell is it doing at Charlie's house? After transferring the cash to the duffel bag, I head back to my garage. There, I put it back behind the bikes and cover it up with the empty suitcases.

Sarah, Emily's younger sister by two years, and almost her twin is sitting on the couch, holding Ava. Ava is playing with her long hair.

I hand Emily her Starbucks drink and ask what's wrong.

'I don't know, I don't know,' Sarah says. Her eyes don't meet mine. Staring off into the distance, she blows her nose and wipes a maverick tear.

'I was on the phone with Colton this afternoon. He was really upset. He was ranting about someone taking his money or something. I thought he was just drunk. He said he lost fifteen grand at a casino last night. Where the hell did he even get that kind of money?'

Sarah shakes her head, unable to keep going. Emily takes over.

'With the divorce and all, he didn't have much of anything left,' Emily says as if I didn't know that already. 'Neither of them did.'

'And if he still had fifteen grand somewhere, that's something that my lawyer would really like to know,' Sarah says.

'So, I don't understand. Did something else happen?' I ask, trying to get this conversation over with.

'Anyway, he was freaking out and he called me. And you know, things between us haven't been the best. We haven't really spoken at all since we separated. So, it was beyond odd for him to call.'

I nod.

'But then…' Sarah's voice drops off.

'What happened?' Ava whispers. Suddenly, all the adults in the room become aware of the fact that a child is listening.

'Oh, honey,' Emily says suddenly. 'No, nothing bad. Why don't you put on *The Little Mermaid* again?'

Ava refuses. It takes Emily a while to distract her enough so that she forgets about Sarah's story.

'Something happened, Noah,' Sarah says. 'He was on the phone one moment, ranting about someone taking his money. And then he was gone. I heard someone with a deep voice tell him to put the phone down. He asked him, who the hell are you? And then he said, please put the gun down.'

Her voice trembles as she says that.

'Someone had a gun to his head, Noah,' Sarah says with tears running down her face. 'And then there was like a tussle. Maybe they were fighting over the phone, I don't know. But then the line went dead.'

I don't know what to say. A thousand thoughts go through my mind in an instant. A part of me thinks that this is all a joke. A really bad joke. Or maybe Sarah is just confused. But after examining her face more closely, I'm sure that neither of those options are true.

Sarah and Colton have had a difficult relationship. At the end, it got so bad that she refused to talk to him without a lawyer present. So, Colton was feeling really off if he actually called his ex-wife for help.

And what about that phone call? Sarah would not be this upset if she, even for one second, thought that it wasn't true. She heard something happen to Colton. But what?

The phone rings and Emily gets up from the couch and leaves the room. I can't make out what she's saying. Both Sarah and I hold our breaths in anticipation.

'Was that Colton?' Sarah asks. Her voice goes up hopefully at the end of the question.

'No, it wasn't,' Emily says slowly, staring at me.

'Em, what's wrong?' Sarah asks. 'Who was it?'

Emily continues to stare at me. I shrug my shoulders and mouth, what's wrong?

Finally, after a few tense moments, Emily says, 'That was the principal. He wants to schedule a meeting to discuss the incident with your brother-in-law during class today.'

My heart skips a beat as all eyes are on me.

CHAPTER THIRTY-TWO

NOAH

'Noah, what happened in school today?' Emily asks me.

I don't know how much time has passed since she had picked up the phone. All I know is that it was enough time for my mouth to get parched.

'Um, nothing, really,' I mumble. I don't know exactly how much she knows. I need to be as vague as possible just in case.

'Did he say why he wants me to come in?' I ask. I'm fishing. The look on her face tells me that she's not impressed.

'Yes, actually,' Emily says, folding her arms across her chest. 'He wants to talk to you about the fist fight you were in.'

I stare at her dumbfounded. I can't believe that he actually said that.

'You were in a fist fight at school?' Sarah asks.

'In the hallway with a guy the kids said was your brother-in-law,' Emily says.

I can't believe she's airing all of this out right now. In front of Sarah, no less! It takes Sarah a few moments to put the story together.

'You were in a fight with Colton?' she shrieks.

'Okay, it was an accident. Nothing happened.' I shrug.

'So, what exactly happened, Noah?' Emily asks.

I'm at a loss for words. I take a step back, trying to collect my thoughts. Why would we get into a fight? I need a legit excuse. It needs to be believable. The most effective lies are the ones that are the closest to the truth.

'He had a really bad night,' I start slowly. I don't have a plausible explanation but sometimes when you start talking stuff comes out that surprises you.

'He spent the whole night in a casino. He lost a lot of money. And he was pissed,' I say. And then something occurs to me. 'How did he even find out where I was?'

'What?' Emily stares at me.

'I'm not supposed to be at work. I just went in as a favor. Did he call here and find out where I was?' I'm turning the whole thing on her. Making her sweat. A part of me feels bad, but it's all I can think to do.

'Yes, he did. He said it was urgent. He had to talk to you,' Emily says.

I feel the tension in the room shifting from me to Emily. Suddenly, I'm not the only bad guy. I'm not the only missing link in the puzzle.

Now, I have to come to her rescue.

'Why didn't you tell me?' Sarah shakes her head.

'I didn't think it was important.'

'He just showed up. I was monitoring a test. He kept knocking on the door until I came out,' I say. 'As soon as I got into the hallway, I knew he was off. He was super agitated. Like really on edge. He kept ranting about how he'd lost all this money at the casino and that it wasn't his fault. And he was asking me for money. He said that if he could just have a thousand or even five hundred then he could get it all back with interest.'

Sarah and Emily don't take their eyes off me. I know they believe me. They believe me because the story is as close to the truth as possible. I'm on a roll, full steam ahead.

'Anyway, we don't have that kind of money. I'm not working now. And even if we did, I didn't think it was wise to give him any. I mean I felt bad that he lost so much, but there's no guarantee that he would get any of it back.'

Sarah's shoulders start to shake as she sobs.

'Oh, honey.' Emily puts her arm around her. 'Please don't cry.'

I pat Sarah on her back. Eventually, she calms down a bit.

'So, what happened then? People saw you fighting,' Sarah asks.

'Well, he just wouldn't take no for an answer. He kept pushing me and pushing me. He was raising his voice. I didn't know what to do to stop him. He pushed me into the lockers and we started to wrestle. I punched him and then he hit me on the head a bunch of times. Frankly, I can't even remember. When the bell rang and kids started to come out into the hallway, it broke us up.'

'Why didn't you tell me any of this?' Emily whispers.

I shrug and look away.

'Because it's embarrassing. Colton's my friend. I know you don't have the best opinion of him because of everything that's happened. And this whole situation didn't make either of us look particularly good,' I say, shaking my head.

Emily pours Sarah a glass of water and forces her to drink it.

'I just can't believe that the principal actually called here and got me in trouble,' I joke. 'Hey, aren't you late for work?'

I look up at the clock. Her shift had started half an hour ago.

'I called and switched with Lisa,' Emily says, still clinging to Sarah. It's hard to tell who is supporting whom at this point.

Feeling strangely proud of my clever cover up, I nod and flip on the TV. It's rare that the TV isn't occupied by one Disney movie or another. The mystery of what happened, if anything happened, to Colton is still not solved, but at least I have a good explanation for what happened at school. To be honest, I have no idea if something happened to Colton. I mean, maybe Sarah is confused. Maybe she misheard something. Or didn't hear it at all. Of course, she isn't really one to freak out or exaggerate circumstances, that's more Emily's department, but still. I just saw him a few hours ago, so what could've really happened? Grown men don't just go missing. Maybe he just doesn't want to be found.

After a commercial break, the local news comes on.

'The body of a nineteen-year-old girl was found today in the woods near Wasilla. She was found in her 2003 Dodge Neon on a poorly maintained road. The police have not identified the body yet, and they are not saying whether her death was a result of foul play.'

I stare at the screen as they cut to the all too familiar patch in the woods near our house. The road leading there was not just poorly maintained, it hardly exists at all. The footage from the helicopter makes it seem like it's barely a utility road.

'I wonder if it's that girl who went missing six months ago?' Sarah asks.

'Who's that?' Emily asks.

'It was all over the news for a while. It was this girl who lived with her sister's family and she might have been pregnant. Anyway, she and her sister had a fight and the police kept saying that she ran off to Florida or something. But her sister gave all of these interviews saying that there was no way that she would do that. She wanted them to keep looking.'

'Oh, yeah, I remember that. What was her name? Julie something?' Emily says.

My hands turn to ice. My heart starts beating a mile a minute. A cold sweat goes through me, leaving huge stains under my armpits.

Sarah pulls out her phone and then hands it to Emily. 'Here, that's her.'

I can't see the screen from behind the couch, and I can't move my feet to get closer.

'Um,' I start, but my voice cracks. I cough to clear my throat. 'Can I see that?'

Emily hands me the phone and then turns back to the television.

It takes me a moment to gather the strength to focus on the screen. When I finally lift up the hand with the phone, it feels like it weighs a hundred pounds.

There are three pictures of the smiling girl on the missing poster. Two are close ups of her face. In one, she is beaming from ear to ear and in the other, she's making a serious sexy selfie face. The last one is a full body shot of her leaning against a wall.

I stare at each one with total concentration. I am looking for any detail that would make the girl in front of me not the girl in the car. In these pictures, she's alive. Animated. Not frozen. But no matter how long I look, no matter how much I try, I can't convince myself that it's not her.

Suddenly, I feel sick to my stomach. I excuse myself and run to the bathroom. As soon as I'm in there, I regret the fact that I didn't go upstairs. This is not going to be a quiet trip. I flip on the ventilation but it only mildly muffles the sounds of my gagging. After a few dry heaves, the contents of my stomach rip all the way out of me and into the toilet.

'Are you okay, sweetie?' I hear Emily somewhere in the distance. She's just around the other side of the door, but it sounds like she's yelling from somewhere outside the house. She says something else that I can't make out as I purge more of my insides into the toilet. I hear myself whimpering in between attacks, but everything in my body seems to be out of my control at this point.

'I'm fine,' I mumble when I think I have reached the end. But just when I think I can't barf any more, I vomit again. And again. And again.

Eventually, it does stop, leaving me exhausted and holding onto the toilet for dear life. When I'm certain that nothing else is going to come up, I wipe my eyes and push myself up to my feet. In the mirror, I see an old man with sallow eyes and skin so pale that it's almost green staring back at me. It's as if I had somehow managed to age twenty years in the last fifteen minutes. Forcing myself to look away, I wash out my mouth and brush my teeth. Then I splash water on my face until I feel almost human.

'Oh, wow, are you okay?' Emily and Sarah are both standing right outside the door. I would be blushing from embarrassment if I weren't so tired and dehydrated.

'Yeah, I'm fine,' I mumble. 'I'm sorry about that.'

'Oh, no, there's nothing to be sorry about. I'm just sorry that it came on like that. Do you think it's something you ate?'

'Yeah, I guess it must be.' I shrug. 'But I'm feeling better now.'

'You are?' Emily asks skeptically.

'Yeah, actually, I think I'm going to run out to Rite Aid and get some Vitamin water or Gatorade.'

'Oh, I can go,' Emily volunteers.

'No, that's okay. I need some fresh air. Honestly, I'd like to,' I say a little too rushed. My voice is a little too forceful, but it's hard to modulate after you've puked out nearly half of your bodyweight in bile. Reluctantly, Emily agrees.

Getting behind the wheel with the duffel bag in the seat behind me, I suddenly feel lightheaded. I force myself to wave and smile since Emily and Sarah are both standing on the porch watching me, analyzing me, looking for any excuse to stop me. I turn on the engine and drive away. As soon as I disappear around the corner, I pull over and throw up again.

CHAPTER THIRTY-THREE

NOAH

After stopping at Rite Aid and drinking a bottle of Gatorade, I feel a little better. I get back into the car with a newfound sense of purpose. So, they've located her. The dead girl. Are they looking for the money? It's more important than ever for me to hide this money somewhere no one will find it. But where?

As I drive further and further north, I suddenly remember Emily's dad's cabin. Of course! Why didn't I think of this sooner? Emily and Sarah's father owns a little one-room rustic hunting cabin. It started off as a place to escape to when things got rough at home, but has morphed into something of a vacation place. He stays there whenever he's up here visiting from Arizona. And no matter how much Emily pleads for him to stay with us, he always prefers that place instead.

I drive as far as I can on the unplowed road before getting out and walking the rest of the way to the cabin. It takes about forty minutes through heavy snow. By the time I get to the front door, I'm drenched in sweat, and I'm cursing myself for even coming here. I look for the spare key in its trusty place under the big flat rock on the other side of the cabin. When I open the door, it smells musty. Every surface has a thick layer of dust on it. But nothing is disturbed. The cabin is locked up for winter, but that doesn't mean that it doesn't get its share of unwelcome visitors. One year, a curious bear broke in. Another year, a group of hikers used the place for a few days. The irony is that the bear caused less damage than the hikers.

This time, the place looks just as it was left. No sign that anyone has been here in months. I look around. One dining room table, two chairs. A twin bed that looks like it would barely fit a grown man. A fireplace. A bench on the side of the room masquerading as a kitchen. There's no fridge, but there are some basics in the cabinet above the hot plate. On the far side is a large wooden armoire. I'm not sure how old this one is, but I'm pretty sure that it has been here since Emily was a kid. It isn't very tall, barely reaching up to my shoulders. I open the two swinging doors and peek inside. It has a few sweaters and pairs of jeans. The two drawers underneath store extra blankets. For a second, I debate whether I should leave the duffel bag in the armoire, but quickly decide against it. Not that many people know about the cabin, but everyone in the family does. Including Colton. No, if I hide the money here, it has to be somewhere safe. I scan the room again. There's just so little furniture here. If only Emily's dad was a hoarder, then it would be easier to hide the bag without anyone noticing.

Then it hits me. What about behind the armoire? It's positioned flat against the far wall. If I put the bag behind it now, then there would be a visible gap between the edge of the armoire and the wall. But what if I moved it a few inches and put it in the corner? Would anyone really notice? And the two sides of the armoire would make a nice secure little triangle, hiding the duffel bag completely. No gap between the wall and the armoire. It's only a few inches away. I'm certain that not Emily, Sarah, nor Colton would remember the exact location of this wooden beast. Emily's dad might, but I'll get the bag out of here before he comes back for the summer.

It's a bitch to move. After ten minutes of sweating and struggling, I finally manage to get it into place. I pick up the duffel bag and drop it in the triangle behind it. When I'm done, I stand back, impressed. Now, that's a hiding spot.

My phone rings, jolting me out of my euphoria.

'Hey, I'm just calling to see if you're okay. You've been gone for a while,' Emily says.

'Oh, yeah, I'm fine. I actually went on a little walk. The weather was so nice. And I needed some fresh air,' I say.

'Um, okay,' she says, clearly unconvinced.

'I'll be home soon,' I say and hang up.

On the way home, I let out a sigh of relief. The money is finally in a safe place where no one can get it. Not Colton. Not the original owners. It's a place that I and I alone know of. But as I get closer to the house, something in the back of my mind starts to nag at me. What the hell was Charlie doing with Colton's money in the first place? Did she really steal it from him?

I pull into my driveway and see her coming out of the house. I want to go over there and demand an explanation. I want to confront her for stealing my money. But I can't. She works for the police department. It isn't safe. It's better to just let this go. It takes all of my strength just to smile and nod to her and head inside.

CHAPTER THIRTY-FOUR

CHARLIE

It takes me some time to get back to work. I dread it. Postpone. Consider quitting. Convince myself that it's going to be okay. Make it as far as the parking lot one day and then call in sick again. I'm not avoiding it because of the money that's sitting in my crawlspace. It has nothing to do with it. I don't really consider it mine and I don't really know if I can even spend a dollar of it. No, this feeling of procrastination comes entirely from the last person I talked to. I relive that conversation over and over again and I can't get it out of my mind. Maybe I should consider spending some of the money, just so I don't have to take another 911 phone call again.

When I'm all out of paid and unpaid days off, I go in. I sit down at the console table. Luckily, it's a slow time and there aren't many people in the office. I can't bear to talk to anyone right now. I feel like I'm going to burst out in tears if anyone asks me how I'm feeling. My fragility is killing me. It's as if I'm made of glass that even the slightest whisper can break.

I stare at the receiver in front of me. I wait. And wait. And wait some more. My hands are shaking. I can't stop my feet from tapping on the floor in a quiet little pitter-patter that only I can hear. My whole body shakes. I'm not sure if it's from fear or my inability to control my physical body. Suddenly, the phone rings. My heart sinks. My mouth gets dry. I try to swallow, but start to cough instead. After taking a sip of water, I answer the call.

'Nine-one-one. What is your emergency?'

'Oh my god, oh my god!' The woman on the other end is hysterical. She's screaming at the top of her lungs. Her voice makes her sound like she's at least in her fifties. Maybe a smoker. Probably carrying a little too much weight.

'Ma'am, what's wrong?' I ask in the calmest and most soothing voice possible. I've noticed that if I quieten my own voice to something slightly louder than a whisper, then the person on the other end tends to calm down a bit and try to match my tone. This makes him or her easier to understand.

'Put that down. What the hell are you doing, James?' the woman yells into the phone.

'What does he have, ma'am? Can you please give me your name and address?'

I immediately know that I shouldn't have asked those questions in succession. I always get better responses when I ask only one question at a time.

'Put that cane down, James!' the woman yells. She gives her name and address while huffing heavily into the phone.

Suddenly, it occurs to me. Holly is Nana's old neighbor. Her little sister, Julie, is missing.

It's up to me to either dispatch or not dispatch police officers to the scene. I decide to stay on the safe side.

'Holly, now listen to me. I'm sending police officers to your house right now. Can you please tell me if you have any weapons there?'

'No. Just James and his cane,' she says angrily.

Hmm, a caning. That's a new one for the books.

'And who is James to you?'

'My stupid husband.'

'And what is he doing?'

'He's coming in my room and hitting me with the cane,' she says.

Something feels different now. James isn't right next to her anymore.

'Where is he now? Is he still in the house?'

'Yeah, he's still here, but I locked the bedroom door so he can't get in right now.'

I let out a brief sigh of relief.

'Now that he's not right there hitting you, can you tell me what's going on, Holly?'

'I don't really know. He just started to go off on me for no reason. He recently had back surgery and I know he's in pain, but what the fuck? What the hell did I do? Plus, he's all mad at our roommate, Jonathan. He lost his job at Rite Aid, and he can't come up with all the rent. So what? We've all been there, right?'

'Yes, of course,' I agree not so much with the statement but just to agree.

'And how many people live with you at your house? Or staying at your house.' I know the general answer to this, I don't know if they have anyone else staying there and the officers need to know the exact number.

'Me, my husband, Jonathan, and Julie,' she says. 'Well, not so much Julie. Not anymore. I don't know.'

'Your sister, Julie, is missing, right?'

Suddenly, loud, heart-wrenching sobs pierce through the silence. I wait for her to gather herself.

'Yes, six months ago. Vanished. Cops think that she ran away, but I know she never would. She loved me, despite what happened. Despite our fights. She would never let me worry like this for so long.'

Holly whimpers and sobs.

'I'm really sorry for being such a mess,' Holly says, blowing her nose.

'No, not at all.'

'It just all came back to me. I saw her car on the news. They didn't call me yet, but I know it's her. I know my little sister's dead.'

Holly starts to cry again. Somewhere in the distance, I hear a muffled man's voice yelling something indistinguishable and pounding on the door. After listening closely, I finally make out what he's saying.

'You called the cops, you bitch! You called the cops on me!'

'Sir, please put the cane down.' The strong confident voice of a police officer comes through loud and clear.

I let Holly go as soon as she confirms that the cops are there and she is safe. After I hang up, I sit and stare at the receiver for a while. I made it. My first call. It wasn't bad. I helped her before anything worse happened. See, it's going to be okay, Charlie, I say to myself. You can do this.

After answering Holly's call, I take ten other calls during my shift. Some are accidents. Others are domestics. Each call comes with its own difficulties, but I power through. No one dies. Everyone gets help. I go home relieved. That was a successful day. A win. I really needed a win.

When I pull into my driveway, I'm on a high. I feel invincible. I'm capable of anything. I can run faster than anyone else. I can sing better than anyone else. Riding this high, I decide to check on my secret stash. The money that I found in Eklunta is enough for me to move to some tropical island, open a bar, and live the life of the lush expat. I can't lie. I like having it. It's probably the only reason I went back to work today. The money gave me confidence. It made me feel like I don't need this job and going in is entirely a choice. Without it, I would've felt like I had no choice. Without the money, I'm sure that I would've quit.

Before crouching down near the back of the porch, I make sure that there are no cars or people coming. The crawl space wasn't my first choice, but I couldn't very well hide it anywhere in the house. My roommates have this annoying tendency of going through my stuff. We share and borrow each other's clothes with very loose return policies. So, whenever they need anything, they just help themselves to my closet. I don't really mind. Frankly, I do the same thing. But that's what made hiding the shoe box inside the house so dangerous. What if one of them wanted to borrow something and went through my other stuff? No, I couldn't have them finding this money.

I lift up the lattice and shine my flashlight on my phone into the darkness. Nothing. I point the light around all four walls and the corners. The shoe box is gone! Missing! I can't believe my eyes. I drop the lattice and look again. I climb halfway in and feel around. Maybe I left it somewhere in the middle. But I don't find a thing.

'Where the hell is it?' I whisper in a panic.

I run back upstairs and flip on my laptop to check the webcam. Danielle's dad insisted that we install two cameras around our house for safety reasons. I didn't see the point as we live in a very safe neighborhood, but he was going to pay for it so there was no reason to complain. I log in and check the side camera. I scroll back through the hours. Nothing. Nothing. Danielle's making out with her boyfriend. Me coming and going. And then I see it. A slim tall man with his head down heads straight to the side of our house. He's coming from across the street. The camera doesn't follow him to the crawl space. A bit later, he comes back on screen. This time he's holding a duffel bag and my shoe box. He turns briefly to look from one side of the street to another and I see his face.

Noah! That son-of-a-bitch.

My fists clench up. Blood rushes to my head. A pang of anger takes my breath away. How dare he? That's mine. I mean, yes, it's technically not mine, but I doubt very much that he has any real right to it. It's a shoe box full of cash there is no good, legal reason to have.

So what the hell is Noah doing with it? How did he even know that I hid it here? Maybe he's watching me. We are always conveniently running into each other. Maybe he's on to me because I know he's up to something.

Suddenly, I hear a door slam shut. When I turn around, I see him outside his house, heading toward his car. Quickly, my temper gets the better of me.

'Hey, Noah!' I run across the street.

'Oh, hey,' he says, clearly startled. 'Um, actually, I'm kind of in a hurry.'

His eyes won't meet mine. He's afraid. I'm intimidating him.

'I just have to talk to you about something. Where are you going?'

'The grocery store. I have to pick up a few things.'

'Perfect, I actually have to get some things, too.' I hop into the front passenger seat. Sometimes, my impulsive nature gets the better of me. Judging from how he's leaning away, he clearly doesn't want me here. Well, too damn bad. I have to find out what happened to my money.

'Um… okay… I guess,' he mumbles and starts the engine.

Now, how do I bring up the money? I can't just ask about it directly. He's bound to have some questions for me that I can't exactly answer.

'So, this is actually a funny story,' I start as we pull out of the development. 'My roommate's dad set up this webcam for us so we can see if any strangers are walking on our porch or whatever.'

His already pale face turns absolutely green as all the blood drains from it. He doesn't take his eyes off the road as he taps his fingers nervously on the steering wheel.

'We all have access to it through our laptops but I don't usually look at the footage. But today, I was kind of bored and decided, eh, what the hell, right? I'll just sneak a peek.'

'Oh, yeah?' he asks, faking nonchalance. 'Find anything interesting?'

'Yeah, actually, I did.'

I stare at him, waiting for a reaction. But he doesn't respond. He continues to stare straight ahead. Okay, I have to just go for it, I decide.

'I saw you there, Noah. Walking around my house.'

'Oh, yeah? Are you sure?'

Now I'm getting mad. Is he really denying being there?

'What were you doing there?' I ask. 'Near my crawl space.'

He doesn't say anything for a few moments. Then he turns toward me.

'What are you doing with my money?' he asks.

This question blows me back a bit. I didn't expect him to come out on the offensive like this.

'Your money? What the hell makes it your money? You weren't even the one who hid it in Eklunta!'

His eyes narrow as he stares into the rearview mirror.

'Are you listening to me?' I ask.

'I think someone's following us,' he says quickly. His eyes shift back and forth between the rearview mirror and the two side mirrors. When I turn around, I see a big black SUV driving right behind us. It's practically riding our ass.

CHAPTER THIRTY-FIVE
CHARLIE

A part of me thinks that Noah is just trying to avoid talking to me about the money. That's something I would do if I were in his situation. But I don't know him very well. And the grave look of concern worries me.

'Why would anyone want to follow you?' I ask.

'I don't know.' He shakes his head. 'I'm going to turn here and see if they stay on our tail.'

Without turning on the turn signal, he suddenly jolts the car to the left onto a small narrow two-lane street. As soon as we're around the corner, I look back. The SUV is right behind us.

'Shit,' he says. 'Do you think they're cops?'

'No. Definitely not.'

'How did you find out about the money, Charlie?' Noah moves his body closer to the steering wheel and tenses his muscles. It looks like he's going to try to outrun the SUV. 'Tell me!'

'I saw that guy leave your house so I followed him. He drove to Eklunta and I saw him hide something there. I wanted to know what it was. How the hell is that your money, anyway? Isn't it his?'

Noah jerks the car onto another road and picks up speed. I grab onto my fastened seat belt to keep myself in place.

'Where are you going?'

'It's all my money. Colton coerced me into giving him a share but it's not his,' he says.

'What the hell is going on, Noah? Where did you get all that money? And why is that car following us?'

I look back. The SUV is still right on our tail. The driver is experienced. Noah is doing his best, but this isn't that driver's first time tailing someone. I was once in a high-speed chase with Stephen. He took me on a regular drive-by, but one of the guys he pulled over decided to keep going so we had to follow him. Stephen walked me through the process of how to best get away from a cop, and surprisingly Noah is following all the rules. That guy didn't escape. With the looks of it, I'm kind of doubting that we will either.

'I found the money,' he says as we run a red light and all the cars at the intersection honk at us. Oh my God, that's it! We did it. But when I glance back, I see that the SUV is right behind us again, leaving a few collisions in its path at the intersection.

'Shit,' Noah mumbles. 'That guy is good.'

'You found the money?'

'Yeah, I found it in the woods.'

Suddenly, something occurs to me.

'Do you think those guys are the true owners?' I ask.

He shakes his head. 'No, they can't be. It was sitting there for like six months. If they missed it, then they would've come looking for it earlier.'

None of what he's saying is making much sense. Adrenaline is rushing through my body at such speed that I feel sick to my stomach.

I look at the speedometer. We're going nearly ninety. Suddenly, the black SUV jets out of its lane and pulls up next to us. There are two older white men in the car in puffy jackets and ski masks. When one of them knocks slightly on the windshield with a semiautomatic, I get drenched in cold sweat. They move ahead of us. For a second, I think they speed up, but then I realize that it's Noah. He's dropping speed. Suddenly, we're going sixty miles per hour then fifty. Forty. When we get to around thirty, he pulls on the steering wheel. Tires make an awful screeching noise as we rotate around and head back in the opposite lane. When I turn around and look, the SUV is somewhere far in the distance.

'Oh my God, you're awesome!' I exclaim. 'How did you get so good?'

'I saw that in a movie once,' Noah says, flashing a smile.

'Really?'

'No.' He shakes his head. 'Emily got me a race driving class as a birthday present last year. It was like a weekend long and the instructor was amazing.'

'Well, you definitely picked up a thing or two.'

Unfortunately, our happiness is short lived. The black SUV quickly catches up with us. And this time, they're tired of games. The window of the passenger side slides down and the semiautomatic points at us.

'Oh my God, he's going to shoot at us!' I yelp and hide in my seat.

'Hold on and crouch down!' Noah yells as he picks up speed.

A hailstorm of bullets smash into the car. The sound of thunder makes me think I'm going to go deaf. I tuck my feet up onto the seat and try to make myself as small as possible.

Whoosh! Whoosh!

'Oh, no!' I whisper as I hear the undeniable sound of air escaping the back tires. The car starts to shake.

'Hold on!' Noah yells. I brace myself against the door. The car is now shaking uncontrollably as another bullet enters the tire by the driver's seat.

'I can't keep going much longer!'

Noah pulls the car over to the side of the road.

'What are we going to do?' I ask, looking back at the SUV, which is right on our tail.

'Run!' Noah says, opening his car door. I jump out of the car and follow him down the empty field. Why didn't we stop somewhere near a fuckin' patch of trees? Shit! I'm not even asking for a forest at this point. Then we could have stood a chance.

I run as fast as I can, but the two men still manage to catch up. One of them pulls on the back of my coat, tossing me to the ground. The other one shoots a gun into the sky.

'Noah, stop!' he demands. 'Or the next one's going into her head.'

Noah's maybe ten feet ahead of me. He stops running and turns around. He folds himself in half as he tries to catch his breath.

'Now, that's a good boy,' the man with the gun says. Jogging toward him, he handcuffs Noah's hands behind his back.

As they walk us back to their black SUV like prisoners, I try to get a glimpse of what they actually look like. They are both dressed in dark clothes. Since they are both wearing black ski masks, I put them at anywhere between twenty-five and sixty. Probably not much older than sixty since they run like young men. One guy has blue eyes, the other has brown eyes. From the little bit of skin around their eyes, I know that they're both white.

They toss us into the back of the SUV. It has dark tinted windows, making it virtually impossible for anyone to see us from the outside.

'Noah, you've been a bad boy, haven't you?' the driver says. There isn't anything unusual about the sound of his voice except for the mocking tone. He also reeks of cigarette smoke.

'I don't know what you're talking about.'

'Oh, c'mon, don't act like that,' the passenger pipes in.

'What the hell do you want?' I ask. I decide that going on the offensive might be my best option.

'With you? Nothing really. You're just collateral damage,' the driver says.

'What? So, why not just let me go?'

'Oh, no, we can't do that, girlie.' The passenger starts to laugh. There's a sinister quality to his laugh, which sends chills through my whole body. 'You might go to Noah's wife or the cops. And we can't have anyone looking for Noah.'

'My wife is still going to be looking for me. I was just supposed to go to the grocery store.'

'With this girl?' the driver asks. 'Oh, no, I don't think so.'

'It's true. There's nothing going on between us. And his wife will definitely start calling soon. She worries a lot,' I say. I have never met Noah's wife, and I don't know the first thing about her. 'Please, just let me go. I promise that I won't call the cops or do anything you don't want me to.'

'I wish we could believe you, girlie. But, you see, everyone in your position would say that. The only way we will know for sure is if we keep you close.'

I breathe in and out deeply to try to calm down. My heart feels like it's about to pop out of my chest.

'What do you want?' Noah asks after a few minutes of silence.

'Oh, you know what we want.'

'The money!'

'I don't have any!' Noah yells.

'That's not true, is it? We all know that's not true.'

'Of course, it's true. I'm a fuckin' high school teacher. I'm on a sabbatical this semester. I make forty-two thousand a year. I don't have any money!'

'Wow, you only make forty-two grand? A year? You need a new line of work, son,' the driver says. 'But that's not the money that we're talking about. We're talking about the duffel bag.'

'What duffel bag?' Noah asks. He actually looks perplexed.

'Wow, Bill, who would've thought? It turns out that Noah is a damn good liar,' the passenger says.

The driver's name is Bill, I chant to myself over and over until it's ingrained in my memory.

'What duffel bag? What duffel bag?' Bill mimics. 'C'mon now, you know exactly what we're talking about. Your brother-in-law, Colton whatshisname, sang like a fucking canary.'

'What have you done with Colton? Where is he?' Noah asks.

'He's fine. He was smart. He told us everything and we didn't even need to hurt him,' Bill says.

'Yeah, that brother-in-law of yours is quite a blabbermouth,' the guy in the passenger seat says. 'We've been looking for that money for six months. We thought it was long gone. But then one of our associates calls us and tells us that there's a drunk in the casino spending thousands and going on and on about how his brother-in-law found this bag of money in the woods.'

'We just had to meet him,' Bill says.

Noah cowers in his seat. He hangs his head down and lowers his shoulders.

What an asshole, he mouths silently.

'So, that's where you come in, Noah,' Bill says. 'Now, are you going to be smart and just hand us the money or are you going to make this difficult?'

'Yeah, we're not bad guys, Noah. You haven't seen our faces, so we have no reason to hurt you. If you just tell us where the money is, then we'll let you and your pretty little friend here go.'

I don't know whether to believe them. On one hand, I know that we shouldn't. They are bad people who probably run drugs and who knows what else. Who the hell else has this kind of money to lose? On the other hand, they did let Colton go. So, why wouldn't they let us go?

'I have no idea what you're talking about,' Noah says.

'Awe, c'mon now. Don't make this harder than it has to be,' Bill says. 'Our boss, and his friend with the hammer, have a way of getting people to tell the truth.'

CHAPTER THIRTY-SIX

NOAH

As we sit in the back of the SUV with our hands tied behind our backs, I run over what I can possibly do to get us out of this mess. Charlie shouldn't be here. It's all my fault. And now, she's probably going to die along with me. No, you can't think like this, I say to myself. There's a way out of almost everything. I just have to find it. I look over at Charlie as Bill and the other guy keep talking. She looks scared, but composed. Her eyes meet mine and we acknowledge our understanding. We're on the same page. One way or another, we have to get out of here.

I've refused to tell them where the money is. I refused to even acknowledge it. This does not make them happy. They threaten me. They tell me scary stories of what their boss's friend is capable of. This may be true. This may not be true. But the money is the only bargaining chip I have. I will use it if it's absolutely necessary, just not yet. Right now, I need some guarantees. I need a guarantee of my safety. And Charlie's.

We drive up a big windy road to the top of a large hill. The hill is surrounded by a thick forest of trees on both sides. It looks like it's government land. I've never been here, but I try to remember as many details as possible. The fallen tree to the right, covered with moss. The red box buried in the snow on the left side of the road about a mile down the road. This is the road back from there.

And Colton's not the only blabbermouth. From Bill and his partner, I learn that their boss's name is Steven Dossey and he owned a big salvage yard. About six months ago, Dossey was found with a bullet in his head, and the money from his safe missing. Apparently, this is the money that I found in the car. Did that girl actually shoot him? I don't dare ask to avoid confirming that I found the money. So far, they don't know for sure that I have the money, and I want them to believe this as long as possible. The guy who now runs the salvage yard is his son Allan Dossey and according to Bill, he isn't as much of a nice guy as his father. I don't know how much of this is true. They are in the intimidation game, and they're quite good at it.

'I don't know what you want from me,' I say. 'Like I told you before, I don't have any money.'

I pause for a second to consider if this is something I actually want to say. Then I go for it.

'But I do know who does,' I say.

They both start demanding the answer. Looking over at Charlie, I wink at her.

'She does,' I say.

'What? What the hell are you talking about?' Charlie jumps back in her seat, incensed. I'm not entirely sure if she's along with the plan, but she's definitely acting accordingly.

'Colton's right. I had the money. I didn't want my wife to find out so I hid it somewhere safe. In her crawl space.'

'Under her house?' Bill asks.

'Exactly. I had a cop come around. I also didn't want them finding the money in case they got a search warrant for something. When I went back to check on it, it was gone.'

'What are you talking about?' Charlie demands. 'You know very well that I didn't take any of your money.'

'Well, actually, I don't. I know that it was under your house and then it wasn't.'

'Listen, I have no idea what he's talking about.' Her voice is getting rushed. Fast-paced. If she's acting shocked and appalled by my lies, she's doing a great job.

'Why are you lying?' she asks with almost tears in her eyes.

You'll see, I want to say. I wink at her and kick the passenger in the face with my boot. He's not wearing a seat belt and his face hits the windshield, leaving a big bloody stain.

Suddenly, Charlie jumps up into my lap and wraps her hands around the driver's neck. She pulls as tight as she can. Struggling for air, Bill lets go of the steering wheel and waves his arms around. The car goes into a total spin. I don't know whether I feel sick to my stomach from the gurgling sound coming from the driver's seat or the 360-degree turns that the SUV is making, but I try to focus on the guy in the passenger seat. When he comes out of his slouch and tries to stop Charlie, I kick him again and again in the face.

Bam! The front of the SUV collides into the tree. Plastic blows up in my face, bracing my impact against the wall. The crash launches Charlie all the way to the front seat.

I don't know how much time passes before the buzzing stops. At first, my eyes can't focus on anything. But soon, my blurry vision dissipates and everything comes into focus. The guy in the passenger seat is hanging halfway out of the windshield. His airbags also exploded and are now pushing his feet into Charlie. Somehow, she managed not to go through the windshield. Instead, she's sitting in Bill's lap. Both Bill and his friend are dead. I'm pretty sure that I'm not. And I have no idea if Charlie is.

'Charlie?' I whisper. My voice is quiet, unsure. It feels wrong to disturb the silence for some reason.

She moans. I let out a big sigh of relief. Okay, okay, she's not dead. That's good.

'Charlie?' I say more forcefully. 'Are you okay?'

'Um, I don't know,' she moans. I lean forward to try to get a look at her. There doesn't seem to be any blood on her. Her eyes open and look at me.

'Can you move? Please move.'

'I'll try,' she whispers. She moves her head with a struggle, wincing in pain. She wiggles her fingers and moves her legs a little bit.

'So?' I ask, unable to hold my anticipation back.

'Um, I think I'm okay. My neck hurts a lot, but otherwise…' She pulls herself up a bit. Like my own hands, hers are still handcuffed just in the front. She searches around for the doorknob with both hands at once. When she opens the front door and scrambles out, the cold air hits me like a brick. But in a good way. It wakes me up. My mind gets sharper in a second. I'm suddenly able to focus better on the task at hand.

I search for the handle with my back to the door. Before I'm able to find it, it swings open and Charlie helps me out.

'What the hell were you thinking?' Charlie asks. 'If I hadn't got my handcuffs to the front, this could've gone way wrong.'

'I had no idea you were going to do that! I just thought we could kick our way to an accident,' I say. 'How the hell did you even get your hands to the front?'

'Yoga.'

I shake my head and smile.

'Okay, where do you think they put the keys?' She goes to the other side of the SUV and feels around in the guy's coat. He and his coat are halfway through the windshield.

'I can't feel anything. And I don't know how to get his coat free.'

'Try Bill,' I say. 'Maybe he has them.'

After a careful search of Bill and all his pockets, Charlie doesn't find a thing. The weather is turning colder and my teeth start to chatter.

'Listen, why don't we just start heading back down? I'm getting really cold, and it's a long way.'

'But what if the other guy has them?'

'They could be anywhere. You can't pull him out of the windshield anyway. And what if they're in his front pockets under the glass? I just think it's a lost cause.'

Taking one last look around, Charlie sighs.

We walk in silence for a bit until the tips of my fingers start to feel numb.

'You know that could've totally gone off the rails, right?' Charlie says.

'What do you mean?'

'You could've been a little bit more explicit about what you were about to do.' The terseness in her voice catches me off guard.

'Are you serious?' I ask. 'What are you, mad at me?'

She shrugs nonchalantly.

'You know, I thought you would be a little bit more grateful given the fact that I just saved your life.'

'Saved my life? Oh please.' She rolls her eyes. 'If I didn't catch that wink of yours, we'd both be dead.'

'So, what would you have me do? Come out and tell you what was going to happen out loud, so that they could hear?' My face flushes with anger.

'And why the hell did you put that money in my crawlspace?' she asks.

'It's pretty much what I told them. Cops were coming to snoop around and I didn't want them finding it in case they got a search warrant.'

Neither of us say anything for a few moments.

'You know, I was quite impressed by the way you jumped into my lap and wrapped your hands around the driver's neck,' I smile.

'It was lucky that I was tied up with my hands up front,' she says. 'I had to do something. I really didn't want to die in that car.'

Charlie shrugs and lets out a deep sigh.

No longer fueled by adrenaline, I suddenly become keenly aware of how human and vulnerable I am. Darkness is quickly falling around us. With the high after all that high-paced action, I suddenly feel at an all-time low. It's difficult to just move my legs forward and everything about the day seems impossible to comprehend. I try to focus my thoughts on something good and pure, Emily and Ava, but even the thoughts of them can't sustain me for long. I can barely focus enough to remember what either of them look like. My house and my family seem like distant memories. It's as if they belong to someone else or they are figments of my imagination, someone I've seen once or twice in a movie a long time ago.

'Are you okay?' Charlie asks, sensing that something is wrong. I nod and look away.

'I'm good,' I add, trying to convince her of something that I myself don't even believe. My chest tightens as my thoughts turn to the inevitable conversation that we will soon have to have with the police. We need a solid explanation for all of what happened, but nothing good comes to mind. I take deep breaths to try to calm myself and as the cold air enters my lungs and then slowly escapes, I finally begin to think this whole thing might be over.

CHAPTER THIRTY-SEVEN

NOAH

As we walk back down the road, my hands get numb. Temperatures are plummeting, and I don't have my gloves on. The handcuffs feel too snug, cutting off some of my circulation. Emily loves going to her hot yoga class four days a week. When my back gets stiff, she's on my case to do stretches and go along with her. Apparently, I wouldn't even be the only guy in the class. There are four or five regular male attendees. Still, I never do go. Now, I wonder if having a little bit more flexibility would help me get out of these handcuffs or at least move them to the front of my body. Charlie, who's walking next to me, doesn't seem to be in nearly as much discomfort as I am.

I've never been down this road, but it's pretty desolate, even by Alaska standards. Not a single car drives by as we descend through the darkness. I doubt that we will see anyone until we get closer to the highway, almost four miles away. Maybe then, we'll have a chance of someone picking us up.

'I'm sorry I stole your money,' she says. The wind blows her long hair into her face and she tucks some of it behind her ear

I nod. I'm thankful for the apology.

'I'm sorry that all this happened,' I say with a shrug. 'Though, honestly, I'm not sure how I would've been able to get out of this mess without you.'

'Do you know those guys?' she asks.

'No, never even heard of them.' I shake my head. 'I didn't know that money belonged to anyone.'

'Apparently, it belongs to their boss.'

We walk a little further in silence. I don't really know what else to say. All I know is that we should develop some sort of plan. We're miles away from my car and my cell phone. If we pull someone over or hitchhike, how the hell do we explain the handcuffs?

'So, how did you find out that I had your brother-in-law's money?'

'Actually, I needed a place to hide my portion. I was afraid that Emily would find it,' I say. I'm careful to avoid all mention of the police officer who came snooping around. As far as she's concerned, I don't know anything about that.

'So, I thought that your crawl space would be a good place. I didn't think you even knew about it.'

'You didn't think I knew about my crawl space?' she asks, incredulously.

Suddenly, I realize that I must sound like a total sexist.

'Well, Emily doesn't. Sorry, I just thought it would be a good place.'

'And then you saw the shoe box?'

'Yeah, imagine my surprise.' I smile. 'The bills had the same wrappers as mine. I had no idea how you got your hands on it.'

'I followed your brother-in-law when he left your house that day. It was a total fluke. I just wanted to see who he was and he ended up driving to Eklunta and hiding the box in one of those burial boxes.'

I nod. I had figured that much.

'So, the only thing I don't get is where the money came from in the first place?'

I consider whether I should tell her the truth. I guess I'm pretty deep in this already and the story is innocent enough. As long as there's no mention of the dead cop, it should be okay.

'I went on a run, kind of off the beaten path. And I stumbled upon this car. It was in an accident. It looked like it had been there for a bit.'

'And the money was just sitting there? What happened to the driver?'

'She was dead. I was going to call the cops but then I saw the duffel bag and it was full of cash.'

'How much?'

Oh yes, that's right. She doesn't know. Only Colton does. I need to keep this to myself.

'A lot,' I finally say.

'Do you know who the dead girl was?' Charlie asks.

'I didn't at first. But then I saw her on the news. They just found her. Julie something.'

Charlie stops and looks at me. Her face turns almost white as all blood seems to drain away from it.

'Do you know her?' I ask, praying that it's not someone too close to her.

'Not really, but her older sister is a friend of my grandma's. They were looking for her for a very long time.'

'I'm actually surprised that they found her in the winter at all. That road didn't look maintained. She'd driven all the way into the trees. I was really sorry to see her there.'

'Why did she have all that money on her?' Charlie asks after a moment. I shrug. I think that we both know that there isn't any honest reason to have that much money in a duffel bag. That's not the kind of money that you can make any legal way unless you're some celebrity or business tycoon.

As we continue further down the road into the darkness, our small silences between two thoughts expand into a general silence. Neither of us says anything for a few minutes, lost in our own minds. I let my thoughts wander with abandon. After a few moments, it settles back onto my novel. It has been going so well, and I need to have the time to finish it.

I am still not settled on the ending. My thoughts on it correspond to my own mood and well-being. When I'm tired and sore, like now, I want to kill the old man off for good. Give him some sort of courageous fight against the mighty sea and then make him go down with the ship. On other days, when I'm feeling more optimistic, I want to give him everything he ever dreamed of – a circumnavigation around the globe with the love of his life.

Glancing over at Charlie, I wonder if she's happy. Is she living her best life? Does she have regrets? Until I found the money, my life was stuck in a rut. I was a hamster running on a wheel, not really getting anywhere. Yes, I love my wife and child. But is that enough? I didn't feel like it was. I felt like there was more to life than working a job you hate and pining for dreams that seem impossible to achieve. And now, I'm so close. I'm so close to having freedom. A life somewhere else. A life without a full-time soul-sucking job. To some, I may sound like an egotist. But we only have one life, right? That we know of. Why not be a little egotistical when it comes down to it? Why not hold out for what's worthy? Why not do daring and exciting things?

'Are you happy?' I suddenly ask Charlie. The words escape my lips before I get a chance to stop them. This isn't the most appropriate time to talk about such philosophical things. Surprisingly, she looks at me and smiles.

'I don't know.' She shrugs. 'But that probably means that I'm not, right?'

'I have no idea,' I say.

'Are you?'

'Sometimes. I'm happy doing certain things.'

'Like what?'

'Writing. When my writing is going well, it's like a high. The words just pour out of me, and I know that there's nothing better in the world to do. At least, not for me. I'm also happy with Emily and Ava. But not how our lives are now.'

'And how's that?'

'We've been in a rut. I hate my job. Emily doesn't really hate hers, but it's exhausting and tiring. She wants to stay home with Ava not just rush around and spend all of her time at the hospital.'

Charlie listens carefully. And then asks, 'So, the money is your way out?'

I nod. 'Ever since I found this money, I felt the weight of the world come off my shoulders.'

'Even with what happened today?' she asks jokingly.

'Well, that wasn't ideal.' I laugh. 'I was scared, of course. But now that it's over, I feel sort of like a badass. I mean, think about what we just did.'

'Killed two guys?' she asks.

'Okay, yes, I guess, technically. But we also fought for our lives and won. I mean how cool is that? I thought that kind of thing only happened in movies.'

'I guess that is pretty cool.' She shrugs. 'I'll give you that.'

'What were you going to do with Colton's share?' I ask after a few minutes.

'I was going to pay for Nana's assisted living home in advance,' she says.

'Wow, that's noble.'

'She has some money saved, but not really enough. And I was going to quit my job.'

'You don't like being a 911 operator?'

She shakes her head. 'It's too stressful. The kind of shit that happens to people, I just don't really want to hear about it. It makes me feel very helpless.'

'Well, you send them cops.'

'Yeah, exactly. I just take down their stories and send help. I think I want to be of more use.'

I ask her what she would do instead.

'I think I'd like to be a police officer. Investigator. I know that a lot of shit comes with that job as well, but at least there's action. You're a little bit more in control. Eh, I don't know. Another part of me also wants to be a lawyer.'

'A lawyer?'

'Yeah.' She laughs. 'It's like a long-running joke in police departments. There's always one or two who are cramming for the bar exam or taking night classes.'

'So, you'd fit right in.'

I think about the kind of cop Charlie would be. Tenacious. Fair. Decent. Honest. There are worse things to be.

'I think any police department would be lucky to have you,' I say after a few moments.

CHAPTER THIRTY-EIGHT

NOAH

'What are we going to tell the police about what happened?' I ask after awhile.

'Do we have to tell them anything?' Charlie asks with a shrug. 'I mean, what if we just pretend that we were never there?'

'I'd love that, but it's too much of a risk. There are two men in that car up the hill. The scene doesn't exactly look like an accident and the cops are likely to collect fingerprints and other samples. We have no idea what they will find in that car that belongs to us. Maybe a few strands of your hair? Probably a whole bunch of our fingerprints. Perhaps even some of our blood.'

'Good point.'

'And they already have our data in their databases. I had to submit my fingerprints to become a teacher and I bet you did, too, to get the job at the police department.'

She nods, despondently.

'Okay, so we have to get ahead of the story. We need a good reason of why we were there. And the closer that it can be to the truth the better.'

'So, we can't just say that we were in a car accident?' she asks. I shake my head no.

'They're going to ask us how we know them. How long we have known them. I think the best thing is to tell them that they tried to kidnap us.'

'But why?'

'Because of the money. I will tell them about the dead girl. I will tell them about how I found the money and everything else that happened after that.'

Charlie doesn't look too sure about this plan.

'What?'

'I don't like it.'

'Why not?'

'We can't just tell them what happened. We have to make them work at putting the breadcrumbs of everything together.'

'Listen—' I start to say, but she cuts me off.

'Don't tell me to listen. Who do you think you are?'

'Okay, I'm sorry,' I say. 'The reason I want to tell them is that the best lies are those that are the closest to the truth.'

'And how do you know that, Noah? Did you read it in one of your lame books?'

She's baiting me, but I'm not going to engage.

'I don't know where I got that from. It's true nevertheless.'

'So, you want to tell them exactly what happened? The whole truth?' Charlie asks. 'Even about me following Colton and stealing his money? And putting it in my crawlspace?'

'Yes.' I nod, keeping my gaze firmly on hers. 'It's a good story, Charlie. It's easy to remember because it actually happened. If we come up with another story, it will have too many loopholes and places for us to mess up.'

She shrugs, only marginally convinced.

'I was thinking that we could tell them that I had it on me when the guys ran us off the road,' I continue.

Charlie shrugs again.

'Hey, if you have a better story, then tell me. I'm all ears.'

She thinks about this for a moment. But doesn't come up with anything.

'They were following us and they knew this,' I go on. 'Then they took us and the money to their boss, Dossey, but we didn't see him. Then they were driving us out somewhere into the country to kill us and that's when we got the upper hand.'

Charlie nods reluctantly. I ask her to repeat the story to me just to make sure that she has it down. It sounds good, but the thing about telling it to the cops is that there are many places to mess up. There are still many mistakes to be made. But for now, we are on the same page.

I keep waiting for Charlie to ask me for the money, but she never does. She took it, so I know that she wants it. But she either has too much class to come out and say something or everything that we've been through has given her a bad feeling about it. I consider my options. I can keep it all, but that doesn't seem fair. I mean, unlike Colton, she actually saved my life. I feel like I owe her something for it. Besides, I've seen enough crime movies and read enough thrillers to know that nothing good comes from someone being part of something illicit and then not taking their cut from it. We have to come up with a good story to tell the police and she needs to be motivated to stick to it long after.

'So, Charlie, I was thinking. I'd like you to have some of the money,' I say. She looks up at me with big wide eyes. She is completely surprised by my generosity. Exactly how much I want to give her, I haven't decided yet. All I know is that it has to be significant.

'Really? Why?'

'Because you really saved our butts back there. If it weren't for you, I don't know what would have happened.'

'Um, I don't know,' she says after a moment. 'It's not like I can't use it, of course.'

'Well, that's perfect then,' I say, feeling a sense of relief wash over me.

'But the thing is that I don't really know how I feel about taking it.'

'But you took it already. From Colton.'

'I know,' she says shyly. 'But I took it back when I wasn't sure what was really in there. I mean, I followed him out there and was just basically spying on him. I was curious about what was in the box and then when I brought it home, it was too late to return it.'

'Well, I would like you to have it,' I say. I didn't think it would be that hard to convince her to take the money. I mean, who the hell would say no to it? But I sense that her hesitation is coming from all the shit that has gone down ever since that money came into her life. And for that, I don't blame her.

'I really appreciate it,' Charlie says after a few moments.

I get the feeling that she needs just a little more coaxing. She really wants to take it, but she's not sure about it and all the bad juju that seems to come along with it.

'I think you deserve it for all the crap that you've been through. Getting kidnapped and almost dying, you know? And for saving my life. Just think of it as a thank you. For everything that you have done for me.'

'Okay,' Charlie finally says. 'I guess that could be okay.'

'I'm going to give you half,' I say decidedly. When she's about to protest, I put my hand up and shut her down. 'It's yours. You can do whatever you want with it. Honestly. And the fact that you will probably use it to pay for your grandmother's accommodation just says a lot, you know? About the person you are.'

Everything that I'm saying is the truth, but there's an underlying reason for my insistence. I need her to tell the cops the same story that I'm going to tell. We need to be on the same side. And her accepting the money will make me feel a lot better about the fact that she is actually standing by me. It's not that I'm trying to pay her off, exactly. But it is.

*

We walk for close to two hours. Every part of my body cries out in pain. I don't know if I can go on like this in the dark and the cold. I look over at Charlie. She also seems to be struggling. She had complained of a headache a little bit ago, and it seems to have got worse.

'I don't feel so good,' she says, suddenly dropping down to the ground.

'Oh, crap, are you okay?'

'Yeah, I think so,' she whispers. 'I'm just really tired.'

'No, Charlie, no, don't fall asleep,' I say, kneeling down next to her and nudging her. If only I had my hands free!

We shouldn't have walked so far. We should've flagged down a car sooner. What was I thinking that we could get all the way to my car?

Charlie's eyes flicker open for a second and then close until I shake her again. She's struggling to stay awake. The impact from the accident probably had much more of an effect than either of us had realized.

'Listen, listen,' I say. 'I'm going to flag someone down. I'm going to tell them the truth. I'm going to tell them that the guys who kidnapped us took the money. Can you hear me?'

I repeat myself a couple of times, trying to ingrain the story in her mind one last time before she passes out, but I have no idea if I'm getting through. This isn't a big variation on the plan, but we should've talked about it. How could I have been so stupid as to think that we would actually get back to my car? No, we needed to get help earlier. And now, there's no way out. I can't take these handcuffs off without Charlie. And without me, I don't think she will wake up. Christ, what a shit storm!

Suddenly, a pair of headlights appear in the distance. They are coming on the other side of the road, so I run across and jump up and down to get their attention. I know that I don't stand much of a chance. I'm a single male. It's pitch black. It's not the seventies anymore. Even though it's Alaska and people do pick up hitchhikers a lot more around here than in the lower forty-eight, the odds are not in my favor. Luckily, the car starts to slow down, eventually drifting to my side of the road. When the driver opens the passenger window, I peer in.

'I need your help. My friend and I were kidnapped. We got out and tried to walk back. But she passed out right over there. I'm still handcuffed. Please, can you call the police?'

The man who pulls over is in his fifties and doesn't look like the type who suffers fools gladly.

'Listen, I know that this sounds ridiculous. But as you can see, I'm handcuffed. I can't hurt you. Just please take a look.'

The man slowly gets out of his car and walks over to Charlie, who is now completely passed out in the snow. After confirming that my story is true, no matter how fantastical, he picks up his phone and calls the cops.

CHAPTER THIRTY-NINE

NOAH

After they take off my handcuffs and the paramedics check me out, they gave me a large gray blanket to wrap myself up in. Two deputies in their mid-forties drive me to the police station. It's a relatively modern building, about two stories high. Unlike a lot of government buildings around here, it has plenty of windows, which I appreciate even though it's pitch black outside.

The deputies walk me to a small windowless room with a table and two chairs. There is a camera in the ceiling, but no mirror. I'm pretty certain that it's an interrogation room. Another cop in uniform, a woman I've never seen before, brings me a cup of coffee and asks if I'm hungry. She offers me a donut they have left over from a party earlier that day and I gladly accept. I'm starving. My stomach is actually rumbling so loudly, I feel the need to apologize for all the noise it's making.

'There's going to be someone in to talk to you soon,' the woman says and closes the door behind her.

I take a bite of the powdered donut and cough a little as the confectionary sugar makes its way into my nostrils. It's a little dry, clearly made at least twelve hours ago, but it is the most delicious thing I've ever tasted. I try to pace myself, but it's difficult. I take a sip of my coffee and close my eyes as the black liquid runs down my throat.

My mind goes to Charlie. Is she going to be okay? She was unconscious by the time the paramedics arrived and they rushed her to the hospital. When one of them tried to talk to her, I heard them say that she was not responsive. Did she pass out from too much physical exertion or is there something really wrong? Maybe she had injured her head in the accident and has been slowly bleeding into her brain this whole time? My mind has a way of going to the darkest place possible if I let it wander too much unsupervised.

Suddenly, the door opens and a familiar face walks in. It's the same cop who I've seen with Charlie. He's the one who came over to my house. I force a smile as he shakes my hand and introduces himself again as Officer Stephen Silko.

'Is Charlie going to be okay?' I ask.

'Unfortunately, we don't actually know yet,' Silko says.

That's when I notice it, the sad look in his eyes. He doesn't just look tired or bored like he looked that day at my house. No, there's an actual sorrow in his eyes.

'So, what happened today, Noah? You don't mind if I call you Noah, right?'

'No, Noah is fine.' I shrug and launch into the story. I've already gone over it in my head a couple of times. The only thing I wasn't sure about was where to start. Do I start in the beginning with the dead girl? Or do I just start with today?

Silko listens carefully as I look him straight in the eyes and relay the events as they happened. Or as I want him to believe they happened. There are things I leave out. The dead cop. Charlie stealing Colton's money. Hiding the money in the cabin. And there are embellishments I add. The two guys in the SUV demanded the money so I showed them where I hid it, in one of the colorful burial boxes in Eklunta. They took it to their boss, and I don't know where it is now. And then I finish up with the truth. When Charlie and I realize that they're going to kill us, we cause the car accident. The bad guys are dead, and we're walking down the road back to my car. Handcuffed. Charlie passes out and I flag down a car.

'So, what was Charlie doing in your car in the first place?' Silko asks after I finish and take another sip of my coffee.

'Well, she's my neighbor. And we're friends. We got close when she told me about that incident at her job about the mother who killed her kids. She was really distraught. She wasn't sure if she wanted to go back to work. And the night before this happened, she just saw me outside. I told her I was heading out to the grocery store, and she asked if she could come along.'

'Just like that?'

'Well, yes.' I nod. That's as close to the truth as I can get it. Making it almost all true.

'Just seems odd,' Silko says, clearly not convinced. 'I mean, she has her own car. It's odd to go to the grocery store with a friend, wouldn't you say that?'

I shrug. 'I don't think so.'

'Noah, did you and Charlie have an intimate relationship?'

My heart skips a beat. Why did he use the word 'did'? Past tense. Does he know something about Charlie that I don't know? She is okay, right? She has to be okay.

'What? No, of course not.' I shake my head. 'I'm married. Happily married.'

Silko's eyes narrow. Clearly, he doesn't believe me.

'She is just my neighbor. We weren't really even friends until recently. Is she okay? She's going to be okay, right?'

Silko looks away. I have no idea how to read him. He's definitely the type to keep his cards close to his chest.

'She has to make it,' I say. 'I mean, she was in that car because of me. She had nothing to do with any of this. The whole thing was just a terrible mistake.'

Silko listens carefully without saying a word. I feel the need to fill the void with more words.

'I really thought that giving them the money would make them go away. But when it became clear that they were not going to let me go, Charlie saved my life. If it weren't for her kicking Bill, there's no way we could've caused that accident and got out.'

After I finish talking, Silko takes a deep breath before excusing himself.

Again, I'm left alone in the interrogation room with nothing but my thoughts. The donut is gone, and the coffee only has the black sugary silt at the bottom. I look around, glancing up at the camera. There are people on the outside watching me. Or will be in the future. For a second, I wonder if they will find my story as convincing as I do.

The walls of the room are painted taupe. I am familiar with this color because when Emily and I first bought the house we had a big fight over it. I never thought that I would be the kind of person to fight over paint colors, but marriage does funny things to you. Over the years, it wears on you and you sometimes become glimpses of a person you never thought you could ever be. Yet, sitting in this taupe-colored room, this fight seems like an old joke and one that's not particularly funny either.

I miss Emily. I miss her crooked smile. I miss the way she laughs at any slapstick comedy. I miss the way she pats my back whenever I'm upset. But mostly I miss all the millions of small moments that we share in our life. Not the fights or the arguments, but all those ways that we're there for each other. If I ever get out of this place, I know that I won't take them for granted anymore. Not even for a second.

Silko comes back into the room.

'Any word on Charlie?' I ask almost immediately. Silko looks me up and down as if he's considering whether he should tell me what he knows.

'She's still out,' he finally says. 'But she's stable.'

I let out a sigh of relief.

'She must've struck her head when we hit that tree,' I say. 'But I'm so glad that she's okay.'

Silko flashes me a reluctant smile. 'Yeah, me, too.'

The expression on Silko's face is not just of a concerned police officer.

'You know Charlie, right?' I ask. 'I mean, she works here.'

He's taken aback by my question.

'Yes, I know her,' Silko says after a moment.

'I'm really sorry.'

He nods.

'Were you close?' I push. His eyes don't meet mine. They dart back and forth from one side of the room to another.

'You could say that,' he finally says, and I decide to let go of any further questioning. I know that they've been seeing each other, but he doesn't have to know that.

'If you don't mind, who was the dead girl in the car?' I ask.

Silko doesn't say anything for a bit, probably debating whether he should tell me anything.

'Julie Reid worked as a drug runner for Steven Dossey. He ran one of the biggest salvage yards in the area and owned a couple of trucks, which he used to deliver drugs all over the state.'

'So, how did she end up with all that money?'

'He was found shot in the head in his office awhile back. Her fingerprints were found on the gun from the scene. His safe was open and whatever money was in there was gone.'

'So, she shot him and took his money?'

Silko nods. 'Most likely.'

'But why?'

'One of her friends said that he had raped her.'

'And she got her revenge?'

'I guess.' Silko nods. 'Something like that. We're not sure where she was headed. But it doesn't look like there was foul play at the scene where we found her. That road wasn't very well maintained, and there was an early season blizzard around the time when she went missing. So, we think that she just got into a car accident and froze to death.'

'What a horrible story,' I say, nodding.

Silko shrugs. 'Shit happens all the time.'

CHAPTER FORTY

NOAH

Silko leaves me alone in the room again. I know that they do this on purpose. They want to watch me. They analyze me from the other side of the two-way mirror. Despite knowing all that, it does not make the experience any easier. Being alone in a police interrogation room is not the most comforting thing in the world, and that's an understatement.

I stare at the walls and crack my knuckles. I don't know whether I should try to look innocent or concerned. The only thing I know for sure is that I shouldn't look guilty. But what does that actually look like? My mind goes to all the videos I've seen on Court TV. Some people simply lay down on the desk while others stretch out and put their feet up on the table. Others look more nervous and pace around the room. And there was that one girl who did cartwheels and yoga poses. All of these are bad options for me.

I put a stern, concentrated look on my face and stare straight ahead. I have to look like I'm taking this seriously, but not like I have anything to hide. As far as they know, I'm just a regular person who got caught up in something bad. This has all been a misunderstanding. I made a few poor decisions initially, but I didn't break the law. I have to get them to believe me.

When Silko comes back into the room, he has a stern look on his face. It's not like he was particularly friendly before, but whatever friendliness he had offered me is all but gone. The expression in his eyes is uncompromising. He flips a file of papers onto the table in front of me. They make a big thump sound, rattling me to my very core. I take a deep breath and brace myself for whatever is about to come.

'I don't think you're telling me the truth, Noah,' Silko says.

'What do you mean?'

'I know about the fight that you had with your brother-in-law, Colton, at your high school. Does that ring a bell?'

'Yes,' I say slowly.

'Well, why have you left that out of your story?'

I shrug.

'I didn't think it was relevant to what happened to Charlie and me.'

'Oh, really? And why is that?'

'I don't know.' I shrug again. 'Colton's not the greatest guy in the world. So, we had a fight, so what?'

Silko shakes his head.

'Colton's missing,' he says after a moment.

'Yes, I know.'

'Doesn't that mean anything to you?'

'Of course, it does. I'm worried sick,' I say. We go back and forth on this until I'm pretty sure we have hit a standstill. I haven't convinced Silko of anything he refuses to believe. But I also know that he has no proof. Of anything. I have no idea where Colton is and neither does he.

'And what if I told you that I think you have something to do with his disappearance?'

I stare at him. 'I wouldn't really know what to say to you,' I reply after a moment. 'I had nothing to do with anything like that. Colton is family. I would never…'

My voice drops off as I consider the eventuality. Silko is just trying to rattle you, I say to myself. I know this, of course, but it doesn't really change anything. It's working.

'Why would you even think that?' I ask.

'Why would he just go missing all of a sudden?'

'Because the same guys who took us probably took him,' I say. 'I mean, they knew we had the money.'

'And you never turned Colton in to Dossey or his men?' Silko asks me, staring straight into my eyes. He doesn't know what he's talking about, but his confidence is disarming. I suddenly feel like he knows everything about me and what I did and he's just waiting for me to come clean.

I take a deep breath and try to center myself. No, he doesn't know anything. He's just a cop. A very good cop and a very good interrogator. That's what they do. If things get really bad, you can always ask for a lawyer, I say to myself. But wouldn't that make me look really guilty? Maybe. But at least you won't actually confess to anything.

You can do this, I say to myself over and over again, silently.

'Noah?'

'I don't like all of these accusations, Officer Silko,' I say, gathering my breath. 'I don't understand why you're implying all of these untrue things about me. I was a victim in this. I didn't do anything wrong.'

'Well, you did take the money and not report the dead girl to the authorities,' he observes. That's a good point, but I can't even give him that. I don't really know if that's a crime or not, and I'm not willing to find out without an attorney present.

'Listen, all of this, it's making it sound like I need an attorney.'

'Why is that?'

'You're accusing me of all these things. I don't know what I'm supposed to do to convince you that I had nothing to do with anything,' I say.

'I wouldn't say that,' Silko says after a moment.

'You wouldn't say what?'

'I wouldn't say I'm accusing you of anything. We're just having a friendly chat.'

I shake my head. 'I've had friendly chats before and I wouldn't say that this is a friendly chat at all.'

'If that's what you think, I can't do anything about it.'

I decide to push him on it a little bit further. 'So, you don't think I need an attorney?'

'You're not under arrest,' he says after a moment.

'So, I'm free to go?'

'Of course. I just thought that you would want to help us out in our investigation into the men you say kidnapped you, but if you don't want to…'

He's toying with me again. He's ignoring and deflecting my questions about the lawyer. I let out a deep sigh. At least, I have a way out now.

'I do want to help you,' I finally say. 'But I don't want to be accused of anything I didn't do.'

'Okay, fine,' Silko says. He smacks his lips and opens the manila folder in front of him. I can't see what's in it because he lays it on the edge of the table and tilts it toward him. But I get the sense that it contains information about this case.

'So, before we let you go, I just want to ask you one final thing.'

I wait for him to continue.

'How do you know Charlie Easton?'

'She's my neighbor.'

'And you would say that you're close?'

I stare at him. 'No, I wouldn't say that at all.'

'Oh, really? I find that hard to believe.'

'Why?'

'She's a pretty girl who lives next door to you.'

'So? Her roommates are pretty, too,' I say. 'But I'm married and I love my wife. And my daughter. I would never do anything to jeopardize that.'

'So, you two never…' His voice drops off. I have no idea what he's referring to.

'I don't know what you mean, but Charlie and I never did anything. We are just casual acquaintances. We barely know each other, actually.'

'And she will confirm this?'

A shiver runs through my body. I certainly hope so. But I keep it all under wraps.

'I'm sure she will. Anything else would be a lie.'

Silko continues to look through the file. I consider my options. Then it occurs to me. What if I were to turn the tables on him?

'But wait, you and her,' I start. 'Aren't you two… together?'

Silko's face drains of all color. When he looks back at me, his eyes don't meet mine. Instead, he looks through me.

'I've seen you come and go from her place,' I say. 'You two are dating, right?'

By the grave expression on his face, I can tell that I have him. Hook, line, and sinker. I didn't realize it at first, but I don't think people at the police station know that they're dating. I mean, she's not a police officer, but there's no way he would be doing the interrogation if the higher ups knew that they were together. It would be unprofessional and considered a conflict of interest.

Just after this epiphany comes to me, another uniformed police officer bursts through the door. He is a few decades older than Silko and with a rather pissed off expression on his face.

'Silko,' the cop says, standing in the doorway. 'I need to speak with you. Immediately.'

Silko's face drops and he follows him out of the room like a child who has just been sent to the principal's office. I try to wipe the smile off my face, but it keeps creeping up around the corners of my mouth despite my best efforts. At last, I decide to simply cover my mouth with my hand so that I'm not caught smiling on camera.

A few moments later, the older police officer returns and introduces himself as Sergeant Grisham. He apologizes profusely to me and tells me that Silko is now off the case. Something about a conflict of interest that he was not aware of up until this point.

'Yes, I understand,' I say, nodding and trying to look as concerned as possible. 'So, can I go now?'

'Yes, of course,' Sergeant Grisham says quickly. I let out a huge sigh of relief. Within a moment, I'm no longer carrying the weight of the world on my shoulders.

'But please make sure to stay in town for a while in case we have any more questions.'

'Yes, of course,' I say casually. 'I don't have any plans to go anywhere.'

CHAPTER FORTY-ONE

NOAH

Emily meets me in the hallway of the police station. She throws her arms around me. Hot tears stream down her face as we embrace, and my own eyes start to water.

'I'm okay,' I reassure her over and over.

'They told me what happened, Noah,' she says, choking over her tears. 'Oh my God. I can't believe that we almost lost you, honey.'

I pull away from her and look her in the eyes. I wipe a loose tear and hug her again.

'I'm fine, really,' I say, mumbling into her hair.

As we walk out of the police station hand in hand, I straighten out my shoulders and feel some of the tension in my neck dissipate. The cold air is refreshing and I inhale deeply, trying to fill my lungs with as much oxygen as possible. This is almost over.

In the car, Emily's mood seems to change course one hundred and eighty degrees. At first, she was relieved to see me safe and sound, but as we drive home, other thoughts start to creep into her mind. After such a long time at the police station, I am too tired to even talk, but I know that I can't get out of this situation that easily.

'What happened, Noah? I mean, who were those guys?' she asks. Her voice is frantic and erratic.

I take a deep breath. I don't know where to start. Do I tell her about the money and the dead girl? Do I tell her about the dead cop? Should I just come out and tell her everything?

'Did the cops tell you anything?' I ask. She shakes her head.

'No, no one has told me anything, Noah,' she says. She's saying my name at the end of each sentence. That's not a good sign.

'And you better start talking. And I mean fast. What the hell were you doing in the car with that girl Charlie? You've been acting weird for days. What's going on?'

Dammit. So, she does know something. Again, my thoughts rush around my mind at a mile a minute. Eventually, I decide to tell her the same thing that I told the cops. I start at the beginning.

'Wait, you found how much money?' she asks.

'Two point two million in cash. I know now that I shouldn't have taken it—'

'Of course not!' Emily interrupts me.

'But at that moment, all I could think about was how all that money was going to change our lives,' I explain. The look on her face says that she doesn't really care.

'You've been lying to me.'

'You're right, I'm sorry. I shouldn't have lied.'

'You stole the money and you didn't report finding a dead body. A dead girl! What were you thinking?'

'I was just thinking about us. I mean, no more mortgage, no more long hours at the hospital for you. No more teaching bored teenagers who couldn't care less about anything that was coming out of my mouth.'

'But why? Why didn't you tell me any of this? How could you lie to me?'

'I wanted to protect you. I didn't know what was going to happen.'

When I continue the story, I reach the moment of truth. The dead police officer. Should I tell her about it or just keep it to myself? So far, no one else knows except for Colton and me. I feel a tightness in my chest and an urge to tell her everything. There's something about keeping a secret that makes you feel a little shitty inside. But no matter how much relief telling the truth might provide me, I decide to keep this under wraps for now. It's not anything that I'm proud of and the fewer people know about it, the better.

I proceed with the rest of the story as linearly as I can. I go over as many details as I can remember, eventually getting to the kidnapping. I don't mention the rendezvous that Charlie and I have at the diner, the night that I bury the body, for pretty much the same reason that I don't mention the dead cop. There are just certain things that would complicate this too much. No, that's not entirely true. There are certain things that I just don't want Emily to know because I know that it will hurt her too much.

'So, Charlie just hopped in your car with you?' Emily asks, long after I'm past that portion of the story. 'I just don't understand why.'

'She needed to talk to me,' I say, shrugging. 'This whole thing got very complicated very fast.'

'Yes, it seems so,' Emily says, skeptically.

I want to continue, but I can sense that Emily is hung up on this point.

'What? What is it? Don't you believe me?' I ask.

She shrugs, looking away from me. 'She's just a little too involved in this whole thing for my liking.'

'I know, don't you think I know that?' I ask. 'Hell, I wish I wasn't that involved in it. I wish this whole thing would just go away, but it won't. I made a lot of bad mistakes, Em. I didn't think this whole thing through. Not that I could really think any of the things that happened through, but I should've known that it was a terrible idea taking the money.'

Emily sighs. I can tell that whatever I'm saying is not enough. Emily is completely fixated on the fact that Charlie and I were found together after the kidnapping. She's putting way more weight on this issue than I thought she would. I have to convince her that there's nothing going on between us. Mainly, because it's the truth. Whatever feelings I had for Charlie have long but dissipated and all I want now is to just get back to my normal life with Emily and Ava.

'Listen, I hardly know Charlie,' I say. 'She was just there. She was involved, but not because I wanted her to be. She got herself involved. I love you, Emily.'

Emily sighs again, but by the expression on her face I can tell that I'm making some progress. And after a few more minutes of convincing, Emily seems to let the topic go for now.

'So, what happened to the money?' she asks after I finish telling her the story that Charlie and I have decided on to be the truth. I've been waiting for this moment, but not with anticipation. I want to tell her that I still have it, but I hesitate because I don't know how she will react to it. If only I could somehow gauge her reaction.

'Well, the guys who grabbed us took it back to Dossey first. I don't have it anymore,' I say after a few moments.

Emily nods. 'It's probably for the best.'

I smile. 'It's the only option I really thought I had,' I add.

'Oh yes, of course,' Emily agrees. 'I mean I wouldn't want you to jeopardize your life any more than you already have just for money.'

The words coming out of her mouth are reasonable and rational. But by the expression on her face, she is hiding something else. Am I seeing it right? Is that a tinge of regret? Maybe even a longing for the fact that I no longer have it.

'What? What are you thinking?' I coax her. It takes her a few moments to reply.

'I don't know. I mean, it's stupid, I know. I know that you should've never taken the money. I mean, it belonged to really dangerous men. But still…' Her voice drops off. I wait for her to continue.

'I just can't help but think about how nice it would be to still have it.'

'Really?'

'Yeah, I know, it's dumb. I mean, people don't just forget about $2.2 million, but still. I mean, if you still had it…'

'What?' I ask with a little smile forming at the corners of my mouth.

'Well, maybe that life we talked about at dinner at the Grape Tap, maybe that could've been in our future.'

'Would you like that?'

She looks at me, surprised. 'Yes, of course. Just the thought of not going back to those night shifts at the hospital, I mean, I love just thinking about that. And imagine all the time that I could spend with Ava. We both could. And maybe we could even move to Key West. I mean, wearing flip-flops all the time. That's not a hard life to get used to.'

'Yes, I think you could manage,' I say.

'I guess it's just nice to imagine yourself in another world, you know?' she says. 'I guess I just wish you told me about it earlier.'

'Honestly, the only reason I didn't tell you was that I wasn't sure how you would react. I wasn't sure if you would want me to put it all back.'

'Yes, I probably would've wanted that. It's dirty money and you, we, have no right to have it. But still… now that it's gone, it's nice to think about all the things that we could've done with it, you know?'

I know exactly how she feels. Imagination is a powerful force. It can take you out of the day-to-day. Imagining a life that was not so much in a rut as mine was before I found that money was the whole reason why I grabbed that bag in the first place. Again, I wrestle with the idea of coming out and telling her the truth. But I decide to wait. There will always be time for that later.

As we drive past the brightly lit gas station, it suddenly hits me. I'm the only person who knows where it is. No one else knows, not Colton, not Charlie, not the cops, not the bad guys. But is that too good to be true?

CHAPTER FORTY-TWO

NOAH

The next few days pass in a blur as I lounge around the house and spend my days in sweats in front of the television. It is on this one lazy afternoon, while drowsing on the couch with a half-opened thriller on my stomach, that someone rings the doorbell. Ava and Emily are somewhere upstairs, so I stagger down the hall to answer it.

'Officer… Silko?' I ask, trying to remember his name. He looks different out of uniform, a bit less intimidating, but not by much.

'I just have a few more things I want to cover with you, Noah,' he says. I'm keenly aware of the fact that he just used my first name instead of last name. He's trying to be casual. He's trying to be my friend.

'Okay,' I say, without making a move to invite him in. A cold gust of wind comes through and he shivers and turns the collar on his coat up.

'May I come in?' he asks after a moment.

I take a deep breath. I definitely don't want to invite him in, but I don't really have much of a choice.

'What do you want?' I ask, once he closes the door behind him.

Silko stomps his feet in our hallway before answering. I purposely stand in the hallway, without inviting him further into the house. I don't want to see him. I've answered all of his questions before and I've been perfectly clear.

'Well, I was just thinking,' he says, unzipping his coat and taking off his hat, 'about Colton. Can you tell me what happened at that fight you had with him again?'

'I already told you,' I say, crossing my hands over my chest.

'Yes, I know. But I need a refresher.'

What a dick, I say to myself, but go over the details of that day at school again.

'The thing is that I sort of think that there was something more to it,' Silko says after a while. I shrug. I'm not really sure how to respond. 'I mean, you two have this fight. It's very public, the whole school knows about it, and then he disappears. Don't you find that odd?'

I shrug. 'I guess.'

'And you had nothing to do with that?'

'Of course not! Who do you think I am? I'm just a teacher. I don't know how to make people disappear.'

'Well, I wasn't implying that. I was just thinking that there was a little bit more to the story than you are saying.'

I take a deep breath.

'Listen, I don't really know how to convince you that I'm telling the truth and I'm a little tired of all the accusations.'

'What accusations?'

'Like this one. I had nothing to do with Colton's disappearance. I have no idea what happened. But it's likely that the same guys who took me and Charlie took him, don't you think?'

'Perhaps.'

Neither of us say a word for a while.

'Is there anything else?' I ask, when I feel my patience growing thin.

'I was just thinking that maybe things aren't exactly as you had laid them out back at the station,' Silko finally says.

'I can't help that.'

'What do you mean?'

'I mean, I can't help what you think. I can only tell you the truth.'

'Which is?'

I resist the urge to roll my eyes in his direction. No matter how little respect I have for him, he's still an officer of the law and I have to act somewhat deferential toward him.

'I told everything already. They ran us off the road. They put us in their car and drove us to someone's house to take the money there.'

'And you had the money with you again, why?'

'Because I was going to put it somewhere else. It wasn't safe at my house anymore.'

'Uh-huh,' Silko says, not particularly convinced. 'And what about Colton?'

'What about him?'

'After your fight, you just let it go?'

'Yes.'

'I find that hard to believe. I mean, Colton insisted that you share some of the money with him, right? He beat you up in front of your students. That didn't make you mad?' Silko says, narrowing his eyes. He's toying with me. He's playing a game. The only way to deal with it is to play back.

'Yes, but I got over it. Colton has a bad temper. I don't. Yes, Colton and I have had our share of problems. He's not exactly one of my best friends or anything.'

'Oh I don't know. I've seen money do crazy things even to people who were best friends.'

I didn't want to give him anything else to go on. It seems like his imagination is already in overdrive.

'Hello?' Emily's quiet voice startles me. It's coming from somewhere down the hall.

Silko introduces himself and tells her why he's here.

'I thought that you got all of your questions answered back at the station?' she asks.

'Well, I had some more,' he says. He's using his intimidating voice, the one that's supposed to put us in our place.

'And now?' Emily asks, clearly unintimidated. 'Did you get them answered?'

'Somewhat.'

'Well, in that case, I'd appreciate it if you were on your way. My husband and I are going out soon and I need him to get ready.'

'Oh, yeah, where?'

'That's really none of your business,' Emily says. I've never seen her like this. So outgoing and adamant, especially with an authority figure. Silko doesn't say anything and instead stands there, challenging her with his gaze.

'Actually, I was under the impression that your sergeant took you off this case,' Emily says after a few moments. I had mentioned this to her earlier, but I guess she remembered.

'Um, that's not entirely true,' Silko says. I'm almost one hundred percent sure that he's lying, and my hunch is confirmed when he makes the move to zip up his coat again.

'But I guess I'll go for now,' he says, as if he's giving us a favor instead of getting kicked out of our home. 'You two have a nice day.'

Later that afternoon, Silko is back. Only this time, he's helping Charlie inside as I watch from my living-room window. She was just released from the hospital. From the way he supports her back and helps her up the stairs, it's clear that they have a long history. I wonder what, if anything she said to him. Sometimes with head injuries, people don't remember anything that happened around the time of the injury. Or maybe she's just not saying. Either way works for me.

As it turned out, Colton wasn't actually missing for long. True to their word, Dossey's men did let him go.

'I still can't believe that you kept all that from me,' Emily says over breakfast.

Ava is playing in the living room, and we're keeping our voices low. She doesn't know anything about this, and we both would like to keep it that way.

'I know.' I shrug, inhaling one of her delicious blueberry and chocolate chip pancakes. She only makes them on special occasions. I guess surviving a kidnapping is special enough.

'I'm really sorry, Em. I just didn't know what was going to happen. I didn't want you to know anything in case anyone came looking for it.'

That answer seems to satisfy her. For better or worse, Emily tends to believe what I say just as I believe what she says. And outside of this incident, that policy has always coincided with the truth. I haven't really lied to her about anything important and, as far as I know, she hasn't either. I hate lying to her about the money. But I want to go to the cabin and check on it first. I have to see that it's actually there, that I didn't hallucinate stashing it away. The incidents over the last few days have made me question my own reality in many ways.

'And this money, you gave it back to them?' Emily asks.

'Yes, I did,' I say after a moment.

She looks disappointed.

'I'm sorry. I just thought that they would let us go, and… it was a mistake.'

'No, you did the right thing, absolutely. You saved your life, that's what's important.'

I nod.

'You know what's silly?' she asks after a moment. 'I wish that I knew about it even for a moment when you still had it. It would've been nice to imagine a world in which we had over two million dollars. I mean… everything would be different, wouldn't it?'

A smile spreads over my face. I had no idea how she would react to the idea of having it. Many wives would've scolded me for putting my life in danger. Or would've been worried about what it meant to have all that stolen cash.

'What would you have wanted to do with it?' I ask.

'Quit my job. You could quit your job, too,' she says very quickly. This is definitely not the first time she has imagined this.

'You could write full-time. I could run a little used bookstore somewhere warm. Maybe Mexico or Belize.'

'You would really want to move there?' I ask. I don't think I've ever been happier before. After all of these years, Emily and I are still in-sync. How many married people can say that?

'Absolutely. I mean I like living here. But the tropics? That would be amazing. And the best part is that the money is stolen so we'd have to go somewhere where we could fit in with the rest of the expats.'

So, that's it. I pour a generous serving of maple syrup over the last pancake on my plate. It's decided. I'm going to check on the money, make sure that it's still there, and then come back and make a plan for how to start a new life. It's probably not something we can do too quickly. The cops are still investigating the loose ends. We can't very well disappear into the night without arousing suspicion. But at least, there will be a plan in the making.

In a month or two, the commotion of the kidnapping should die down. I'll finish my book. Emily will give notice at her job, and we'll move somewhere else. We'll start a new life. She'll pick the place. We'll tell everyone that we're going on a long and well-deserved vacation, and we'll never come back.

After doing the dishes, I kiss Ava on the head and head toward the front door.

'Where are you going?' Emily asks.

'Just for a drive. I want to get out of the house,' I say. She looks me up and down. The lies from the last couple of weeks have definitely added up, but she lets me go without another comment. I do want to go on a drive. But I also want to go check on my money. I have to make sure that it's still there. Hidden and safe. And that I didn't dream up this whole mess in some delusional episode.

On the way to my father-in-law's cabin, 'Sweet Child o' Mine' by Guns N' Roses comes on the radio and I turn it up to full blast. I sing along at the top of my lungs, but can't hear a thing over the roaring stereo. I tap my fingers on the steering wheel in anticipation. I can't sit still. I'm practically dancing in my seat. I zoom through all green and yellow lights. Every red light that I encounter takes excruciatingly long.

When I finally pull up to the cabin, my heart drops. Colton's car is parked out front.

CHAPTER FORTY-THREE

CHARLIE

I haven't talked to Noah since the accident. My memory of what happened is hazy from the car crash. The bang to the head kept me in the hospital for a few days and I need him to fill in some of the points. But I can't very well do that while Stephen is watching my every move. There are things that he doesn't know, and it would be better if it stayed that way. Stephen helps me up to the door with his arm firmly around my back. He has been beyond helpful in this whole experience. But also smothering. He's always watching me. And not just in that comforting, supportive way. He's watching me like a suspect.

I think on some molecular level he knows that I am not telling the truth about everything. He just doesn't exactly know where I fit in. At first, I thought he suspected that there was something going on between Noah and me. But now it feels more like it's something else.

I sit at the kitchen table cradling a cup of tea. Stephen helps himself to some biscuits. After taking a bite, he looks up at me with an inquisitive expression on his face.

'So, I was just wondering,' he says. 'Something about this whole thing is just not adding up. I mean, you and Noah, you said that you barely know each other.'

Here it goes again. A part of me thought that we had put this behind us, but now I know that it was just too good to be true. I roll my eyes and take another sip.

'What? What's wrong?'

'I just don't understand why we have to keep going over this, over and over again. I mean, I answered all of your questions already. What else do you want?'

Stephen shakes his head. 'Well, I don't really understand what the big deal is. I mean, don't you want to know more about what happened?'

'No, frankly, I don't. I couldn't care less. I've had enough with all the interrogation. I already told you everything that I'm going to tell you. I already told you the truth.'

I feel my blood pressure rising, but I take a deep breath to try to calm myself down. I'm still taking a full dose of the pain medication that they have prescribed me at the hospital and my mind isn't entirely where it should be. Suddenly, I feel dizzy and everything before me starts to look blurry.

But Stephen doesn't seem to notice a thing.

'I don't understand why you wouldn't want to know more about what's going on.'

'I already know everything.'

Stephen takes a deep breath. 'Okay, let me just come out and say it then.'

I sigh deeply and wait for him to continue.

'It's just that you and Noah, your statements are just too… spot on. It could only mean that you have somehow came up with the story together—'

'Or that we are telling the truth,' I cut him off. That's it. I've had enough of this. I get up from my chair and put my cup of unfinished tea in the sink.

'Listen, I want you to leave,' I say without turning around.

'What?'

'Thank you for everything that you have done for me. For bringing me back from the hospital and taking care of me, but I would like you to leave now,' I say sternly. My voice is firm and unwavering.

'But, Charlie—'

'I'm sick of it,' I say, finally turning to face him. 'I'm sick of these questions. I'm sick of being a suspect. Your sergeant took you off the case and here you are harassing me with all this. I already told you everything that I'm going to tell you and that should be enough for you. But it's not. So, I want you to leave.'

Stephen shakes his head. He gets out of his seat slowly and heads to the mud room where his coat is hanging.

'I'll call you later,' he says, putting on his boots. I consider that for a moment.

'No, I don't think that's a good idea,' I say. Stephen looks up at me, dumbfounded. He really didn't expect that answer. A part of me is surprised as well.

'What do you mean?'

It wasn't supposed to come out this way, but this is as good a time as any.

'The thing is that I don't think this thing between us… I don't think it's working out,' I say. As soon as the words escape my lips, I feel a big weight lift off my shoulders. It's like I had something heavy and unwieldy pressing down on me for a very long time and in one moment it vanishes.

'We were never really serious, right?' I continue. 'You said so yourself. We were never exclusive.'

'Is that what you want?' Stephen asks.

'No, not at all. I want the opposite, actually. I don't think we should see each other anymore at all.'

'But why?'

'Because we're not that great together, Stephen.'

'I thought we were fine,' he says quietly. I don't know what else to add. I just want him to leave my house. I can't handle him watching me anymore. I can't handle his questions and his nosing around.

'Charlie, please.' He comes up to me, putting his arms around my shoulders. 'I'm really sorry about all the questions. I was just worried about you. A lot more than I ever thought I would be. I mean, when I heard you were in the hospital and what had happened, I thought that I would lose you and I couldn't deal with it.'

I look down at the floor and pull away from him.

'I'm really sorry, Stephen,' I say after a few moments of silence. 'I just can't do this. And it's not because of the accident or all the questions. It's just something that I've been thinking about for some time now. I just don't think we're good together.'

Standing by the window in the living room, I let out a big sigh of relief. That has been a long time coming and I'm glad that I finally put an end to it. I should've done it earlier, but better late than never. The sound of an engine starting up draws my attention to the house across the street. A few minutes later, probably after the car is sufficiently warm, Noah comes out of his house and gets behind the wheel.

As soon as I see him, I put on my boots, grab my coat and hat off the rack, and leave the house. But I'm too slow and he has already turned at the corner. Burying my hands in my pockets, I find the keys to my car and hop in.

I haven't talked to Noah since the night I was taken to the hospital. The fact that we are both at home is a good indication that we both told the same story to the police. Despite that, I still have an inkling to talk to him. I need to know how he is and how the interrogation went. I also want to tell him about me and Stephen. And then, of course, there's the money. I didn't want to accept Colton's share at first. But I knew that he wouldn't trust me as much if I had turned it away. I know too much about this whole situation and if I don't get at least some of the money, he would not trust me. Of course, I'm not taking it entirely for altruistic reasons. I already got the second letter from Nana's assisted living facility about a bill that I have yet to pay and there are only more on the way. Even if I don't necessarily want to accept the money, I know that I have to.

I don't really know why I'm following him except that I want to talk to him. I don't have his number and I don't feel comfortable going over there and asking to speak to him. Besides the money, I also want to know exactly what he told his wife. We should be good with the cops for now, but did he tell Emily anything more than what he had told them? I really hope not.

Driving a few cars behind him, I follow him as he drives further and further north. He turns off the main highway and loops around various narrow two-lane roads. There are no cars around us now, so I stay even further back. A couple of times, I think that I lost him only to have him emerge just ahead of me behind a bend.

When he turns and slows down onto a poorly maintained road about the size of a street alley, I wait at the corner and watch. Somewhere in the distance, he parks by another car and heads toward the only cabin for miles. I wait until he disappears inside before getting out of the car and hiking up to the cabin. My feet descend far into the deep snow, making each step laborious. When I reach the cabin, I wait. Snow begins to fall, and the sun disappears behind a veil of twilight. Suddenly, the unmistakable sound of a gunshot pierces the silence.

CHAPTER FORTY-FOUR

NOAH

When I open the door, it creaks but not loud enough to startle Colton. I watch for a few seconds as Colton slams around the cabinet doors, furiously seeking something.

'What are you doing here? People are worried about you. The police are looking for you,' I say. He stands up, narrowing his eyes.

'I'm looking for the fucking money. What did you do with it?'

'It's not here. You know that,' I say as calmly as possible. Colton's eyes are bloodshot. The buttons on his shirt aren't fastened correctly, and the shirt is wrinkled as if he had slept in it for days.

'You have it!' Colton runs up to me, sticking his finger in my face. For a second, it looks as if his eyes are about to pop out of his skull.

'I don't have the money, Colton. You sent those thugs after me and they fucking have it!'

'What?' Colton takes a step back.

'Oh, c'mon, please?' I roll my eyes. 'The only reason they found out I had the money is because of you and your blabbermouth. The casino? Remember? You told them about me.'

'So, what? They threatened my life!'

'Well, they did the same to me, and they very nearly killed me.'

'But you didn't have to give them the money,' he says on the verge of tears.

'Oh, yes, I did. Of course, I did. They would've killed me if I hadn't.'

No one says anything for a few moments. I'm pretty sure that I have convinced him. I mean, of all people, he should know how scary Dossey's men are.

Colton shakes his head.

'You fuckin' betrayed me,' I say. 'You ruined everything.'

'Well, what the hell was I supposed to do? They tossed me into their SUV and said that they were going to kill me.'

'Why were you even running your mouth in the first place? I mean, what the hell were you thinking?' I ask. 'This is all your fault. They didn't know anything about us having the money. And we could've got away with it. Now, it's all fucked.'

'I wouldn't have said anything,' Colton says, 'if you hadn't taken my money.'

'For the last fuckin' time, I didn't take your money.'

Colton goes over to the half-drunk bottle of whiskey on the counter and takes a swig. Then he grabs the shotgun off the wall and points it at me.

Staring into the barrel, my heart skips a few beats. My chest closes up, and I can't take a full breath.

'Colton, what are you doing?' I ask, mulling over each word deliberately. I don't know whether it's loaded, but I can't risk saying anything offensive or out of order. 'Please, put the gun down.'

'No, I won't,' he says, swaying a little as he talks. He isn't firm on his feet, but I don't know if I'm quick enough to grab it away from him before he pulls the trigger. I try to reach for it but he fires off a shot into the wall behind me.

'The next one is going into your head if you don't show me where the fuckin' money is,' Colton says.

I take a deep breath. This is it. It's now or never. Am I willing to die for that money? No, of course not. But that's not what this is about. This is a bluff. Colton doesn't know that I have it. Not for sure. The story of me giving it over to Dossey's men is strong. It's got a solid foundation. I just need to convince him of this somehow.

'Colton—' I start, without having any idea how I'm going to follow that up.

Suddenly, the front door swings open and a female voice startles me.

'Put that down!' she says. It's Charlie, pointing a handgun at Colton.

The surprised look on Colton's face quickly dissipates.

'He has my money and he's going to die if he doesn't tell me where it is,' Colton says. His voice is firm and severe and I know that he means every word of it. He did kill the police officer in cold blood, what would stop him from doing the same to me?

'Put that down,' Charlie says again, taking a small step forward. Suddenly, Colton starts to laugh. It's a loud, bellowing laugh coming from somewhere deep inside of him. To say that it's unsettling would be an understatement.

'Put that down,' Charlie repeats herself. But Colton's laugh only gets louder. The shotgun moves with each wave of laughter, no longer pointing directly at me, but still in my general vicinity.

Charlie shoots off a round into the ceiling and then points the gun back squarely at Colton's chest. The sound of the gunshot makes my ears ring as a loud high pitch sound settles somewhere into my eardrums.

'You think I'm kidding?' she asks. I've never seen her so serious or put together. Gone is the frightened girl afraid to answer a 911 call. In this moment, she's in full control. There isn't a tinge of fear in her eyes. There is something else there. Something very unsettling. I think about it as the moment drags on and then it hits me. It's determination.

Even though Colton's far from being in his right mind, he seems to get this, too. He stops laughing and glances at me, then at Charlie, and then back to me again. Finally, he puts the shotgun back down on the table.

Charlie and I let out a sigh of relief. Charlie relaxes her right arm from its strict horizontal position. Her arm folds at the elbow before she points the gun down at the floor.

'Who are you?' Colton asks.

'I'm Noah's neighbor. I followed you that day you drove to Eklunta. I waited for you to leave and then I took your money. Noah had nothing to do with that.'

Colton furrows his brows as if he doesn't understand what she is saying.

'I just wanted to tell you that I'm really sorry about that,' Charlie says. 'Also, Noah is telling you the truth. When Dossey's men kidnapped us, giving them the money would have made them let us go. Unfortunately, they had another plan.'

Colton shakes his head.

'No, that's not true.'

'Yes, it is,' Charlie says.

'So, where is the money now?'

'I have no idea. The two men who kidnapped us dropped the money off with their boss. It was only after that we found out that they had no intention of ever letting us go.'

Colton stares directly into Charlie's eyes. But Charlie doesn't look away.

'You're lying!' he says, grabbing the shotgun from the table. Before he has the chance to aim and shoot, Charlie unloads her gun into his chest. Colton's knees bend, and he drops to the floor. Little spots of blood grow from the size of needle pricks to grapefruits on his shirt. Blood gurgles out of his mouth. His eyes roll to the back of his head as the life drains out of him.

CHAPTER FORTY-FIVE
NOAH

Everything about the world stops suddenly after the gunshot. Charlie and I stand staring at Colton's lifeless body for a few moments without saying a word. The moment doesn't feel real. It's as if it's happening to someone else and I'm just watching it on television. The trance breaks when Charlie takes a step and the floor of the cabin creaks. Suddenly, something occurs to me.

'He was going to shoot me,' I say, choosing each word slowly and deliberately.

'I know.'

'You saved my life. For the second time, actually.'

Charlie doesn't respond. I'm not sure why, but I suspect it's because to admit that she did would be to admit that she was the one who killed him.

'I didn't mean to kill him,' she says after a few moments.

She turns away from me and bends in half, burying her head in between her knees. I listen to her deep heavy breaths and wish there was something I could do. After a few moments, I walk over, kneel down next to her, and put my arm around her shoulders.

'You did what you had to do to save me, Charlie,' I say. 'I just want you to know that I'm really grateful for that.'

She nods slightly, but the sobbing does not stop. 'I just can't believe that I did that,' she mumbles. 'Maybe I shouldn't have been so impulsive. I should've waited for a bit. Maybe he would've come to his senses.'

I try to imagine how that scenario could have gone and realize that it's a fiction.

'No, you did the right thing. Colton would've killed me if you hadn't shot him first. Trust me, he is not the type to hesitate or to give anyone the benefit of the doubt.'

She doesn't ask how I can be so sure and I don't explain, but my mind flashes back to the officer he shot and left bleeding in the snow.

I give Charlie some time to calm down and pace around the room, trying to figure out what to do next. A few moments later, she wipes her tears and stands up to face me.

'Are you going to be okay?' I ask.

'What are we going to do now?' she shrugs and asks instead.

'I don't know.'

'Maybe we should call the police,' Charlie says after a few moments of staring at Colton's body.

I consider that option. But it sounds like a terrible idea.

Reading the sour expression on my face, she says, 'What if we call in anonymously from a pay phone or a disposable phone or something? We can say that we heard some shots fired in the area.'

On the surface this doesn't sound like a bad plan, but in the pit of my stomach I know that it is. Then I remember Colton saying that pay phone calls can be tracked, that's if you're lucky enough to find one.

'The thing is that this cabin belongs to my father-in-law. So, the police would inevitably come around to me asking questions. On top of that, Colton's my brother-in-law. Well, ex-brother-in-law, but we're still family. It would just be too suspicious if I was somehow connected to his death, even if only on the periphery.'

Charlie nods.

'Plus, the cops already know that Colton and I got into a fist fight at my school not long before he disappeared,' I say. 'And I got the sense that your boyfriend already suspects that the story I told him about our kidnapping isn't entirely true.'

'He was never my boyfriend,' Charlie says. 'And now, we're done for sure.'

'Well, I'm not convinced that will make him any more amenable in understanding our little predicament here,' I add.

'So, what do you suggest we do instead?'

'That I don't really know,' I say, looking around the cabin. I'm not clear as to what I'm looking for. There has to be an answer to our problem here somewhere.

'All I know is that we have to make it look like we were never here,' I say after a moment. 'Colton was never here and we were never here with him. This never happened. It would just be too suspicious if we were somehow involved in this on top of being kidnapped and being responsible for those two deaths as well.'

It takes a few minutes to figure out where to start.

'We need to dig out the bullet,' Charlie says. 'They can identify the type of gun that has been used by the bullet and the casing. If they don't have these two things, and they do end up finding the body, that will make things much harder on them.'

She walks up to me and hands me a knife.

'What do you want me to do with this?' I ask, taking a step back from her.

'Dig the bullet out of his chest.'

The monotone tone in her voice tells me that she's completely serious about this. Reluctantly, I take the knife and take a step toward Colton's body. There's a large pool of blood underneath him and the entry point is right by his shoulder.

While I debate how exactly to do this, Charlie walks around the room, looking down at the floor. She crawls under the table and emerges with something in her hand.

'Found it.'

'What is it?'

'The casing.'

I shake my head. Why couldn't that be my job?

'Wait, before you touch him,' Charlie looks under the kitchen sink and hands me a pair of disposable gloves, 'put these on. Just in case.'

I put them on and repeat my question again.

'Because I saved your life. It's the least you can do.'

Well, I guess she has a point there.

Colton's dressed in a thick sweater and I'm not entirely sure how to go about digging out the bullet through it. Like an expert surgical nurse who is there to anticipate the surgeon's every need, Charlie hands me a pair of scissors. I cut through the sweater, exposing the wound. Frankly, it doesn't look that bad. Deep, yes, but not like it should've killed him. But what do I know about medicine, right?

I press the blade to his skin, but hesitate for a moment. My stomach rumbles and I feel like I'm about to throw up. I close my eyes and take a deep breath.

'Wait, maybe these will help,' Charlie says, handing me a pair of tweezers. She also put on a pair of gloves. 'I spotted them in the bathroom. Maybe you can use them to pull it out.'

There's something about focusing on the tweezers that makes some of my nausea subside. I focus my mind and dig in. The bullet didn't go that far in and I poke at it with the knife. I try putting the blade a little bit under it, but it doesn't budge. Finally, I use the tweezers. I fish around for it for sometime before it finally comes out.

'It's all about having the right tools, huh?' Charlie makes a joke. I drop the bullet in her hand, pull off the gloves, and step outside. The cold air is the exact thing that I need. It hits me hard and I open my arms wide and let the gusts of wind slam into me over and over again.

This is going to be okay, I say to myself. You're going to be fine. After a few minutes when my fingers start to feel tingly from too much cold, I make my way back inside. Much to my surprise, I see that Charlie has already wrapped Colton's body in the rug. I help her place him on the children's sled that is kept out back. Having done all that, she's on her hands and knees cleaning and scrubbing the floors.

'Thanks for doing that,' I say, putting on a fresh pair of gloves.

'No problem. He's a heavy son-of-a-bitch, but I managed to get him strapped down to the sled. My only worry is that even if we get this place super clean, as if none of this ever happened, someone will notice that the rug and the sled are missing. Any chance of that?'

I shake my head. 'Not likely,' I say, shrugging. 'This place sits empty most of the year. And it has had more than a couple of break-ins. Sometimes people just come here to ride out the storm, but don't actually take anything. But we've had others take the television and other stuff like that. One time, someone broke in and just stole the comforters.'

The clean up takes a lot longer than I thought. Just when I think we're almost done, we find something else we forgot to scrub and we spread around the perimeter to make sure that we don't miss a spot. A couple of hours later, we are finally finished.

'So, I want to ask you something,' I say, about to take off my gloves.

'No, don't take them off yet,' she says. 'I don't want you touching anything in this place with your bare hands.'

'Good point,' I say. I tie up the garbage bag full of soaking paper towels and old rags, which are covered in blood. 'I was just wondering how you ended up here in the first place.'

Charlie wipes her forehead with the back of her hand. 'I followed you.'

'But, why?'

'I don't have your phone number and I didn't want to just knock on your door and run into your wife,' she says. 'I haven't seen you since I was in the hospital and I guess I just wanted to make sure that we were still on the same page.'

She probably means the money. She's wondering when I will give her her part. I wait for her to bring it up, but she doesn't.

'I mean, I knew that we must've told the cops the same story because they let us out. But I just wanted to make sure that's what you told your wife as well.'

'Emily?'

She nods and waits.

'What do you mean?' It takes me a moment to realize what she's asking me.

'Does she know anything else about… anything?'

'No, absolutely not.' I shake my head. 'It's not like I didn't want to tell her, but I just thought it would be safer to keep her out of the loop for now.'

'Good, that's good,' Charlie says. 'Now let's deal with Colton.'

CHAPTER FORTY-SIX

CHARLIE

A big part of me still hasn't fully grasped the fact that I just killed a man. A human being. I may have done it to save someone else's life, but that hardly seems to matter now. I mean, I just killed someone. Me. A girl who cries at rescue animal commercials on television. Being a 911 operator, I'm used to dealing with emergencies. Well, not so much dealing with as numbing myself to them. People call in, freaking out, and it's my job to calm them down. It's my job to ground them and to tell them that it's all going to be okay. I'm their voice of reason. Or maybe unreason. Because I don't really know if it's all going to be okay – and many times it's not – but I have to make them believe it in order for them to do what I ask them to do until the police arrives. Whenever people call the station, they are calling for backup. The cops are essentially the cavalry, they come to save the day. But in this situation, the police are the last thing I want. If they show up, or even catch a whiff of what happened here, it's all over. No, there's no backup here. No one to rely on except ourselves.

This isn't the time to break down or lose myself in wallowing. I know that, of course. If I want to even have a chance at getting my old, normal life back, the police can't find any of this out. I know that. That's why I'm on my hands and knees scrubbing the hell out of this damn cabin, trying to remove every speck of evidence of what happened here. The blood is messy and gross, of course, but at least it's visible. It's the fingerprints that are the hard ones. I try to remember every single thing I touched in the cabin. My mind runs in circles as I walk through each moment since my arrival. But instead of focusing on what I touched and where I could've left my prints, my thoughts just keep going back to a few moments before I fired the gun.

Maybe I shouldn't have brought it with me in the first place. I don't really like guns, unlike most people in this state. I don't collect them. I didn't even get it for protection. Frankly, I have no good excuse for bringing it along except that I had a feeling that something bad was going to happen. But maybe that's why I should've left it in the car in the first place.

I consider this possibility as I walk around the cabin, wiping the windowsills even though I'm positive that I've never touched them. I try to convince myself that bringing the gun was a bad idea, but I can't. Not fully. I can't convince myself because without it I'd probably be dead. The look on Colton's face was terrifying and depraved. He was angry and if I hadn't shot him, he would've shot Noah. And probably killed him. And once there was one dead body on his hands, then he probably wouldn't have hesitated to kill me either. I was a witness, after all.

Standing in the middle of the cabin staring at Colton's body wrapped up in the rug and secured to the sled makes me feel oddly disconnected from the moment. On one hand, I'm here and, on the other, I'm not. I feel my mind floating away, going someplace far away. It's an ability I developed when I was a little girl. Whenever my parents fought and I no longer wanted to be stuck in the house with them but I couldn't escape because the house was too small and the walls were too thin, I would just disconnect from the world. My body would remain in place, but my mind would take me someplace else. Somewhere beautiful and kind. Someplace that's always warm and I could walk barefoot on the soft green grass and be surrounded by a million wildflowers.

Noah puts his hand on my arm, startling me. I even jump back a foot. 'Are you okay?' he asks.

'Yes, I'm fine.' I nod.

'I was just wondering what you think we should do now,' he says.

I try to collect my thoughts and focus on the task at hand.

'I don't really know. I guess we can take him out back. There are miles of wilderness out there.'

'Yes, I know, but we can't exactly bury him anywhere. The ground is rock hard.'

'What if we just leave him out there somewhere? Maybe under a fallen tree or something? The animals will probably get to him before spring.'

'Yeah, most likely. I mean, the wolves and the coyotes are hungry this time of year,' Noah says, considering the proposition. 'The only problem is that what if they don't? I'm just worried that some hunter or a hiker with a dog will stumble upon him. And we are very close to our father-in-law's cabin.'

Noah has a point. People are always finding dead bodies in the most unlikely places. It would be a risk. On one hand, there are miles of wilderness so the likelihood is quite small, but you can never really account for luck. No, it would be best for all if this body is never found. And for that, we need a much better plan.

Noah paces around the room, trying to come up with an alternative plan.

'Okay, this may sound like a crazy idea,' he says after a while. 'But there's the frozen lake out back. So, what if we use some of this old ice fishing equipment, make a hole in the ice, and dump him in the lake?'

'I guess that way no one will find him for sure until after the ice melts.'

'That's what I'm thinking.'

'But what happens then? Don't bodies float?' I ask. 'People go fishing in this lake all the time.'

'Yes, ice fishing, so they won't find him then. And once the ice melts, that will be a long time from now. Besides, we can find something to weigh him down.'

I try to remember what exactly happens to bodies in water. I'm a big crime fiction reader, but I've seen a few police procedurals on television and in the movies. I remember that some bodies float up after decomposition. It has something to do with gases escaping after death, taking the body up to the surface. But I'm not certain about any of this.

'If we do this, I think we will have to weigh him down with something. Just in case,' I say.

We head outside to see what we can find around the cabin. Luckily there's a big, heavy metal chain that someone once used to pull something.

'This will work,' Noah announces and hands it to me. He heads into the shed out back and emerges with a thin screw-like device.

'What's that?'

'An auger,' Noah says. 'I've used it a few times with my father-in-law. We're going to use it to cut through the ice to make the fishing hole.'

'Do you think that's wide enough?'

Noah examines the diameter and compares it to the size of the body. 'It should be plenty,' he says after a moment.

When we finally have everything we need, we set out for the lake. I have a knot in the bottom of my stomach from worrying about running into someone. I keep looking around to make sure that there's no one around, but luckily for me the cabin is in a fairly isolated place.

'Don't worry so much,' Noah says when we step onto the ice. 'Even if someone were to see us, that's why you're carrying the bucket and the fishing poles. We're just going fishing.'

It's as if he can read my mind. I inhale deeply and try to put my worries aside. But still, they creep up.

'But what about this?' I point to the sled that he's pulling. 'All I see when I look at it is a dead body wrapped in a rug.'

'But that's not what they're going to see. Even we even do manage to run into anyone, all they're going to see is a rolled-up rug. We'll say you wanted to bring it out because you wanted to have somewhere warm to sit. People who ice fish come out with all sorts of things.'

His confidence puts me somewhat at ease. I nod and decide to focus my energy on the task at hand. Ten minutes later, Noah stops and says that this is as good a spot as any. I look around. The lake is completely frozen over. Whiteness spreads for what seems like miles in all directions. There are trees around the perimeter, but we are the only living things for as far as the eye can see.

Without saying another word, Noah turns on the auger and presses it to the top of the ice. It roars into action and starts to penetrate the top layer. The machine is so loud, my heart sinks to the pit of my stomach. I keep looking around, waiting to get caught.

'Don't worry,' Noah yells without turning the auger off. 'We're just out here ice fishing.'

I nod and wrap my hands around my body. I guess he's right, but it doesn't feel like that. It's well below freezing out, but I am covered in sweat. I can feel it seeping through my clothes, making me colder and colder with each minute that we're out here. I know that this feeling of dread won't go away until we're back at the cabin.

Once Noah hits the water, he pulls the auger out. I stare into the hole. The water is murky at first, but then it quickly clears up and I can see straight to the bottom.

'The water is too see-through,' I say. 'What if someone comes out here…'

I can't finish the thought. It's too horrible. But Noah shakes his head.

'Don't worry, the current will pull him away.'

'But it's a lake.'

'Well, then not the current but just the displacement of water. Besides, the chance of someone coming out here to this exact same spot is highly unlikely. But I'll cover up the hole with some of this ice if it will make you feel better.'

I nod and watch him wrap the body with the heavy chain. With great effort, he wraps the chain around the body a couple of times and wraps one side under the other.

'This should pull him down.'

I nod. The chain does look substantial. Without further ado, Noah pulls the body toward the hole in the ice. I help him along. It doesn't make much of a sound as it disappears below the surface. I look into the hole to make sure that it's gone and I don't see it at the bottom. It must be somewhere under the ice already, headed toward the bottom, but not directly here. True to his word, Noah takes some of the ice and snow generated from cutting the hole and places it over the opening. I stand here watching him, and he does a very good job of camouflaging the opening.

'Okay, let's go,' Noah says, putting the auger on the sled and turning back toward the cabin. Without saying anything, I follow along.

There isn't much to say at all. I want to be just about anywhere but here. I try to escape it by thinking about something else, but for once in my life my ability to simply not be somewhere I don't want to be fails me. I can't force myself out of this moment and just have to endure it.

I pull my fingers out of my gloves and fold them under the palm section. My fingers are ice cold and it feels nice to press them against something warm. I shuffle my feet all the way back to the edge of the lake because picking them up is just too difficult. It feels like everything that we've just done is wrong, but it is the only thing to do.

'Are you okay?' Noah asks.

I shrug, not knowing how to answer his question.

'I just feel a little lost,' I say. 'This whole thing just feels very wrong, you know?'

He nods.

'But also like there's no choice.'

'Yes, that's how I feel, too,' he says after a moment. 'I mean, going to the police isn't going to make anything better. It's not going to bring Colton back. And it might, or it will, probably get us in a lot of trouble.'

'Well, mainly me,' I say. 'I mean, I was the one who shot him.'

'To save my life.'

'I guess.'

'No, don't underestimate that, Charlie. You saved my life. And I'm grateful for that. I am, really. I mean, if you hadn't done what you did, I'd be dead. Emily wouldn't have a husband anymore. And Ava would grow up without a father.'

I shrug. All that seems too abstract and academic at the moment. All I can feel is the blood that I have on my hands.

'And the thing is that you would probably be dead, too,' Noah says after a moment.

'What do you mean?'

'Well, you would've seen him shoot me, for basically no reason. He was in a rage, and he's not the type to leave witnesses. Especially not ones he doesn't really know.'

He's right. Of course, he's right, I say to myself. Maybe it was for the best. Or if not for the best, but for the better. I mean, what is the alternative?

When we finally get back to the cabin, Noah turns to me and says, 'I think we should agree that we were never here. At all.'

I nod.

'I think we did a good job of cleaning everything. There shouldn't be any fingerprints anywhere. And they will have no reason to suspect that you were here at all.'

'Yes, I think you're right.'

We stand around at the back of the cabin for a few moments unsure as to what to do next.

'So, I think this is goodbye,' Noah says. 'This has been… interesting.'

I fake a smile.

'I just want to thank you again.'

'For what?'

'For following me and for saving my life. And I will get you your portion of the money soon.'

The money. Yes, of course. So, there is something I've been meaning to talk to him about.

'Actually, I don't think that's such a good idea,' I say.

'What are you talking about?'

'Well, I don't want to take it. I'm sorry, but I don't want a share. I don't even want a dollar.'

'Charlie—'

'No, don't,' I say definitively. 'My mind is made up. I don't have anything against it, I just feel like a lot of bad things happened once I agreed to accept it. And I don't think I want to have it.'

'But you need it. You're paying for your grandmother's assisted living facility.'

'I'll figure it out,' I say. 'I can get another job.'

'Charlie, I don't think this is very wise.'

'Noah, please, listen to me. You don't have to worry. Your secrets, or rather, our secrets, are safe with me. You don't have to worry about me going to the cops or anything. But if it's okay with you, I don't want the money. I just don't want it in my life. Okay?'

By the skeptical look on his face, I can tell that it's not entirely okay. He's about to say something else to try to convince me, but in the end he is courteous enough to let it go.

'Okay, if that's what you want,' he says.

'It is.'

EPILOGUE

CHARLIE

The next four months passed without incident. For a while, I kept waiting for the police or Stephen to show up at my door asking questions. And when they found Colton's body a month ago, I was almost certain that it would be only a matter of time before they came knocking. But as time passed, no one came. No one asked me anything. Not even about where Noah went.

Noah put his house up for sale a few weeks after our time at the cabin. The neighborhood is up and coming and it's in a good school district, so it sold pretty quickly. Noah and I made a concerted effort to not speak to each other again, but right before the moving truck pulled away, I waved goodbye to them and asked where they were headed. Emily said they were driving all the way down to Key West, Florida. Maybe that's the best thing for them. It's nice to make a change, especially after everything that's happened.

I haven't seen Stephen much except for in the professional setting and we have never discussed our relationship again. That was a relief because as far as I was concerned there was nothing else to talk about. Whenever I saw him around the station, he always had a morose expression on his face. I attributed this to the fact that we weren't seeing each other anymore, but later learned that he was struggling to deal with the fact that his friend, Officer Teaghan, was still missing and they couldn't find any trace of him anywhere.

We did run into each other once after they found Colton's body and I asked him about the case. He said that a hiker and his dog found him along the edge of a lake somewhere up north. He was wrapped up in a rug and had a big chain around him to keep him under like an anchor. My heart sank at that moment and I thought that I was done for. But I kept my mouth shut while Stephen kept talking. The working theory that the department had going was that Dossey's men kidnapped and killed him, and that was exactly the plan they had for me and Noah. They did an autopsy in hopes of finding some evidence to support their theory, but Dossey's men were meticulous, even dug out the bullet from his shoulder so they couldn't identify what kind of gun they shot him with.

When I asked him if that's what he thought happened as well, he nodded and shrugged and begrudgingly agreed. I was surprised to see that Stephen seemed to be satisfied with that explanation. I let out a sigh of relief because Stephen isn't the type to really be satisfied with anything, and if he was then the case must be as good as closed.

I arrive at Nana's assisted living facility with a heavy heart. I have to walk past the front desk and explain, yet again, why I'm late with the payments. The woman there doesn't much care for my sob story. Everyone has one, right? She typically sighs and puts me down for a late payment. There are a certain number that I can accumulate before they start to send out those letters and start the eviction.

It's on days like this that I really regret not taking a portion of that money Noah found. I know that it doesn't really belong to me, but it's not like I'd be stealing it from some orphans or a school for the blind, right? That money was dirty and it belonged to some bad men who tried to kill me. I could think of it as payment for all of my troubles, but only if I convinced myself that I got into that trouble in the first place as a result of the money. Nevertheless, on days like today, when I know that I owe money that I can't possibly pay, I really wish that I had taken it. I did take on extra shifts at work but besides leaving me exhausted and with even less free time, it didn't do much in covering the assisted living fees.

I take a breath before I walk through the doors. I'm not really sure if any of these conversations do any good, but I feel the need to at least apologize. Explain. Say something. I don't want them thinking that my grandmother and I are just a couple of freeloaders.

When I get to the front desk, I see an unfamiliar face. They usually have a few people in rotation, but this woman must be new.

After introducing myself, I quickly launch into my story. They cut my hours at work. I'm going to the police academy soon and after I graduate, I'll definitely have the money.

'Um, excuse me, miss.' The pudgy middle-aged woman with a large hairdo lifts her finger in the air to stop me.

'What did you say your name was again?'

'Charlie Easton.'

'Oh, yes, I thought that was familiar. Though, to tell you the truth, I thought you'd be a man.'

I nod and shrug, waiting for her to continue.

'Actually, I just updated the records. We received a check this morning that covered the fees for the next year,' she says.

My mouth nearly drops open.

'What?' I mumble.

'Yes, right here.' She points to the computer screen under Nana's name. 'You're all covered until next year.'

I stare at her dumbfounded. Is she for real? When I finally get a hold of my senses, I decide that the best way to proceed is to simply agree, smile, and go in and visit my Nana. Perhaps, this was just one of those very convenient computer glitches that only happens in movies?

I don't visit with Nana for long. She's distracted because she's getting ready for the dance tonight, and I'm distracted because my mind keeps coming back to the mysterious payment. After we say our goodbyes, I head out to the car with my mind still running in circles.

How could I be all covered until next year? I was behind on the payments for sometime and now, all of the sudden, magically, I'm up to date? What was that woman even talking about? No, she must be looking at someone else's account. This all must be just one big mistake.

When I get home, I check my mail expecting to see another past-due letter from the assisted living facility. But instead I find a large yellow envelope without a return address. The first thing I pull out is a computer printed letter addressed to me from a bank in Panama. The bank manager thanks me for setting up a trust with them and lays out the steps for accessing my numbered account.

My numbered account? I read the letter so fast that it barely makes any sense. The thing that I keep going back to is the figure at the bottom: $400,000.

Someone had put $400,000 into an account for me. The same someone who paid my grandmother's assisted living fees. There is only one person in the world who would do that.

I sit down at the kitchen table and stare at the letter. My hand runs over the envelope. That's when it occurs to me that there's something else in there. I open the flap and pull out a book. It's entitled *The Old Man and his Sailboat* and the author is N. C. Laird. Inside the flap, it says, '*Dear Charlie, I finally finished it. Noah.*'

I read it in one sitting. The book is about an old man who forsakes his boring life in his later years, builds a sailboat, and takes off. The boat becomes his obsession, causing his wife to leave him. But he doesn't really care. He has a dream of sailing to California. When he reaches North Carolina, he meets a woman who he falls in love with. Together they go all the way around Cape Horn and back up to California. The journey is not without a lot of close calls and near misses – they are on the brink of death a number of times, but in the end, they eventually make it. It's a happy ending.

I close the book and run my fingers over the number $400,000 on the trust fund paperwork.

'That son-of-a-bitch.' I start to laugh.

A LETTER FROM K.T. FINCH

Dear Reader,

Thank you very much for taking the time to read *Finders Keepers*. I was inspired to write this novel because I love stories about ordinary people who are placed in extraordinary situations. We all face challenges in our lives and it is these points of inflection that really define who we are. Some of us become better people as a result of the drama that we face and some of us, unfortunately, become worse versions of ourselves. But in either case, without these challenges, we would never know what we are truly capable of.

If you would like to keep up-to-date on all my latest releases, just sign up on the link below.

www.bookouture.com/kt-finch

I started writing this novel, my first foray into crime fiction, when I became pregnant with our child, Tristan Finn. I was bed-ridden for nearly four months – and the only thing that made that time bearable was this story. The process of writing *Finders Keepers* was my escape from the dreariness of everyday life and, for that, I will be forever thankful.

I hope you enjoyed reading it. If you did enjoy it, I hope you take a few minutes to write a review. I love hearing what my readers think and reviews are the main way that other readers discover new books.

Also, I love to hear from my readers! Please reach out to me on Facebook, Twitter or email.

Thank you again for all of your love and support. I really appreciate it.

K.T. Finch

www.ktfinch.com

@ktfinchcrime

KTFinchCrime

ACKNOWLEDGEMENTS

I would like to express my gratitude to Helen Jenner, my editor at Bookouture, for all of her hard work and guidance during the editing process. I would also like to thank Natalie Butlin for seeing potential in this book when it was originally self-published and inviting me to join the Bookouture family. Finally, I would like to thank everyone at Bookouture for everything that they do and for their ongoing enthusiasm.

Also, a huge thank you to my wonderful husband, Kevin Doran, for all of his support in every aspect of our lives as well as for his help in developing and plotting the story. You have always understood my insatiable need to write and supported me in this pursuit back when it was only a dream rather than a reality, and for that I will be eternally grateful.